COWBOY
ANGST

COWBOY ANGST

Jasen Emmons

SOHO

Special thanks to Norm Anderson and
Marcus Ratcliff

The following lyrics are quoted from by kind permission: "These Boots Are Made For
Walkin'" (Lee Hazlewood) © 1965 Criterion Music Corp. © Renewed 1993 and
assigned to Criterion Music Corp.; "Love Shy" (Sandy Rogers) reprinted by permission of Metro-Goldwyn-Mayer Inc./© 1986 Cannon Film Music. All rights reserved.

Published by
Soho Press, Inc.
853 Broadway
New York, NY 10003

Library of Congress Cataloging-in-Publication

Emmons, Jasen, 1963–
Cowboy angst / Jasen Emmons.
p.   cm.
ISBN 1-56947-021-9 :
1. Country musicians—Montana—Fiction.   2. Young men—
Montana—Fiction.   3. Cowboys—Montana—Fiction.   I. Title.
PS3555.M5225C69   1995
813'.54—dc20   94-9854
                                                                        CIP

For my mother and father
and for Joanne

COWBOY
ANGST

One

I was sitting on a padded stool at Fat Sam's Saloon, tapping out paradiddles on the bar. The owner, Ray, was next to me, a squat man, all breasts and belly, sweating heavily into his madras shirt.

"I understand this is the end of your band," Ray said. "I know you want to go out with a bang. Who doesn't? The reason I hire you is because you fill my bar with people who enjoy dancing. But when they're always dancing, they're not drinking. And when they're not drinking, I'm not making dick. Understand?"

"I understand, Ray."

"Play more slow songs. People can drink during a slow song."

"No problem."

"Are we clear on this, Dennis?"

"Very clear, Ray. We got carried away last night. I apologize."

We had ripped through the first two sets without playing a single slow song and were well into the third set when I saw Ray balancing perilously on a chair at the back of the crowd, waving his stubby arms. When he saw that he had my attention, he drew a forefinger across his throat. I had a vision of him as Humpty-Dumpty in a Hawaiian shirt and huaraches, and I told Montana to sing "I Fall to Pieces" as the next song. Ray'd smiled and sunk from sight.

"We're here to make money," Ray told me now. "I pay you to bring people in and make them want to dance, and they pay me to drink my booze. You make money, I make money, everyone goes home happy."

"The American way of life," I said brightly.

"The only way of life. Now play slow songs and make ole Ray happy."

"Done."

We shook hands and I went to find Montana, who'd said she'd meet me on the deck. I wondered if I'd miss Ray and his bar. Probably not Ray. I would miss playing gigs for the sororities at Colorado State that held their autumn barn dances at Fat Sam's. All those sleek, eager girls decked out in boots and borrowed chaps, four or five of whom inevitably ditched their dates shortly after arriving or simply lost them in the shuffle of rampant swapping that went on; unencumbered girls, almost hysterical in their zeal to have a good time, who were usually up for a quick boink in the parking lot with a musician between sets.

I didn't see Montana on the covered deck that looked west over the Medicine Bow Mountains. The sun was a deep ocher and sat low and heavy on the horizon. People were leaning out over the deck railing to catch the last hour of its heat on their faces. I looked at the dark serrated outline of the mountains against the sky and suddenly missed home. I wanted to be in Prairie View, looking at the high sweeping arc of the Highwoods and Little Belt Mountains, to be walking alone in the rolling hills outside town enjoying the wide horizons. During college I'd spent four consecutive summers in Prairie View working for Cascade County Weed Control walking along gravel roads spraying pesticide on leafy spurge and spotted knapweed in the ditches. My parents had always thought it was a ridiculous job—roadside weed killer—but it paid $8.50 an hour, which went a long way toward placating them. For me it was an excuse to spend time alone in the country. Who else spent that kind of time outside anymore? Sportsmen? Cowboys? Maybe you had to be involved in raising or killing something—weeds, game, livestock—to get out these days. I thought riding a horse in the open country was the single greatest draw of an overly romanticized occupation; its greatest drawback the silence that seemed to go along with it. Certain people in my family had a cowboy's inclination toward reticence. I wasn't sure it was a positive attribute.

After fourteen months of supporting myself playing gigs in anonymous bars and clubs, I thought two or three weeks of walking alone in familiar territory would go a long way toward bringing a sense of clarity to my life that I'd lately felt was missing. Like whether I was starting law school in a month because I wanted to or because I'd convinced myself I wanted to.

I found an empty table and sat down. In a few minutes I saw Montana step out onto the deck. She spotted me and smiled. Then strode toward the table with squared shoulders and a straight back, chin slightly raised. Her straight brown hair was cut like a helmet around her tanned face and moved lightly as she walked. She was tall and wiry and had an aura of resilient wildness that excited and frightened men. Over the last six years, Montana had become the star attraction of the band.

When we were both freshman, I'd wanted to play rhythm and blues. The first person to join the band I was forming, a bass player named Bill Adams, said he wanted that too. We found a guitarist named Tom Zarle who played slide and pedal steel, but he knew only country songs. Bill and I said he'd learn. A female

5

guitarist and vocalist joined and then she and Tom Zarle formed an alliance, claiming there was more of a demand around Fort Collins for a solid country band than any blues band. The woman, Janey Bowman, was the only one among us with a good-enough voice to sing lead. Once Janey realized this, she said she wouldn't do anything but country. All this before we'd played a note.

I saw my hopes of ever playing in a blues band slipping away. They ended when a keyboard player named Ed Clayton, who could also sing lead, joined and sided with Tom and Janey. Bill Adams said he wanted to play country too.

"It's your band, Dennis," Janey said, "and you can do what you want, obviously, but the four of us are going to play country. So what do you think?"

"I guess I'm destined to play country," I said. "But I get to choose the name."

I came up with Cowboy Angst. I liked the irony and figured that anyone booking the band who was confused about its meaning would feel reassured by the word *cowboy*. Janey told us that from then on we were to call her by her stage name: Montana Wildhack.

It was a start. By the end of the school year, I'd been converted; I didn't want to play anything but country.

"Just saw Ray on my way back from the bathroom," Montana said now, pulling up a chair and sitting down. "He asked me to sing every Patsy Cline song I know. I told him to piss up a rope."

I rubbed my face and laughed.

"What?"

"I just spent fifteen minutes promising him we'd play lots of slow songs tonight. He complained that people didn't drink enough last night because they were too busy dancing. Tonight he wants slow songs and heavy drinking."

"Slow songs and heavy drinking."

"Right."

"Do you think Ray's a heavy drinker?" Montana arched her eyebrows. She had a delicate nose and green eyes that changed color with the light.

"I think Ray's plain heavy. Heavy drinker, heavy eater, heavy man."

"Heavy heart?"

"I don't even like to think about his poor heart."

"I said good-bye to Clint this afternoon. Sent him back to the ranch. He was pissed about it, but I told him tonight was the last time I'd see you for a while and I didn't want him here. He gets so possessive when you're around, and it's annoying."

"What are you saying?"

"I need to stay at your place tonight. Is that all right?"

"Sure."

"You know what Clint asked me?" Montana said. "He wanted to know if I was going to sleep with you."

"Clint did?" I said. Did Clint know something I didn't? Was this something he *thought* should happen or was *afraid* would happen? What would he do if he caught us in bed? Would he weep? Bludgeon me senseless? Shoot me? He'd probably shoot me, then bludgeon me senseless. No weeping. "What'd you say?"

"I said no."

I was disappointed she said it with such conviction. "Do you think he'd kill me if we did?"

"Clint?" Montana said. "No, he's not that violent. You just think he's mean because he doesn't say much."

"That's certainly true," I said, picturing Clint, a tall, rangy cowboy, so self-contained you could almost hear him ticking. My brother, Miles, was the same way. Whenever I was around Clint or Miles, I felt an eerie anticipation of impending fury about to erupt, like a bronc and its rider exploding from a rodeo chute. God help the unlucky bastard who was on hand when it happened. Montana was attracted to men like that. I wondered if making love to her would be worth the risk of a severe beating at Clint's hands. On the whole I thought it would be worth every broken bone. I felt giddy.

"What do you want to open with?" I said.

"Let's start with 'Love Shy,' 'These Boots' and 'Walkin' after Midnight.' Make Ray happy."

"Good. I need to go find those other guys," I said. Both of us stood up.

"Come here," Montana said, pulling me toward her. I slipped my arms around her shoulders and drew her close. She held me tightly and pressed the side of her head to mine. "Dennis?"

"Yeah?"

"You're shaking."

"I get nervous before these things."

I walked into the bar and began to weave through the crowd. I felt like a boxer headed to the ring, a slight flutter in my stomach, a tremor in my hands. Acquaintances and well-wishers yelled my name and slapped my back. I really didn't care for backslappers. If I'd ever made it big in country music, I would have hired an entourage of short-necked gymnasts with over-developed lats to take the blows of my ardent admirers.

I stepped outside to the open courtyard, still bright with late evening sunlight, a large square with the feel of a beer garden, dotted with small white islands of corrugated steel tables and chairs, and I surveyed the crowd: cowboys with straight backs, their Stetson straws tipped in front to cast shadows over their eyes; cowgirls in sleeveless western shirts that showed off their brown wiry arms and flat stomachs; tanned college students wearing Jams and flip-flops, staring at their reflections in one another's sunglasses; Deadheads in tie-dyed shirts; three girls in climbing shorts and Day-Glo bikini tops, with lime green triangles of sunscreen on their noses, pink circles on their cheeks, and a pale blue dot on their foreheads. Modern war paint: What I'd give to be the hunted. People appeared to be drinking heavily and I imagined Ray panting every time a cash register rang.

I found the other band members leaning against the stage, tucked diagonally into a corner. All three were new to the band, maintaining Cowboy Angst's six-year revolving-door tradition. Montana and I were the only original members.

"We're starting with 'Love Shy,'" I said.

"'Love Shy?'" Gavin, our twenty-two-year-old bass player, was still learning all the songs.

"Sandy Rogers. Six-eight time." I sang the first two lines.

"Jesus, no wonder you don't sing backup."

"You know the song or not?"

"I know it."

"Good. Then we're playing 'These Boots' and 'Walkin' after Midnight.' Ray wants more slow songs. What do you want to open with, Mike?"

"Let's start with 'Sweet Mama.'" He was our other vocalist and keyboardist.

A heavy woman in a black Resistol hat bounded on stage and tapped the center microphone twice. "Can you hear me?" she shouted.

Several people booed. A drunk yelled "Nooo!" and broke into a hyena laugh.

"Did Ray mention anything about a farewell bonus?" said Brian, the pedal steel guitarist.

"No."

"Just checking."

"Thanks for coming out to Fat Sam's tonight," the woman on stage said. "Now I'd like you to welcome, for their last time together, Fort Collins's very own . . . Cowboy Angst!" The crowd cheered. A group of friends yipped and howled.

"Here we go, boys," Mike said, leading us up the stairs.

I walked behind my drums and sat on the small cushioned stool, taking a deep breath to steady myself. My hair fell a couple inches past my shoulders and I tied a bandanna around my head to keep it out of my eyes. Sunlight bounced off the smooth black surface of my drums and their silver rims. I stroked each head, played a crescendo roll on my snare and ended with a rim shot. When I saw they were ready, I clicked my sticks together and we went into "Love Shy." The song had a swing rhythm. As I played on the ride cymbal and snare, I could see people begin to sway from side to side. By the time we were three-quarters of the way through the song, a crowd had gathered before the stage, moving in a mesmerizing wave.

A cheer went up as Montana walked on stage dressed in black, her sombrero tilted to one side. Talcum powder had been tapped over the floor around her microphone so her boots would slide, and she twisted on the balls of her feet to test it. She strapped on her acoustic guitar, turned and grabbed the microphone.

"You know there's a battle goin' on out there," she sang in her full, throaty voice.

Only I knew how far Montana had come as a performer. The first time we'd played to an audience, when we were both freshmen, she had opened her mouth to sing and nothing happened. The band came around for her intro again. Not a sound. On the third try she managed to mumble a few words. The other singer took over until the break, when Montana cried and said she'd lied about singing in a band before. No kidding. Now she could handle anything.

"I'm a little love shy."

I noticed the cowboys and cowgirls standing on the perimeter of the crowd, drinks in hand, sizing things up. I knew the song was too slow for them this early in the evening. They wanted the formality and grace of two-stepping and jitterbugging, not this mindless swaying.

When we went into "These Boots Are Made for Walkin'", the cowboys led their partners to the floor. I was playing on the hi-hat and snare, sweat already beginning to work its way down my back. I looked over at Gavin, who pursed his lips in time to the music. He smiled at me, then resumed his facial contortions. Couples swung away from one another and snapped back at the point of tension, swung out and the women twirled like ballerinas. On the turns the cowboys' free hand was always where it needed to be the moment their partners reached for it. Their faces were focused and made me smile, impressed as always with how serious they were.

Now that everyone was dancing, Montana didn't want to slow down. She scratched "Walkin' after Midnight" for "You Ain't Woman Enough." Mike kept up the pace. It wasn't until he closed the set with "Way Downtown" that we realized what we'd done. We turned and looked at one another like delinquent children.

"He's going to lynch us," Gavin said. "I mean it. He's going to be pissed. And you guys don't care, do you?"

"We had to warm them up," I said. "They were sluggish."

"I've never seen such a sluggish crowd," Montana said.

"They're thirsty now," Mike said. "Don't they look thirsty?"

"I've never seen such a thirsty crowd."

"Here comes Ray."

"Would you say Ray looks unhappy with us?" Brian said.

"I'd say Ray looks pissed," Mike said.

"Take care of him, Dennis," Montana said, squeezing my arm.

They scattered. I walked slowly down the steps where Ray stood waiting. I wiped my damp face with a towel and looked at him; his face called to mind a human pumpkin with triangular slits for eyes.

"You're going to tell me you were just warming them up, right?"

"Exactly. They were a little sluggish at the start there, Ray."

"Sluggish?"

"I've never seen such a sluggish crowd. Three slow songs and we would have been right down the tubes. Nothing would've jump-started them after that. Now look at them. They're in a frenzy. They want to get loaded and dance. Your bartenders can't serve them fast enough. You're making money hand over fist, Ray. You're kickin' ass. *We're* kickin' ass! I'll bet you ten bucks this is one of the biggest-grossing nights of your life."

"Ten bucks?"

"Ten bucks," I said, caught up in my own enthusiasm.

"You're on." We shook hands.

"Trust me, Ray. We're professionals."

"An occasional slow song, that's all I'm asking."

"No problem."

"I hear you're going to law school," Ray said.

"I start next month at George Washington University in D.C."

"You'll make a great lawyer, Dennis. You're completely full of shit."

"Thank you, Ray."

The sun had slipped below the Medicine Bows, now black against the pink sky. The outside lights were turned on. I saw Montana wave from a back corner, and I began to move through the people seated at the tables. I walked behind the trio in bikini tops and slowed to see how they had them fastened. All three had the neon strings tied with six or seven granny knots. Veterans.

I sat next to Montana at a table of friends who were listening to Brian and Mike talk about past gigs. I leaned toward her and said, "I miss Montana."

She frowned. "I haven't even left yet."

"The state. Home."

"Oh. Really?"

"I was standing on the deck looking at the Medicine Bows and all of a sudden I wanted to be back in Prairie View."

"You miss your parents?"

"No, I miss the mountains. And the prairie."

"What's wrong with these mountains?"

"Nothing. They're wonderful. They're just not home."

"There are no mountains in D.C.," Montana said.

"Yeah, well, there's none in Austin, either."

"Austin's nicer."

"If you don't mind a city full of redneck cowboys."

"Better than a city full of fat-ass politicians." She had taken my hand and was digging her fingernails into the skin.

We glared at one another for a moment.

"Come to Austin with me," Montana said.

"I can't."

"Yes, you can."

When it was time to play, I sat behind my drums and dug through a canvas bag for a pair of sticks. The July night had turned dark but was still hot. A luminous half-moon floated low on the horizon, mysterious and cool. The courtyard lights on their tall metal stanchions cast orange cones of light that flickered with bugs. Mike opened with "Streets of Bakersfield." People began to drag tables and chairs away from the stage so there would be more room to dance. Montana sang three Patsy Cline songs in a row and couples held one another and shuffled in short, tight circles. Mike brought them out of their reveries with "Tiger by the Tail" and kept it up until Montana slowed things down again. Then, she said, "We're going to play a song now to see how fast you folks can dance." She turned to call out the tempo and we started "My Baby Thinks He's a Train." People began to two-step, the better pairs gliding and turning with ease, sliding effortlessly out of one another's way. I picked up the pace after the chorus. A few less-practiced couples collided and then frowned at their feet as if wondering whom they belonged to. Faster, and more and more couples began to redline, a few of them going over the edge and reeling into the tables. After the third chorus, we played all out, only one couple able to keep up. The crowd circled them and clapped as they floated and turned with the grace of an Olympic ice-skating pair. When the song ended, the young man and woman grinned self-consciously, their faces red and sweaty.

I went to the bar and ordered a large glass of water. Montana was talking to a cowboy with red hair. A redheaded stranger. I wondered if I would have slept with her by now if I were a cowboy. My brother, Miles, had been a cowboy and now he was a cop. My father was an attorney, but his stance in life was essentially that of a cowboy. Why wasn't I a cowboy? I played in a cowboy band. Even gave it a cowboy name. A little irony for all you cowboys. What would it be like to make love to you, Montana? Would it be as good as I think it would? Part of me wanted to know and part of me was afraid to find out.

"What're you doing over here all alone?" Montana said. Her sombrero was pushed back on her head.

"It all seems so much more final when Mike and Brian start telling stories about what we've done. And they've only been in the band for a year. After this, it's all memories. Just another phase in our lives."

"It doesn't have to be that way."

"Right now it feels like it does."

I knew where this was headed and wanted to avoid it. We'd been fencing about my decision to quit and go to law school since I'd applied in January. Montana said I was wimping out and sucking up to Mom and Dad. Which is not how I saw it. She said I hadn't given my music career nearly enough time to develop into something. How long did you have to stick with it before the decision to quit wasn't considered wimping out or sucking up? I'd been in Cowboy Angst for six years. Did the first five not count because I'd been in college? How long, Montana? Seven years? Ten? When you turned thirty? Hank Williams was dead by twenty-nine. Stevie Wonder was eighteen years into his career by thirty.

"You don't have to go."

"I want to go."

"I don't believe it. If you really wanted to go, you'd be sitting with the guys right now talking about all the great times you've had in the last six years. You wouldn't mind looking at it as a phase because you'd be ready to go on to the next one. Like they are. Mike's going to vet school, Brian's going to grad school, Gavin's going to preach the insulation benefits of wall-to-wall carpeting."

"What an awful job."

"What do you call being a lawyer?"

"Noble. Well-paying."

"You're full of shit."

"Ray said the same thing."

"Don't go, Den. You'll hate it."

"It's in my blood."

"Bullshit."

"I'll represent you when you become a big country star and your two-timing, whiskey-addict cowboy-husband demands a divorce for neglect because you're always on the road. He'll ask for half your annual income, the six-thousand-acre ranch and four of your seven Cadillacs. I'll fly down to Austin from Montana and tell him that I won't allow my close friend and favorite client to be treated in such an underhanded, despicable manner. And that when I finish with him he'll be lucky to get out with his embroidered boxer shorts and fuchsia-tinted boots. Because that, my dear, is the kind of attorney I'll be. Vicious, savvy."

"I'd rather have you as my drummer than my lawyer."

"That kind of talk will get you nowhere. You're supposed to tell me to study hard but always take time to smell the roses."

"What I'd like to do is kick your ass, but I'm not sure it would do any good," Montana said, putting her face close enough that I could feel her breath.

She had full lips that looked swollen, the upper lip tapering in the center to form two halves. I wanted to kiss her. Tilt my head and kiss her hard. Did I want to do this so badly because I knew she was going to Austin and nothing could come of it? I had a habit of pursuing women who were already involved with someone else or were about to move far away. At parties I could, without asking for a show of ring fingers or itineraries, pick out every fiancée and Peace Corps volunteer headed for Gambia or Gabon. But lately I'd started to realize I wasn't doing anyone any good behaving like this.

"What are we going to do about us?" Montana said.

"I don't know."

Whenitwastimeforthefinalset,wehuddledonstageto decide what to play. Montana wanted to play as hard as we knew how. Brian said he still thought Ray might give us a bonus if we played enough slow songs. Gavin agreed. Mike and I wanted to ease into it for the first twenty minutes and then cook for the last forty.

We played "Waltz across Texas" and "Tennessee Waltz." I watched couples speak to one another's ears as they whirled around the floor. Single men appeared from the shadowy peripheries of the courtyard and took women in their arms. I imagined all the lines that were being whispered, the plans that were being hatched.

Mike said, "We're going to play a song made famous by Jimmy Swaggart's first cousin."

We kicked into "Great Balls of Fire" and were off and running.

I was euphoric. I was playing with my right hand on the bell of the ride cymbal, left hand on the snare, right foot working the bass drum pedal on the downbeats, left foot working the hi-hat pedal on the offbeats. It was so ridiculously easy, so wholly natural and innate, so joyful and freeing that I couldn't imagine why everyone couldn't play the drums. You didn't even have to think. Your hands and feet did everything for you without being told. Two rim shots, a flurry of sixteen notes on the tom-toms, crash cymbal, ha!

We tore through one song after another and I was oblivious to everything but the band. I watched Gavin's lips puckering wildly, Brian bending low over his pedal steel, Montana holding her guitar high on her heart with her left arm extended, twisting on the balls of her feet, Mike tilting his head back as he played. On the final song, Montana and Mike sang a duet and afterward I whipped my sticks into the air, watching them float end over end and drop into the crowd. I came out from behind my drums and joined the others on the edge of the stage. We had our arms around one another and bowed in unison as the crowd gave us a rousing ovation. A series of floodlights were thrown on, and with their glare returned a sense of reality that had been suspended for a few hours. People squinted and checked their watches, made arrangements for rides home, patted their bodies for paper and pen to jot down phone numbers, searched for coats and purses and began to file out.

"Well, that was fun," Gavin said as the courtyard was emptying.

No one knew what to say. We looked lost, confused, as though we'd wandered on stage by mistake.

"Let's pack up," Montana said.

I dismantled my kit, packed it in cases and put it in the back of the Angstmobile, my orange VW van, then went inside and found Ray at the bar counting receipts.

"Big night, Dennis," Ray said, glancing over at me.

"I win the bet?"

"Too early to say." He unzipped a canvas money pouch and counted out $625. "There you go, kid. Best of luck at law school."

"Thanks." We shook hands and I turned to leave.

"Wait, I almost forgot," Ray said, standing up on the brass foot rail and flopping over the counter. "Here you go." He handed me five White Owl cigars. "A bonus for the band."

"They're going to love these, Ray."

In the parking lot I gave everyone $125 and paused before saying, "There's a small bonus, too."

"I *knew* it," Brian said. "I love Ray. I love you, Ray!"

I handed out the cigars.

"This is it?" Brian said. "*This* is the thanks we get for giving Ray the best night of the year? Let's torch the place."

Montana climbed in the Angstmobile and we drove the thirty-one miles down Poudre Canyon to Fort Collins. At the house I stood in the kitchen drinking a beer as she showered.

When it was my turn, I showered and shaved before the fog-smeared mirror. I was six feet tall and weighed 165 pounds, one of those tall, thin musicians with long hair and pale skin whom people immediately suspect of a serious drug habit. What are you going to do? I asked the face. I'm not going to do anything. It's all up to her.

I carried a six-pack of beer into the bedroom and found Montana sitting up in bed wearing one of my white T-shirts, her limbs tanned and mysterious. I could see the ruby tip of her cigar glowing in the dark.

"A little night music, *monsieur?*"

"*Oui-oui, mademoiselle.*" I passed over Marvin Gaye and

Percy Sledge as too . . . romantic and settled on Roy Orbison. Roy began to sing "Crying" and I said, "Dance?"

"Love to," Montana said, turning back the sheet and swinging her legs out onto the floor. Her T-shirt ended an inch below the top of her thighs and gave the illusion of underlying nakedness. I began to seriously doubt my ability to stay in control.

We slow-danced in the center of the room. I held my hands low on her back. Montana's arms were coiled around my bare shoulders, one hand holding her cigar. Roy Orbison was singing "Dream Baby."

"How many times have you done this?" she whispered.

"What?"

"Brought a woman home and played Roy."

"Never. You're the only woman I know who likes him. Little too *doo-wah* for the ladies."

Montana rested her head against my neck and shoulder, her hair damp and cool against my skin. When she spoke again I could feel the vibrations of her throat against my collarbone. "Dennis?"

"Yeah?"

"Why do you think we were never lovers?"

"I don't know." I really didn't.

"Did you ever think about it?"

"Oh yeah."

"When?"

"Tonight when we were standing by the fence and you leaned close to say you wanted to kick my ass. I wanted to kiss yours."

Montana laughed. "Why didn't you?"

"I was too busy debating whether or not it was a good idea."

"You decided it wasn't?"

"No, I ran out of time."

"Why wouldn't it be a good idea?"

"I'm not a cowboy and I've got a lousy track record with women."

"You really believe I only date cowboys?"

"Judging by what I've seen."

"Well, you're wrong."

"Okay."

"You think I'd let you slip away like you have with all those other girls?"

"I'm not sure it's a matter of letting."

"Wouldn't happen with me."

"I'd love to believe that."

"Come to Austin with me and find out."

It had come back to this.

"You decide," Montana said. "I'm going to sleep." She kissed me on the cheek, snuffed out her cigar and climbed into bed.

I turned off the stereo and sat in bed with my back against the wall. I opened a beer. Montana lay on her stomach with her face turned away from me. I couldn't tell if she was asleep. Probably she was. She was convinced she was right and I was wrong, and she'd sleep like a brick while I sat by and got quietly smashed. What a rich, fulfilling life I led. Drinking in bed next to a beautiful woman I was afraid to lay a hand on for fear I'd fuck up our friendship.

I was avoiding the real issue and knew it. Goddamnit, why did this alluring possibility have to spring up at the last moment? I already had enough doubts about my decision to go to law school without this. I'd known Montana for five years and tonight was the first time she'd ever asked me why we'd never become lovers. Why now? Why not last September when I was studing for the LSAT or in January when I was mailing my applications? Say I went to Austin with Montana and we became lovers. Boyfriend and girlfriend. A couple. What if it didn't work out? That could happen. What if it not only didn't work out, but we actually started to dislike one another? How would that affect us musically? Would that disintegrate too? Then where would I be? A drummer who couldn't sing in a city I didn't know. But if I didn't go with Montana, would I lose her forever?

My decision to go to law school had gained so much momentum that I was being swept along by its force, unable to stop it even if I wanted to. Weary and depressed, I watched the morning light creep up the lawn until it filtered through the bedroom window. The paperboy coasted by on his ten-speed and whipped a rolled newspaper at the neighbor's front porch with the accuracy of a blind man. Seconds later I heard my paper hit the side of the house. I hoped that I was more on target. But I had no conviction that I was.

That afternoon I said good-bye to Montana.

Two

I flew home from Washington, D.C., on the last day of May, a liar and a failure. The closer I drew to Prairie View, the clearer this became.

Two weeks into the second semester of law school, I had suddenly dropped out. Then waited a day, a week, a month, to tell anyone in my family. The longer I waited, the harder it became and the more lies I had to tell until five months had now passed and I was headed home, afraid of a hero's welcome.

There was a brief stop in Bozeman where most of the passengers wearing boots and hats got off. A very short while later we landed in Prairie View. I let everyone else go ahead. The flight attendant at the cabin door asked if I was okay. I nodded and walked solemnly up the ramp and into the terminal, scanning the crowd for my parents. A dozen red and silver balloons floated ahead of me and a makeshift banner I couldn't read was taped to the wall. I felt self-conscious and edgy, not sure I could go through with this. I breathed a little easier after I read the banner:

WELCOME HOME TO PRAIRIE VIEW!!
WENDY & JIMMY
WE LOVE YOU TWO!!!

Wendy was hugging someone and sobbing while Jimmy shook an older man's hand and scuffed the floor with his boot tip, chin down in embarrassment.

I passed through the crowd without spotting my parents, turning in a circle and wondering if they'd forgotten I was arriving today.

"McCance!"

I flinched and turned to see my brother push away from the wall he'd been leaning against and move toward me. Miles was wearing his deputy sheriff uniform and obligatory dark aviator sunglasses. He was two inches shorter than me but built like the 180-pound judo master he was, trained to break bricks and bones with all parts of his body. He had a Fu Manchu that made him look like a forlorn cattle rustler, and he was wearing a holstered .45 that tapped rhythmically against his right thigh as he walked. I had a moment of panic wondering what he was doing here. Had he, somehow, discovered I'd dropped out? I told myself there was no way he could know, but I didn't believe it.

"What are you doing here?" I said, a note of fear in my voice that I was sure he'd pick up on. We didn't shake hands, simply headed for the escalator.

"Mom and Dad are busy and Anne's at the dentist."

"Anne's home?"

"She drove into town last night. Hurry up and get your stuff. I'm still on duty for another fifteen minutes." Miles walked out to his sheriff's car with the white star on the door, parked extralegally out front.

When my duffel bags appeared on the carousel, I lugged them out to the car while Miles sat and watched. I opened the passenger door and said, "Do you want me in back with my bags or should I sit up front?"

"Just get in the goddamn car, Dennis."

There was a radar mounted on the dashboard. Out on the road its glowing red numbers climbed rapidly as it tracked an oncoming car at forty-seven miles per hour, then dropped off as the driver hit the brakes. As we passed, the violator looked down in guilty supplication. The road curved away from the airport and I looked south across the sprawling prairie to the majestic sweep of the Little Belt Mountains, the dark timbered sides gun-metal blue in the late afternoon sunlight, the crests still white with snow.

As the interstate descended, Prairie View was off to our right, richly green from a winter of heavy snows that had fallen and melted up until mid-May. Houses stepped down Airport Hill in a series of tiers and fanned out across the river floor to the tilting cottonwoods along the banks of the Missouri, quietly winding its way through the center of town. The original town site began on the opposite bank. Thousands of elm and pine trees formed a green canopy that stretched to the city's eastern limits. Beyond lay the prairie, covered in thick geometric blocks of brown and green grain fields that flowed away from Prairie View in all directions over rolling hills that ran unimpeded to Canada but in every other direction were soon halted by mountains. To the east were the Highwoods, their bald spots still coated in snow, long flat clouds anchored above them.

Miles's silence was making me nervous. He seemed to be waiting for me to say something. Maybe he was expecting me to tell him how happy I was to have finals over. Or rub it in that I was in law school while he was pulling over drivers with broken taillights. If I didn't say anything he'd suspect something was wrong. Nothing would make him happier than discovering I'd not only dropped out but lied about it.

"How's the patrol business?" I finally said.

"Fine." Miles looked straight ahead, hands at ten and two, ever vigilant.

"Better than being the jailer?" All new deputies had to serve as jailer during their first year. Twelve months watching bored criminals and empty hallways on a wall of black-and-white TVs. After that you could remain a jailer or go on patrol. Miles had been on patrol for a little over four months.

"Different."

"Different," I said, thinking Miles was a little different. Putting a guy who was full of bottled-up rage in a car all day with the express purpose of arresting people seemed like an unhealthy idea to me. Then again, the reason I found it so disturbing was knowing that Miles had once told a family friend that one of his goals as deputy was to arrest me. The friend laughed when he told me, but I failed to see what was so funny.

We passed the Big Sky Dog School, a fenced backyard where a trainer wearing a protective leather sleeve held out his forearm for a slobbering Rottweiler to attack. The animal didn't appear to need any encouragement. One yard over, a black Labrador sat sunning himself on top of his kennel, head on his paws, sleepily watching. My kind of dog.

I reached for the barrel of the shotgun angled on the middle of the seat, and Miles said, "Just sit there with your hands in your lap."

"That's quite a shotgun, Miles. What is it, a twelve-gauge pump with a ventilated barrel?"

"Bingo."

"Have you gotten to use it yet? Had any speeders who refused to pull over, so you had to shoot out a tire? Do they teach you things like that in sheriff school? Actually that probably never happens in Montana since the fine's so cheap. You know, there were people in D.C. who wouldn't believe me when I told them it's only five bucks in the daytime. They really nail you back East. Particularly Pennsylvania from what I've heard. Big fines in Pennsylvania. Hundred, hundred and fifty bucks a pop."

Miles swiveled his head toward me, eyes hidden behind his sunglasses, and I stopped. I realized I was babbling; this was our pattern whenever we were alone together. I'd start off waiting for Miles to say something, and when that failed I'd try to prompt him with one or two questions. If those didn't do the trick, and they rarely did because I never felt as though I knew what Miles cared about, I'd start jabbering away.

He turned off the interstate onto Dingfelder Avenue West, driving past anonymous cinder-block motels with signs promising HBO in every room. Faded Toronados and Lincoln Continentals were backed up to the numbered doors. Past the appliance stores and tire outlets with their tall glinting windows, the fast-food joints and service stations. We crossed the Missouri and drove beneath the railroad overpass where someone had spray-painted in black: Had enough?

When Miles pulled up to the curb of my parents' three-story blond brick house with its groomed lawn, he didn't take the car out of gear, simply turned and stared at me for a moment. "Watch your step this summer" was all he said.

"OK," I said, nodding at my cowardly reflection in Miles's sunglasses.

I climbed out, piling my bags on the boulevard. Miles drove off without so much as a honk. I carried my bags inside and dropped them in the front entryway.

The house was filled with the warm aroma of freshly baked bread and the sound of someone hammering. I found Anne in the kitchen pulverizing zwieback toast with a ballpeen hammer. Her shoulder-length auburn hair was pulled behind her ears with a navy blue ribbon, her tongue sticking out in concentration. She had a square, windburned face and narrow brown eyes like mine. She was tall and slim, dressed in faded Levi's and a red denim shirt. The sleeves were rolled above the elbows, her forearms tanned and freckled.

"Anne."

"God, you scared me, Dennis." She set the hammer down and hugged me. "Sorry about letting Miles pick you up. I made a dental appointment a couple weeks ago and forgot that's when you were coming in. How was it?"

"Not too bad."

"Sorry."

"I know you don't want to hear this, but you're starting to look like a sheep rancher."

Three years after Anne graduated from Bowdoin College, when she was working at Houghton Mifflin in Boston, she met a man named Jack Siegrist, who was two years older, an attorney in a small firm in the city specializing in environmental law. After their fourth date Anne called home, crying. "I've fallen in love with the man I'm going to marry, Mom," she said, barely able to get the words out between sobs. "That's wonderful," my mother said. "He's from Montana!" Anne wailed.

Jack Siegrist was from Grass Range, a town in central Montana of 180 people. Jack's older brother, David, had been raised to take over the family's sheep ranch, and when Jack outstripped his junior high school classmates, his parents packed him off to Exeter and then Dartmouth. Jack had reassured Anne that he had no desire to live in Montana, let alone Grass Range; he considered himself an easterner who had mistakenly been born in Montana. They were married in Boston six months after their first date and rented a narrow yellow walk-up in Cambridge. Boston was the only place to live, Anne said.

Three years later, David, who'd taken over the ranch after the elder Siegrists retired to Arizona, was killed in a hunting accident. On the final day of deer season, David still hadn't filled his tag yet; he climbed a pine tree, either to spot deer or for the element of surprise, no one knew which. It was believed that he dropped his rifle, which hit the ground and went off, shooting him in the leg, causing him to fall out of the tree and snap his neck.

Mr. and Mrs. Siegrist had grown attached to their life of late mornings, hot weather and next-door neighbors, and they asked Jack to take over temporarily. He told them it wasn't possible. Life for him and Anne was centered in Boston; he knew next to nothing about sheep. Mr. Siegrist said if Jack wouldn't run it, they would have to sell a five-hundred-acre ranch that had been in the family for three generations. An immeasurable amount of Siegrist toil had gone into making it what it was today, but, if that didn't mean anything to Jack, one of the neighbors would snap it up. Jack knuckled under.

"It's all temporary, Anne," Jack had said. "My parents are in shock about what's happened. They don't trust anyone outside of the family to run the place. God only knows why they'd trust me, as little as I know, but what can I do? It's only until we can find someone else to run the place. I swear. I don't want to live in the West any more than you do."

Anne had called home for support. My parents had a good laugh on a daughter who'd sworn off Montana by age sixteen.

Anne finally relented when Jack promised that within a year they would find someone to lease the ranch and they would return to Boston. They'd been in Grass Range for eight months now.

"Have you found anyone to take over yet?" I said.

Freshly baked loaves of bread sat on wire cooling racks, sending up heat waves. Stainless steel cookware hung from handles overhead. I noticed my mother had taped my first semester report card to the refrigerator, the 3.2 grade point average circled in red ink. "What are you making?"

"Cheesecake," Anne said, mixing the crushed zwieback with sugar, cinnamon and melted butter. "Jack's still trying to work out a deal with the rancher to the east of us. His parents have said they'll split the lease money fifty-fifty with us, which will be a nice source of income. And Miles says if this deal falls through, he knows a couple people who might be interested."

Before he quit to become a deputy sheriff, Miles had been working as a hired hand on a cattle ranch near McLeod, between Livingston and Big Timber. It was only after he'd grown tired of taking orders and realized he'd never be able to afford his own ranch that he'd moved back to Prairie View and joined the Sheriff's Department. Around the same time he'd also taken the LSAT, thinking if he did well he might go to law school at Missoula, an idea my parents fully supported. They offered to pay his tuition, but his scores had been dismally low and the idea had been quietly dropped. My mother had always referred to Miles's ranch job as "playing cowboy," and she'd told me she thought being a deputy was only more of the same. (She didn't say this to my father, whose own father had been a cop in Helena for twenty-five years.)

"Now tell me about law school," Anne said. "Did you get the care package I sent? I thought you'd need a boost during finals."

"That was great. Thank you." She'd sent two dozen chocolate chip cookies, a pound of gourmet coffee and packets of black tea. I'd given it all to my housemates, unable even to look at these treats without feeling guilty.

I'd never intended to lie to Anne, but when she called shortly after I'd dropped out and asked how school was going, I realized I couldn't tell her the truth without also telling everyone else in the family. It wouldn't be fair to burden her with a secret, and she'd pressure me to tell my parents. Even if she didn't, sooner or later my mother would discover that Anne had known all along and not said anything, and my mother would never forgive her. So I had lied and said school was okay. Later whenever we talked on the phone I tried to steer the conversation away from law school or gave vague replies. Lying to her had been easier on the phone, when I couldn't see her face. Now that I was home I realized what a terrible mistake I'd made and how betrayed she was going to feel when I told her the truth.

I looked out the window above the sink and saw the automatic sprinkler system kick on, shooting long graceful arcs of water from strategic locations in the lawn.

Looking at the lawn, I realized the tree that used to stand in the center of the yard, ruining what would have been the neighborhood's finest football field, was now only a dark circle of earth.

"What happened to the oak tree?" I said, turning to Anne.

"It was hit by lightning and died, so Dad had someone take it out."

I looked out the window again, then did a lazy drumroll on the wooden counter. "I'm going to play my drums for a while."

"You haven't told me how finals went."

"Too early to say," I said, feeling cryptic. I'd never meant to lie to her.

"Are you all right?"

"Yeah." My mood was spiraling downward, a drizzly precursor to the bottom dropping out. I was hoping to fend it off with my drums.

"I want to hear all about it while I'm here."

"You will," I said, moving toward the hallway.

"Welcome home."

I had the third floor entirely to myself, two large rooms on either side of the stairway with angled ceilings that caused people to gravitate to their centers. My bedroom was on the south side of the house. Across the hall was the designated Music Room where I kept my drums and stereo. My mother had had an electrician install a light in the Music Room that could be flipped on and off from the kitchen, indicating lunch, dinner, phone call, visitor, Anne playing a joke. It saved on leg wear.

I dumped my bags in the bedroom and went to the Music Room. I'd shipped my stereo home the week before so it would be here when I arrived. It was now sitting in heavily taped boxes on the floor. My drums were in hard round carrying cases, stacked in a corner.

Five months earlier I'd played a New Year's Eve gig at the Knights of Columbus Hall with the Cloverleafs, a local band I'd been in since high school. During one of the breaks that night, I'd been accosted by a comely blonde in her forties wearing a white John B. Stetson hat. She drunkenly told me that for a drummer in a country band, I sure as hell didn't dress like one. I was wearing a khaki Boy Scout shirt, washed-out Levi's and Adidas tennis shoes. I'd heard this complaint before and was tired of explaining that I thought most snap-button shirts were tacky and cowboy boots impossible to play in. I'd learned to simply agree that my cowboy attire was sorely lacking.

"Personally I think you're kinda cute," the woman said thickly. She was sinewy, like someone who has spent hours bucking hay or splitting wood.

"Well, thank you, ma'am." Slipping into my aw-shucks politesse. I'd seen her dancing with her husband.

"Actually I think you're real cute," she said, sliding a hand along my right thigh and giving it a thoughtful squeeze. "And I see you've got nice strong legs."

"Like them?"

"You know it," she said, looking me straight in the eye.

Women became aggressive much too late in life. Unfortunately, the last time I'd slipped outside with a woman in Montana, an unhappy boyfriend materialized and would have thrashed me if his girlfriend hadn't intervened. I was also trying to be faithful to a local girl named Susan Hall, whom I fell for whenever we were both in town.

"Well . . . ," fishing for her name and eyeballing the crowd for a charging husband.

"Cheryl."

". . . Cheryl, I'd love to buy you a drink and chat, but it's about time to start the next set. Maybe at the next break." I stood to make my escape. Cheryl stepped into me and grabbed my crotch.

"Ooops," she said, staring up from under the shadow of her brim.

"Watch those hands," I said, trying to grin. Where was hubby? She let go and I slipped into the crowd and back to the sanctuary of my drums.

Throughout the next set, Cheryl made eyes at me over her husband's shoulders. I didn't know where to look. At the break I asked the lead singer, Patti, to bring me a glass of water.

I was sitting on the floor against the wall when I found myself looking at a pair of polished horned-back lizard boots. I glanced up and was momentarily blinded by the stage lights. When the spots cleared from my vision, I saw Cheryl's husband, a small, wiry man in his mid-forties wearing a matching white Stetson.

"I don't know who the fuck you think you are, kid, but if I catch you lookin' at my old lady one more time, you're gonna be takin' a dirt-nap. I'll walk right out to the pickup and get the two-seventy and that'll be it. Ya know what I'm sayin'?"

"Yes, I do," I said, picturing the customary gun rack with an assortment of rifles to choose from.

"Good, 'cause I'm gonna be watchin' you from now on."

"I understand," I said. My foot was shaking double-four time.

I played the next set staring at my drum pedal and drove home on a circuitous route of alleys and side streets that would have baffled even the most gifted FBI agent.

The next afternoon I flew back to D.C., believing I was looking forward to the second semester of law school. Now that only looked like relief at getting out of Prairie View alive.

I slit open the taped stereo boxes with a letter opener, Styrofoam popcorn billowing out onto the hardwood floor, and set up the stereo and speakers facing away from the east wall, a favor to the next-door neighbors, Mr. and Mrs. Peppenger.

I pulled out the largest black case from the stack, removed its lid and lifted out the bass drum. The Ludwig logo was printed in black across the top of the taut white head. Below it were two pieces of white construction paper taped over the center. The leader of the Cloverleafs, George Muzzana, always requested that I cover the black letters that said Cowboy Angst.

George had introduced me to country music. I'd tried to join a garage band, Skank Patrol, my sophomore year of high school, but my parents told me I was too busy with symphonic band, jazz band, cross country and homework. When George called one day and said his country band, the Cloverleafs, needed a drummer, they decided I wasn't too busy. George was forty-six and said he would be personally responsible for my welfare. I told them the only reason they were letting me play in this band and not Skank Patrol was because of Mr. Muzzana. It had nothing to do with how busy I was.

"Exactly, Dennis," my father said. "Now do you want to play with the man or not?"

"Of course."

"You have our blessing," he said. "Bang away."

I'd played well enough during the first gig that George asked me to join permanently, so I'd drummed for the Cloverleafs throughout high school and whenever I was home from college, playing in small towns like Dutton, Fairfield, Fort Shaw.

As for looking after my welfare, George had immediately taken me aside and said, "You buy your own beer, and if you get busted, I know nothing about it. You get shitcanned by some cowboy whose girlfriend gave you a hummer, I know nothing about it. Thrown in jail, same deal. Got it, cowboy?"

George drove us to the gigs in a dented gray Suburban he'd bought from his employer, the phone company. He was a serious drinker, which made the return trips an adventure, and two wrecks during my junior year of high school finally put an end to his chauffeuring. One Saturday night in Sand Coulee he drove through a thirty-yard stretch of someone's white picket fence that cost fourteen dollars a foot to replace; the following Saturday outside Belt he drove through the guardrail of a small bridge into a dry creek bed. Patti, his daughter and my classmate, who sang and played keyboard, was knocked unconscious by the corner of her father's steel guitar case. I loosened my front two teeth when I slammed into the metal back of the passenger seat. The county charged George a thousand dollars. At the next gig he passed a cowboy hat after each set asking for donations to help replace the rail. He turned over the keys to me because I never drank while playing; my sense of timing grew exponentially worse with each drink.

I took my time setting up my drums. I hadn't touched them in five months, and I was enjoying the process of assembling a well-known instrument: pulling out the thin metal legs from the belly of the bass drum, a feather pillow resting inside to deepen its sound; clamping the drum pedal to the chipped wooden rim of the bass, the hard white cotton beater gray from thousands of thumpings; slipping the two black tom-toms onto the angled U-shaped post in the center of the bass drum; extending the three storklike legs of the floor tom; resting on its stand the silver snare drum with the center of its white head a filmy gray where countless strokes had beaten away the outer coating; putting the dull gold cymbals with their circular ridges like a tree's growth rings onto their telescoping metal tripods through the hole in the middle of their cupped bells; and adjusting all of it here and there until, sitting on the small cushioned stool, I had it just right.

I grabbed a pair of wooden sticks with nylon tips and began stroking each drum slowly, listening to its sound and feeling the vibrations through my hands, stopping to tighten loose heads with a small metal key, then playing louder and faster.

"I'm back, baby," I said, stroking each drum. "I'm back. I went away but now I'm back. I'll never leave you again, I swear."

I put on the Allman Brother's *Live at Fillmore East,* turned up the volume considerably and returned to the stool. Waiting for the band to be announced, I played a crescendo roll on the floor tom and yelled, "Mr. and Mrs. Peppenger, I'm home!"

An hour and a half later when the light from the kitchen flashed on and off, on and off (Anne!), I had a blood blister the size of a dime on the inside of my left thumb, two blisters on the middle fingers of both hands, pain in my right wrist from keeping time on the ride cymbals, and sore groin muscles from working the hi-hat and bass drum pedals. It was wonderful. Absolutely wonderful. Ninety minutes of rhythmic violence crashing cymbals and pounding heads.

And then I remembered where I was. My anxiety immediately returned. My stomach pitched and rolled. I went into the bathroom and splashed cold water on my face hoping to make myself look eager and alert. Instead I saw the sullen face of a liar. If I went downstairs looking like this, my parents would know something was wrong. I tried smiling; it resembled a grimace. You can't look sullen, I told the face. You look sullen and they're going to nail you.

I bandaged my fingers and walked downstairs. It was after six, sunlight flooding through the large stained glass window above the second floor landing. My mother was waiting for me at the foot of the stairs.

"There he is," she said, squinting up into the sunlight at me.

My mother had the wide strong face that all three children had inherited, cool blue eyes and crow's feet, and she wore her hair short and off her face in a style that suggested she didn't want to waste excess time on it. She was fifty-seven, but looked forty-eight, tops.

"Hi, Mom."

"You look good, Dennis. Even shaved and got your hair trimmed. I'm impressed."

She hugged me.

"How was school?" she said, walking next to me toward the dining room, right hand resting lightly on the small of my back as if guiding me.

"OK." Once you began, there was no end to these lies.

"Do you think it went as well as last semester?"

"Hard to say." We were standing in the dining room, the table set with the fine china last used at the hometown wedding reception for Anne and Jack, and I was relieved that I didn't have to look at her when I spoke.

Anne came through the swinging door from the kitchen carrying a salad. "Sounded good, Dennis."

"Very rusty." I held up my bandaged fingers to her. Then pointed at the table. "What's the occasion?"

"The end of your first year," Anne said, striking a match to light the two centerpiece candles. "Let me grab everyone else and we'll be set."

She disappeared into the kitchen and a moment later burst through the door backward and pivoted, carrying a large bowl of steaming pasta. Miles walked in, followed by my father carrying a bottle of wine. They were similarly built and looking at them together was like time-lapse photography, showing the young man at thirty-one and later at fifty-eight.

My father had narrow, scrutinizing brown eyes and thinning gray hair with a bald spot that would have been hidden had he been Jewish and worn a yarmulke. He'd fallen out of shape in the last few years, thickening dramatically around the middle, which alarmed my mother, but you could still detect a certain power and quickness in his arms and shoulders that hinted at his past as a scrappy street fighter.

My two uncles had told me stories of how my father had learned to box in the Helena parochial schools where he'd been an Irish Catholic punk and A student with an explosive temper who liked to mouth off to the Brothers. Discipline was after-school boxing matches in the gym with the Brothers wearing twenty-ounce gloves. My father'd had the choice of either shutting his mouth or learning to fight. He chose the latter and achieved legendary status as a senior when he became the first student in Saint Joseph's history to KO a Brother. He was drafted two weeks after graduation and sent to Fort Sill, near Lawton, Oklahoma, for four months of training. Afterward he was shipped to Korea and spent ten months in an artillery battery firing a 155-millimeter howitzer. When he was discharged after fourteen months, he enrolled at Gonzaga University in Spokane on the GI Bill. He continued getting in scrapes, displaying a talent for convincing cops that he hadn't been at fault, that he'd only been defending himself. Whenever the topic of his fighting came up, he liked to point out that he'd never once been arrested or spent a night in jail.

By the time he entered law school at the University of Montana, the fighting had tapered off. He was older, less volatile. And he was dating my mother, who wouldn't put up with it. Not that he was beyond an occasional relapse. Last year he'd had a heated courtroom confrontation with a local attorney named Frank Ronan, who suggested that my father had instructed his client to perjure himself. Afterward in the courthouse hallway my father backed Ronan up against a wall and said if he ever said something like that again, my father would throw him down the elevator shaft. Ronan was sufficiently rattled to yell for the bailiff.

"Well, how did finals go?" my father said, gripping my hand.

"I don't know," I said, turning toward the kitchen door as it swung open to avoid meeting his eyes.

Jack walked in and shook my hand. He was tall and had the broad shoulders and narrow hips of a rower from his days as the five seat on Dartmouth's heavyweight eight. His black hair, cut short, was shot through with more gray than I'd remembered seeing at Christmas.

"Grace?" my father said when we were seated. We bowed our heads while he recited it. I glanced up before he finished and found Miles watching me, studying my face, and I had a nauseating feeling that he knew, had known the moment he saw me at the airport. I looked down at my plate.

After my father finished, he filled everyone's wineglass and then raised his own. "To Dennis and the successful completion of his first year of law school." He looked at me. "You're through the toughest part now."

"Yeah?" I could feel Miles's eyes on me, and I knew I either had to buck up or announce right now that I'd been lying to all of them for the past five months.

"You'll discover it gets much easier after this. Right, Jack?"

"Much easier," Jack said, making a face of mock horror.

"I hardly had to study at all after the first year, did I, Helen?" my father continued.

"Hardly at all," my mother said, dryly. "Miles, why don't you pass the bread. Anne made it this afternoon."

"You sure look well rested for someone who just finished finals," Miles said.

"I slept on the plane," I said, shoveling noodles into my mouth and losing a piece of bacon. Maybe if I kept my mouth full, the conversation would turn to something besides me.

"I was always well-rested when I came home after finals," Anne said.

"Sure, you slept ten hours a day during your entire break," said my mother.

"Have you given any more thought to my offer?" my father said. He'd called me in early May and said if I didn't have anything else lined up for the summer, he'd be happy to put me to work at the firm doing research. "I spoke with the other partners and they all said they have work they could give you."

"Why didn't you get a law clerk job in D.C.?"

"Miles, only idiots and interns stay in D.C. over the summer," I said. That was a mistake. I didn't need him pissed off at me right now. But I refused to let him tell me what I should be doing. He couldn't even get *into* law school.

"So why aren't you there?"

I ignored him and speared a carrot on my plate.

"Dennis?"

I looked over at my mother.

"Your father said you could work at the firm if you'd like."

"I know. Thank you."

She leveled her clear blue eyes on me.

"Take a few days off and decide what you want to do," my father said. "It's your decision. I know we could find plenty of work for you, and I guarantee it'll be more stimulating than walking in the country all day killing weeds."

"You're beyond that now," my mother said.

I was home.

Three

They wanted you to quit. They overloaded you with information, reading assignments, nomenclature, then called on you at random to stand up and recite it. Women cried in the hallways before and after class. Men cursed under their breath, clenched their fists, kicked lockers. The woman who sat next to me in Contracts didn't return after the first week. The man who sat in front of me in Torts quit after the second week. They left quietly, telling no one. Their names were struck from the roster, their seats sat empty. I looked around and wondered who was next.

During the first month of classes I always felt on the verge of throwing up. My stomach was nervous the entire semester. I was in constant fear that I wasn't going to make it, that I would be called on in class and not know the answer, that I was falling behind and would never catch up, that I wasn't studying enough, that everyone else was studying more.

My father called once a week from the office to ask what I was learning, launching into arcane explanations whenever my an-

swers sounded muddled or obtuse; explanations that illumi-
nated nothing. My mother always asked if I liked it, a question
that seemed irrelevant. It wasn't a matter of liking or disliking it.
No one liked law school; it was something you had to get
through in order to become an attorney. It was a question of
survival and determination. They wanted you to quit, and you
didn't want to give them the satisfaction.

There were no midterms on which to gauge your progress,
only final exams in December, and I was afraid I might be
fooling myself about how much information I was retaining,
that only in December would I discover how little I understood.
I devised a strict routine that I followed religiously, concerned
that if I strayed from it once, I'd never return to it. I kept track of
the number of hours I studied every day, adding them up on
Sunday and trying to study more each week, posting the totals
on my library carrel: forty-nine hours, fifty-three hours, fifty-five
hours. The numbers reassured me; they were proof that I was
doing everything I could to survive, that if I didn't pass, it wasn't
from a lack of effort or self-discipline. The week before finals I
topped out at seventy-one hours.

My first exam was in Contracts. There was a separate room
for those of us who wanted to type our exam and we filed in on
Monday morning, silent and ashen. The monitor handed out
the test and told us to begin. I was just starting to read the
second paragraph when the person sitting next to me began
typing at a blistering rate. My entire body broke out in a sweat.
After all those hours in the library I knew I was going to flunk. I
ran out of the room and threw up in the bathroom. I kneeled in
front of the toilet for several minutes, panting, and finally
thought, This is crazy. You've never been more prepared in your
life. Don't fuck up now. I returned to the room, which was
humming and clacking like a secretarial college. The monitor
met me halfway to my seat and said, 'Where do you think *you*

went?' '*I* went and threw up.' After that I was calm. I figured it couldn't get any worse.

I flew home for Christmas, exhausted. My parents kept assuring me that the first semester was the roughest. Grades weren't important. The important thing was just to get through it. If I got through this, the rest would be easy. I wasn't sure if they were preparing themselves or me for the worst.

I returned to school and approached the wailing wall with two classmates; we fell silent as we drew closer, moving mechanically like soldiers about to be executed. The grades were listed by social security number. No one touched the wall. I found my number and scanned across the page. I was listed as having received one A and four B's. I stepped closer, checked to make sure I had the right number and followed it across: one A, four B's. No one had spoken. We turned to leave, afraid to look at one another. Walking outside I said I needed to use the bathroom and would catch up with them. I ran back upstairs and traced my finger across the page to confirm it: one A, four B's. I expected to feel elated, triumphant. But my only thought was that now I would have to keep going.

When I called home with the news, my mother's voice grew faint, then shot back in a high-pitched tremolo. My father spoke with more raw excitement than I'd ever heard him use with me. They kept telling me how wonderful this was, how proud they were of me. "You're going to be an attorney, Dennis!" my mother cried, as if believing it for the first time. I suddenly realized how little they'd thought of what I'd been doing before and how much it meant to them that I succeed. Instead of being pleased I resented how happy and excited this made them.

I wanted to say something that would snap them back a little, tell them I'd joined a band and was going to be playing gigs on the weekends. I was sorry I'd done so well because from now on just getting through would never be enough. The first day back in class my Torts professor fired a question at me. I had no idea what the answer was. I stood up and said, "Pass," the first time I'd ever had to do that. I went to the library in the afternoon to begin studying but kept finding reasons to get up. I went to the bathroom, visited with classmates, got a book from my locker. After the third trip I told myself I couldn't leave my seat for the next hour. I didn't have to study, but I couldn't do anything else.

I struggled to immerse myself in my old routine, feeling like I was slipping into a harness. On Thursday I stared at the column of numbers posted on my carrel. Out of curiosity I added them up, then worked out the daily and weekly average for the semester, followed by the total number of hours I would spend studying over the next two and a half years. I looked at the figures and began to see how I would spend the rest of my life. I would study seven hours a day for the next two and a half years and spend at least eight hours a day in the summers doing legwork and research as an associate for a law firm. Once I graduated I'd immediately start studying for the bar, then spend eight to twelve hours a day doing research for as long as I practiced law, keeping strict accounts of my billable hours, down to six-minute intervals. There would be no catching up or getting out from under it; if that ever happened, it meant I didn't have enough work. My father was constantly juggling cases, moving from one to the next, taking on more clients all the time, delegating nothing, trusting no one else to do his research. The other senior partners were only going through the motions, coasting until they could retire. They kept bankers' hours, took long lunches, talked about how sick of it they were, how they'd quit tomorrow if they could afford it. They were amazed and a little shamed by my father's work ethic and his obvious enjoyment of legal practice

My father was already talking to me about joining him when I finished. He was excited about bringing me into the firm and guiding me, sharing his knowledge. And yet I could already see how I would disappoint him. It wasn't the hours I was afraid of. I'd spent years practicing my drums without ever feeling obligated to do it. Although maybe that didn't count. Maybe playing my drums wasn't the same as doing research. Maybe from now on nothing would hold my interest as strongly as drumming did. And yet my father clearly had that passion for his work. I'd seen him in the evenings half-asleep before the television, his eyes watering when he yawned, and then he would say it was time to go back to the office for two or three hours and suddenly be alert and ready to work. It would never be like that for me. I would be like his older partners, weary and full of regrets, hanging on because I didn't know what else to do or couldn't afford to quit. And my father would always be there as a reminder of my shortcomings as an attorney.

It was already dark outside, rain striking the library windows. I realized I wasn't going to make it, that I didn't want to make it. I was ready to go quietly like the others, sink from sight like a stone.

I quit going to class. I slept late, read the paper, roamed the house like a specter. My three law school housemates asked what I was doing. I said I didn't know. My study group said if I didn't start showing up, they were going to find someone else to replace me. I told them that would be a good idea. My advisor called and asked me to see her before it was too late. In her office she asked what was wrong. Why wasn't I going to class? I said I didn't want to be an attorney. She pointed out how well I'd been doing and said there was still time to salvage the semester. I said I'd think about it and thanked her for her interest.

When my father made his weekly call, I said I was having a difficult time. "But it's exciting, isn't it," he said. "You're learning a lot." I knew if I quit, these weekly talks would stop and I'd miss hearing him so eager to discuss what I was doing.

On the last possible day I dropped out of law school and received a refund check for six thousand dollars, which I deposited in my savings account. Lying in bed at night I rehearsed over and over in my head what I would say to my parents. When they finally called, I was about to break the news when my mother told Miles to pick up the phone. The moment I heard his voice on the other end, I knew I wouldn't tell them. I refused to give him the satisfaction of being able to say he knew I wouldn't last. Instead I heard myself saying that law school was fine, just fine, how were things in Prairie View?

Soon after I officially dropped out, my housemates crowded into my room late one night and stood close together to suggest solidarity. They asked how I was doing, then said they'd talked it over and decided I would have to move out. They admitted they didn't have any legal right to force me out, but they'd let me move in with the understanding that I'd be going to law school. It wasn't anything personal, they just didn't think it would work out, now that I'd quit. I said if they didn't mind, I'd like to stay through the end of the month so I could look for another place. They said sure, no problem, visibly relieved that I wasn't going to be difficult. No rush, really, although there was another law student who would be dropping off a few things next week. Before leaving they shook my hand and wished me good luck.

My days had taken on a quality of unreality, as if what I was doing was someone else's life, not my own. I found a job as a salesclerk at Olsson's Books and Records on Dupont Circle that paid $2.50 less an hour than Weed Control. Most of my coworkers were recent college graduates with no more immediate ambitions than to be able to cover their rent and go out after work. The music clerks were audiophiles with extensive CD collections who tried to stump one another with the names of producers and sound engineers on obscure recordings. They read all the music rags, knew who was in the studio or on the road. Three of them owned guitars and they were always talking about starting a band, but no one wanted to rehearse. A couple of women in the book section had large trust funds and were always threatening to quit, letting everyone else know that they didn't have to work. A group of us drank at the Fox and Hound every night after work, then drifted up to Adams Morgan, sharing cab rides home at three in the morning or going home with strangers. The next day we compared notes and hangovers, cross-referencing what we'd done, drank and said. It was the first time in over a decade that I didn't have to study or practice my drums, and I went to bed every night feeling as if I'd forgotten to do something.

After several weeks at my new job, I finally called Montana.

When I told her I'd dropped out, she asked if I was serious, then held the phone away from her and let out an Indian war whoop. "That's the best news I've heard in months." She said now I didn't have any excuse not to move down to Austin. Pause. "You are moving down here, aren't you?" I said I hadn't told my parents yet, and I also had a new job.

"You haven't told them yet?"

"No."

"Why not?"

"I don't want to disappoint them."

"How do you think they're going to feel when they find out you've been lying to them?"

"Listen, I know it's fucked up. You don't need to tell me that. OK?"

"You have to tell them, Dennis."

"Yeah, well, maybe you'd like to do it for me."

"Don't get mad at me. I didn't tell you to drop out. Although I'm happy you did."

"What am I going to do if I move down there? I haven't practiced since August and you're already in a band."

"Don't worry about that. Just tell your parents you quit and get down here. We'll worry about the rest of it later." But I couldn't bring myself to do it.

When my father couldn't reach me at home, he assumed I was spending all my time at the law library. At first I'd been afraid he'd ask me a question about law school that would make it clear I wasn't attending class, but our conversations had shifted more toward his own law school stories and discussions about what he was working on at the moment. He sent me excerpts from briefs he'd written, court transcripts and depositions. I read them closely so we could discuss them when he called. He explained what he was planning, how he was going to out-maneuver the plaintiff. I enjoyed our talks, but as soon as I hung up I was filled with self-loathing.

Winter passed. The heat and tourists arrived. Montana had quit asking me when I was going to tell my parents, but there was now a note of disappointment in her voice whenever we talked, as if I'd let her down or wasn't the person she'd thought I was. It bothered me and I quit calling her and started writing letters. In April she sent a postcard saying that in case I was interested she was no longer in a band; they'd broken up. By then the late nights and daily hangovers had begun to sour on me, but without them to fill up my spare time I was overcome with panic about what I was still doing here. I'd had to cut deeply into my savings—though I wouldn't touch the tuition money—in order to stay afloat, and it was clear that before too long I'd either need to find a better-paying job, quit drinking or go home and tell my parents the truth. I knew there was only one choice, but I wasn't sure how to do it.

Then one morning in early May my father called and offered to put me to work doing research at the firm over the summer. Unless I had something else lined up in D.C. No, I said, I didn't have anything else lined up. My father said great, we'll see you at the end of the month. At lunch I bought a plane ticket home and told my supervisor I'd be leaving in three weeks. I felt calm, clearheaded, ready to face my parents.

Now that I was home I was more afraid than ever. I got up and went to play my drums.

The Big Sky had fallen. Deep ominous clouds had collapsed on Prairie View, their soft dark underbellies almost brushing the treetops. I showered and went downstairs, my spirits raised momentarily by two hours of practicing. The large house was quiet, the tall windows letting in flat gray light.

My mother had left a note on the kitchen table reminding me to put my breakfast dishes in the dishwasher and run them. She'd been the director of the Neighborhood Housing Service since I'd been in high school. The organization helped lower-income residents upgrade their homes by supplying paint, insulation, storm windows, lumber for new fences, trees, flowers, shrubbery. Below my mother's note was one from Anne saying she'd gone to visit a friend. I rounded up breakfast and the Prairie View *Gazette*.

Hot times in the city. An unknown man wearing a large white cowboy hat had fired two shots from a pistol into the air to stop a parking-lot brawl among three men and a woman swinging a broken wine bottle. The gun-toting hero had knocked her unconscious with the butt of his pistol and driven away in a red Cadillac. Nine local high school girls, all smiling with painful sincerity and sporting Farrah Fawcett's mid-seventies hairdo, had been chosen as contestants for Miss Prairie View. In City Court, four people had pleaded guilty to driving while under the influence and been fined three hundred dollars, and five people had pleaded guilty to driving while privilege was suspended and sentenced to two to four days in the Cascade County Jail.

I wandered outside to look at the hole in the yard where the oak tree had been. When we were growing up, Miles had done all the yard work, meticulously mowing the lawn in strips that always ran lengthwise north to south. He used hand clippers around all the trees and edged the perimeters at least once every two weeks. People walking to William Dingfelder Park, named after the city's founding father, often complimented us on the yard. On Thursday nights in the summers when the municipal band performed at the park band shell, Miles would stand in the yard, armed with a garden hose and fire nozzle, shouting at anyone who tried to cross the lawn, "The sidewalk's free, the grass isn't," and spraying any cars he thought were speeding.

When I was twelve and Miles was eighteen, he said it was time for me to take over the yard. He explained in great detail how often to mow, how high or low to set the mower according to the season, how often to edge. I got off to a rocky start by saying, "It's only a lawn, Miles." He didn't see it that way. I mowed sideways east to west, purposely leaving an inch of uncut grass between every row, and only trimmed around every other tree. The following week Miles was back on the job. He kept doing it until he left for college, after which my father hired a professional lawn service to take over.

I stood and looked at the dark circle of soil where the oak tree used to tower, eighty-odd years of growth KOed by fifteen million volts. The death of the tree had come twenty years too late to be of any use for neighborhood football games, and now with it gone the west side of the house looked naked and cold. My mother would hire someone to plant a new tree, a twig compared to its predecessor, and sixty years from now, when I was eighty-five, whoever lived in the house would be able to enjoy its shade.

I suddenly had an idea. I got in the car and twenty minutes later had bought a one-inch-caliper oak sapling for $44.99, regular $54.99, which the nursery salesman had repeatedly guaranteed me was Montana-grown. He sounded like a dope dealer. I raced home in my father's Volvo and began running back and forth between the yard and the carriage house for a different shovel, more peat moss, a hose, wanting to finish before anyone else came home. When I'd planted the tree, I drove a wooden stake into the grass and ran a wire from it to the delicate trunk, afraid that one good breeze would lay it on its side. I took a few steps back, brushing the soil off my hands on the back of my pants, and began circling the tree, admiring it from every angle, occasionally stealing in to press down loose peat moss with the sole of my shoe, and then continued walking around it, pleased with this small present.

I was stretched out on the deep leather couch in the front room. I'd been reading, but judging from the cocoon of drool that had formed around my right ear I'd apparently dozed off. The room was dark and full of shadows. I saw my mother standing in the front-room doorway, a dusky figure with one hand on her hip. I realized I shouldn't be lying on the couch. Any sign of indolence now would come back to haunt me when she learned I'd dropped out.

"Productive day?" she said.

"Not overly productive, no."

She walked into the room and sat in the wing chair. She crossed her legs and draped her fingers over the ends of the chair's arms. My mother had an elegance and hauteur absorbed from her father, Patrick Quinn, who had owned a men's clothing store in Missoula for thirty-seven years. He passed himself off as a lone aristrocrat in the fashion void of Montana, and insisted his grandchildren call him Patrick because Grandpa made him feel old. He was eighty-one now and favored blue blazers and crisp gray trousers.

Everyone in the Quinn family had worked at the store, called Quinn's. My mother started out pinning shirts and pressing suits before moving onto the sales floor when she was sixteen. To this day she described men according to their clothes. Her own mother, Irene, was a small, vigorous woman who spent most of her adult life in the back of the store as the tailor. She had a keen business acumen and closely controlled the money, reining in her husband's plans to move to a larger location or open a chain of stores across the state. The store had fluctuating fortunes, and my grandmother steered her three daughters away from the business, encouraging them to go into something that offered a steady income and security. Something like teaching or nursing.

My mother received a scholarship to Gonzaga University in Spokane, where she was in the freshman class with my father, who arrived from Korea at the start of the second semester. She thought he dressed like a hick and acted like a hooligan. She refused to have anything to do with him for four years. She graduated *summa cum laude* and returned home to teach at Hellgate High School. My father started law school at Missoula that fall, quit fighting and after six months finally convinced my mother to go on a date with him. Two and a half years later she married him. For the first few years that they lived in Prairie View, my mother taught English at the public high school and was the primary breadwinner while my father struggled to get his law practice off the ground.

"What *did* you do today?" asked my mother.

"I practiced for four hours and did a little reading." I patted the book lying on my chest. "I also planted an oak tree where the old one used to be."

"Did you really?"

"Go look."

"I believe you," my mother said. "That's wonderful. Thank you, Dennis."

"You're welcome." It had been stupid to think I could make this easier by planting a tree. No gift would ever make her forgive what I'd done. It would only look like bribery.

"Have you thought about your father's offer?"

"Yes."

"We discussed it again this morning. We both think it's time you began thinking about your career. Your résumé has four years of Weed Control, Dennis. That sounds like a bad joke. Your father thinks . . ."

"Don't do that to me."

"What?"

" 'Your father thinks . . .' You always do that to me. You get an idea and you introduce it by saying, 'Your father thinks . . .' If that's what he thinks, why doesn't he tell me? I could go to him right now and say, 'Dad, Mom says you think I should work for the firm this summer,' and he'd say, 'No, you don't have to.' "

"Exactly, Dennis."

"So?"

"You don't *have* to. But he would *like* you to, and he feels it makes much more sense at age twenty-five to be doing legal research than strolling around the countryside killing weeds. This is not *my* idea. I don't need to speak for your father. It's just that it would be nice if you told your father you wanted to work for him this summer rather than him having to insist on it. Which he won't do. He would like you to ask."

"Fine." I knew I shouldn't have said anything, that this could only hurt me, but it irritated me too much to let it pass.

"Is Anne home?" my mother said pleasantly.

"No."

"It's men's night at the club and your father took Jack with him. I thought the three of us would go out to dinner."

"She just pulled up," I said, watching Anne park the ranch truck. An umbrella lay across its gun rack. She came up the front walk, disappeared from view, and in a moment reappeared in the doorway.

"Why are you sitting in the dark?" Anne asked.

"We're trying to cut down on the electric bill," my mother said.

"How was your visit?"

"Unbelievable," Anne said, bending to turn on a lamp. She sat down across the room from me. "This place never fails to amaze me."

My mother laughed through her nose.

"Remember Renee Peterson?" Anne said.

My mother nodded.

"No."

"She was one of my high school friends. Thin brunette. Big smile. Giggled all the time. We sat next to one another in band."

"Is she the one who moved her flute like she was paddling somewhere?"

"Right," Anne said. "I saw her downtown yesterday and we decided to get together for lunch. After we caught up on everyone else, Renee told me she'd been married for five years to a guy from Fairfield who sold farm chemicals. She's working as a teller at First National. About a year ago, she and her husband, Roger, weren't getting along. Renee said they hardly saw one another because he was traveling all the time with his job and then refereeing high school basketball games every weekend from September to February. She hates basketball, doesn't know a foul from a free throw. When he was home he didn't talk. She finally got him to see a marriage counselor. The counselor asked her what kind of changes she'd like to see in Roger. Renee said she wanted him to be more open with her. The counselor asked Roger the same question. He said, 'I wish she'd try caring more about basketball.' Renee moved out and filed for divorce. She got the house and ten thousand dollars. Guess what she did with the money?"

"Went to referee school," I said.

"No," Anne said. "She got breast implants."

"What?" I laughed.

"Four thousand dollars for bigger breasts."

"No way."

"I swear to God. She told me she'd always felt insecure about having small breasts, and she decided that since she had the money this was the time to do it."

"How are friends supposed to react to something like that?" I said. "This fascinates me."

"Obviously," my mother said.

"She showed them to me," Anne said.

"You have *got* to be kidding," my mother said.

"No. She wanted to know whether I thought they looked natural. She just had it done a few weeks ago, and no one's seen them yet."

"How'd they look?" I said, imagining howitzers aimed at the sky.

"Big."

"Just big?"

"They look fine, I guess. Big and firm. There's a small scar, but the doctor says it'll go away," she said.

"I'm going to open a checking account at First National tomorrow," I said.

"Say one word to Renee and I'll kill you, Dennis."

After dinner I called George Muzzana to see what he had lined up for the summer. Mrs. Muzzana told me he was in Saint Ignatius Hospital's Detox Center. He'd fallen off the stage at the Cloverleafs' last gig a month ago in Conrad, cracked three ribs and decided it was time to take the cure. She was glad I'd called. The band had a gig coming up this Saturday at Buckaroo's and

George had asked her to find out if I were home; he thought I might be working for a congressman this summer. I said I'd love to play and hoped George was all right. "If this works," Mrs. Muzzana said, "it'll be the best fall he's ever taken."

I hung up and roamed the house, restless and bored. On my third pass through the front room, Anne looked up from her book and bared her teeth. My mother didn't bother looking up from her book. "Go for a walk, Dennis. You're annoying us."

I got a jacket and my Walkman with Vivaldi's *Four Seasons*. Thick black clouds snuffed out the light of the moon. I walked by homes with their curtains and blinds drawn, yellow light leaking out around the edges. Homes with smooth dark lawns, birch and pine trees, with elms on the boulevards that had orange dots spray-painted on them, meaning they were diseased and doomed. Past the sandstone Cascade County Jail and Courthouse. Miles's stomping grounds. By Saint John's Cathedral with confession from three to four on Saturdays, a weekly opportunity to clean one's slate. Forgive me, Father, for I have sinned. By a house with a living room bathed in aqua light that made me pause, waiting expectantly for the owner to frog-kick past the window, pursued by a manta ray. A black sedan rolled silently up the street, but there were no other pedestrians, everyone having gone inside and battened down the hatches. Past an institutional green house that belonged in a Charles Addams cartoon, with a black wrought iron fence around its flat roof where the mysterious family poured cauldrons of boiling oil on the Amway salesman. I looked over my shoulder. For what? For Miles, darting from tree to tree? Olly olly oxen free, Miles. I don't want to play anymore. I'm tired of this game. I cued the violins and then stood on the sloping lawn of a large white house, transfixed by the violent splashes of light from a television screen.

On the return trip it began to snow, not unusual but still a pleasant surprise, thick wet flakes that melted as soon as they touched the sidewalk and street but lay heavily on the grass. Vivaldi's "Winter" was slowly building, and I waved my arms madly as I brought the orchestra to the peak of a crescendo and led them down, then up again. The toes of my shoes were soaked, my hair covered in snow.

Once I told my parents I'd quit, there would be no reason to stay here. If I did, I'd always be the wayward son who tried to follow in his father's footsteps and failed. I saw myself working as a salesclerk in a local record store, directing customers to the latest Garth Brooks offering. On the weekends I'd play gigs with the Cloverleafs and pick up divorced women who would ask which high school I'd attended. My parents would be embarrassed by my job and the stories that would filter back to them about my escapades; they'd apply pressure and try to direct me into a more suitable line of work, maybe something with an ad agency or an insurance company. Whatever I might do here, I'd always feel like returning was an admission of failure, a sign that I hadn't been able to make it anywhere else and now I'd returned to my hometown where my parents knew people and could make things easier. Look at Miles. That was the only reason he was here.

Miles had been an industrial arts major at Montana State and spent his summers in Bozeman framing houses. After graduating he looked for a job as a junior high or high school shop teacher in the area, but there was little turnover and he wasn't hired for the one position that was available. My parents suggested he broaden his search and offered to talk with the district administrators in Prairie View, but Miles refused to let them help; he liked living in Bozeman and he didn't want anyone pulling any strings to get him a job. He resumed framing houses, substitute teaching in the winter when there wasn't any construction. He kept his teaching credentials up-to-date and continued applying for openings, but nothing came of it. Four or five years passed. He began to suffer from lower back pain and in the mornings he couldn't make a fist for the first couple hours because his hands ached so badly from swinging a hammer all day. A doctor told him he could expect to suffer from severe arthritis if he stayed with his job much longer.

Throughout this time Miles had been riding horses with a friend who worked as a ranch hand, and when a rancher near McLeod offered Miles a job, he took it. That had lasted for three years before he began casting around for something else. When his shot at law school failed, he seemed to ratchet back his expectations. He contacted the State Highway Patrol, but they had a hiring freeze in effect. He spoke with the Gallatin County Sheriff's Department, but they had a one-year waiting list.

My father offered to talk to the sheriff in Prairie View. Miles said he didn't want my father asking anyone for any favors. My father told him to relax. All he planned to do was ask the sheriff if he had any openings. A few days later my father called Miles and said if he was interested, there was a slot. Miles asked if he'd pulled any strings. Absolutely not, my father said, although I later learned from my mother that a year ago he'd represented the sheriff in a bitter custody battle with his ex-wife over their two teenage daughters that had turned out well for the sheriff.

Shortly before Christmas Miles had loaded his belongings into his pickup truck and returned to Prairie View to become a deputy sheriff. He lived at home for the first month while he looked for an apartment, the longest period he'd spent in Prairie View since leaving for college. He was short with anyone he bumped into who asked what he was doing in town, and he stayed in his basement bedroom most of the time with the door locked, coming upstairs for meals or to walk over to the Y for judo practice. He didn't seem able to relax until a year later when he moved into the house he'd built outside of town where he could be alone and not have anyone ask what he was doing back in town.

If I stayed here, I thought, walking up to my parents' house every day would be a reminder of all that I'd failed to accomplish, all that I'd failed to achieve.

Four

Anne and I were driving to visit Miles at his house, nine miles southwest of Prairie View. It was Anne's idea. Jack had flown to Billings that morning to attend a two-day computer seminar for ranchers. He'd asked Anne to go, but she balked at spending two days learning software programs for sheep.

A little over a year ago Miles had bought a two-story log homesteader house for twenty-two hundred dollars, dismantled and hauled it to a three-acre lot he owned, then rebuilt it. The exterior was completed, the chinking in place, and now he was working on the interior, one room at a time.

We were headed south on Horse Trot Way, the road wet and humming beneath the truck tires. The sky was slate gray, the sun a white disk drained of heat. We crossed the city limits and the houses abruptly thinned out. The road dropped to the river floor, tall grass fields keeping pace on both sides of the truck, then climbed, fell and climbed again. When we crested the hill, the country opened out onto the vast expanse of prairie that rolled south until it became the smoky blue sides of the Little Belts. I opened my arms to embrace it. "Oh, I missed this."

Anne laughed and turned west onto the gravel road, clutching the wheel with both hands as the tail rattled and slid, then turned south onto Flood Road. On our right, pale green foothills sloped gently to the road and continued down the opposite side to the banks of the Missouri, dark and serene.

"Did you miss this when you lived in Boston?"

"I still live there, Dennis."

"I forgot. Sorry. *Do* you miss this in Boston?"

"Actually it took some getting used to," Anne said, swerving to miss a pothole. "The ironic thing is that for the first couple months after we came back I felt vulnerable not having next-door neighbors. I was used to being surrounded by this soft hum of activity from them, and suddenly I'm out in the boonies listening to coyotes howl. It's eerie. I'm used to it now, but for a while I couldn't sleep if Jack wasn't in the house."

"All this is why I liked Weed Control so much. You're out in the open, lost in your own thoughts."

"You can't tell me Susan didn't have something to do with it."

"Well, that's true."

During my second summer with Weed Control the boss had paired me with Susan Hall, who showed up for her first day in pressed khaki shorts and a polo shirt. I had no idea what she thought Weed Control involved. Time to work on her tan, maybe. I handed Susan one of the white astronaut suits we had to wear and said I'd be happy to walk and spray for the first four hours. She said she thought it made more sense to divide the day into two-hour shifts. Fine, whatever. On the drive out to our area, I asked where she went to school. With precise elocution she said, "I'm at Smith." I wanted to club her. Instead I asked when she'd flown home. Anything so I wouldn't have to hear how wonderful Smith was. "Two weeks ago. My boyfriend drove me to the airport." My boyfriend drove me to the airport? Who the hell said anything about a boyfriend? I hated her and made a vow that no matter what else happened that summer, I was going to sleep with her.

After a week we discovered we were both English majors, and we began discussing books. Susan was reading Jane Austen that summer. I said she was one of the premier stylists ever, something I'd heard Anne once say. Susan ate it up. I was reading a Dickens novel. Susan said her mother wouldn't let her read Dickens in high school because all of his characters were caricatures.

She found out I had a band at college, but I knew better than to mention that it was a country band. One afternoon when I'd been listening to a country station Susan had said, "How can you stand that cowboy-hat music?"

Three weeks went by talking about books and her boyfriend, Trent, who was going to lacrosse camp all summer so he could make varsity that fall. He hadn't been calling and Susan was furious. I said Trent was probably exhausted from working out. All during this time I'd been looking for an opportunity to make a pass, but I lost my nerve and procrastinated, waiting for the ideal moment. Finally one rainy day while eating lunch in the truck, I leaned over and kissed her on the mouth. Susan frowned at me and said, "What are you doing?" I blushed. "I think it's obvious what I'm doing. I'm making an ass of myself." We returned to our lunches.

A week later Susan said, "You're really attracted to me, aren't you?"

I denied it.

"Yes, you are."

"No, I'm not."

"Then why did you kiss me?"

"It seemed like a good idea at the time."

"I have a boyfriend."

"No kidding. Has he called lately?"

"Did you think you could kiss me just because it seemed like a good idea to you?"

"Who cares? That was a week ago. A small peck on your frigid lips."

"I'm not frigid."

"I didn't say you were."

"You just did."

"No, I said your lips were frigid."

"But you meant that I am."

"I did?"

"You're wrong, you know."

"I guess I'll never know, since it seems like a very bad idea now."

Then we were kissing. There was a frenzy of clutching. I unzipped her suit half-expecting her to stop me and say, "That's enough. Now you know I'm not frigid." Instead she began rooting around in my shorts, and soon we were pulling off one another's space suits and Susan was sitting in my lap looking out the back window, clutching my head and telling me to keep an eye out for cars. Who could see anything? Afterward I walked behind the truck, grinning. I could not stop grinning. Susan kept leaning out the window telling me to knock it off, but she was doing the same thing. That night I found bruises on my shoulders where she'd gripped me.

We did that nearly every day. At noon whoever was driving would pull the truck as far off the road as possible; we'd slip out of our astronaut suits, fuck and then eat lunch. For the first two weeks after I returned to Colorado State, I got a hard-on every day at noon.

I'd last seen her at Christmas when she was home for a week. I was drinking at a bar downtown when she walked in with two friends, stamping the snow from their feet and rubbing their arms against the cold. I knew her friends from high school, and they didn't care for me. Susan waved at me, but it was an hour before she left her friends and joined me at the bar. We moved to a booth and sat facing one another. Susan began telling me about her boyfriend in San Francisco, a third-year ophthalmology resident named Tim she'd been dating for two years. She said he was either on call or asleep, and they hadn't seen a movie or gone out to dinner in five months. I listened and nodded. Around one o'clock she noticed that her friends had left, and she asked if I could give her a ride home.

Outside it was brutally cold, the wind stinging our faces and cutting through our heavy coats. Halfway to my van we began to run. The passenger door was frozen shut. At her parents' house I ran in place waiting for Susan to climb over the driver's seat. I moved to hug her and believed I saw her tilt her head slightly. It was all I needed. I kissed her, drawing her close. We stood by the side of the van in the wind until Susan opened her eyes and said, "Your nose is bleeding." She led me inside, the first time I'd ever been allowed in the house.

I was standing before the bathroom mirror shoving rolled Kleenex up one nostril when Susan came in after changing out of the turtleneck I'd bled on. She placed her hands on either side of my face and kissed me on the mouth, then ran her fingers through my hair and down the length of my back. I kissed her pale neck, struggling to breathe through one nostril. In a few minutes I had her shirt off and was about to suggest we close the door before the next stage when she whispered to my ear, "You have to go."

"I do?"

She nodded and twisted away from me, sinking her fingernails into the heel of my palms. She pulled on her shirt, not bothering to button it so that it trailed behind her as she guided me in the dark to the front door. She bit my ear and said she wanted to see me tomorrow night. Then she pushed me out the front door and I was running down the driveway in the biting wind and cold to the van.

Mrs. Hall had Susan booked for the last three nights that she was home. Cocktails with neighbors, dinners with family friends. She would call me at eleven o'clock and give me an address, then tell her father she was meeting friends and slip away before anyone could protest. I would be waiting down the street in the Angstmobile. We would park somewhere, like teenagers, with the engine and heater running, lying together in the back beneath the weight of a half-dozen wool blankets and holding one another like the survivors of a shipwreck. Susan would never let us go any further than we had the first night, as if what we were doing was all she could forgive herself for without feeling she'd betrayed her boyfriend. Her restraint only made it more powerful and alluring, a promise of things to come.

"What's going on with you and Susan these days?" Anne said.

"Nothing. I haven't talked to her since January. We never do a very good job of keeping in touch. Although I did write her a letter last night." Now that I was home I missed her.

We passed a faded white sign that said Westwind Estates. It was a small community of perhaps twenty houses built within a two-mile radius. Miles's house and six others formed the nucleus. Three fenced yards held horses of questionable lineage. Both times I'd visited—once with my parents when Miles had just begun construction and again at Christmas with Anne when it was completed—I'd imagined the neighbors as antisocial survivalists who prided themselves on their self-sufficiency and eagerly awaited Armageddon. That would be their opportunity to shine, a chance to show up all those men who hired people to change the car oil, fix the leaky faucet, reshingle the roof, mow the lawn. Men like me who had no idea how electricity worked and only cared when it didn't. I had a soft spot for E. M. Forster, who was said to have believed that telephone wires were hollow.

We pulled onto Miles's lot, three acres of towering arthritic cottonwoods and sharp-pointed yucca. The house sat on a rise facing west. Dormer windows jutted out in all four directions. The square weather-beaten logs had been stained mahogany, the cedar shingled roof still bright and golden. Miles's black and red two-tone pickup, ideal for a Scotchguard salesman, was parked in front.

Miles walked out on the front porch and leaned on the railing with his forearms.

"Hey there," Anne said, walking up the embankment to the house.

"What do you think?"

"It looks great, Miles."

"Dennis?"

"Yeah, it looks good. How long ago did you do it?"

"Last month."

"It's nice," I said, slipping in the mud and cursing.

"Why don't you take your shoes off," Miles said before we went inside. A pair of muddy boots were standing by the door. Anne and I took ours off. I remembered Miles once telling me that a good way to prevent fights at parties was to make people remove their shoes; they felt vulnerable without them. Miles thought of those things.

The front room ran the length of the house and was un-finished, a temporary workroom of orange electrical cords, an air compressor, table saw, staple gun, stacked lumber and drywall. Bent nails and sawdust had been swept into a large pile.

"Do you want something to drink?"

"I'll have a beer if you've got one," I said. "Anne, why don't you have a beer."

"I'll have a beer," Anne said.

When Miles left the room, I leaned into her and said, "Is that Miles or just a look-alike?"

"I know you're nervous, Dennis, but be nice. Try not to be too flip."

"Who's nervous?"

"You are. I know Miles does this to you, but just try and be polite. OK?"

"OK."

Miles returned with our beers. "Why don't I show you the upstairs first. I've got all the rooms done and I just finished laying the floor."

He and Anne walked up the stairs as I trailed in their wake. "Do you still have to finish these?" I said.

"What?"

"The stairs. The vertical part you can see into."

Anne eyed me over her shoulder.

"That's how they're supposed to be; it's called open riser," Miles said.

I raised my eyebrows and palms to Anne: How'd I know?

"Wow," she said, seeing the upstairs walls, which were painted a rich warm blue.

"Mom helped me pick that out. I was going to go with white, but she thought a deep blue would make the house feel warmer. I had my doubts, but now I like it."

"It's wonderful."

"Yeah? Good."

At the top of the landing was a large rectangular window

looking out onto the sandy backyard and thirty-foot sand dune. "I want to find a stained glass window to go there," Miles said. Then looking down, he went on, "This is my tongue-and-groove hard northern maple floor. Built on the duracushion system. You put a rubber cushion underneath two-by-fours, lay cheap pine one-by-sixes over that at a forty-five degree angle, and then lay the tongue-and-groove maple straight over that. The floor's about four and a half inches off the ground. That way you're off the floor joists, so it's warmer. It also has more give to it."

I hopped up and down in my socks. "Kind of looks like a gym floor with those long narrow strips."

"It's beautiful," Anne said.

"Thank you. I'm going to put this on the first floor as well. I tried to get the wood as bleached as possible so with the dark walls everything would look bigger."

We moved down the short hallway, stopping to look at the bathroom, two smaller bedrooms and the master bedroom. All the rooms had the dry aroma of freshly cut lumber. Miles's room was spartan, a queen-sized brass bed, dresser and bookcase. While he told Anne how he'd built the closet, I examined his book selection. On the top shelf were several of Hemingway's books. I took out *The Sun Also Rises*. Bill Gorton was admiring stuffed dogs and telling Jake Barnes that the secret to his success was to never be daunted. It was a swell novel.

Miles and Anne had finished inspecting the closet and were discussing the brass bed, which he'd found at a junk store. I put the book back and went to the closet. Everything in it was carefully arranged. All the pants were hung in the center, with long-sleeve shirts on the left, short-sleeve shirts on the right, buttons facing toward the pants, all hangers facing east. Directly below this, Miles had three pairs of cowboy boots lined up next to two pairs of athletic shoes and then two pairs of dress shoes, their laces tucked inside. For the sake of symmetry I thought Miles should either throw out one pair of boots or put them in the middle. Everyone in the family except me kept a closet like this. I still hadn't unpacked yet, which was pushing my mother toward the edge. *Your father thinks you should unpack your duffel bags . . .*

"Dennis, we're going downstairs," Anne said.

I followed them down to the study where Miles showed us an antique rolltop desk he'd recently bought. The previous owner had painted it black, and a small patch had been scraped away to reveal oak.

"It's going to be a lot of work stripping it," Miles said, pulling the top down and pointing out all the joints.

"Shouldn't let it daunt you, Miles."

"I'm not daunted by it. I'm just not going to get around to it until the rest of the house is finished."

"Never be daunted by stripping, particularly in front of a lady. Love to strip in front of ladies. Think it's swell."

Miles frowned.

"What have you been up to?" Anne said.

"Been reading a little Hemingway."

"I see. What's next, Miles?"

He continued watching me for a moment, then said, "You saw the kitchen at Christmas, so let's go to the basement. I haven't done anything to it, but I'll show you what I'm planning."

We passed through the kitchen and walked downstairs where the temperature dropped step by step. Miles had mounted a leather speed bag in one corner and a canvas heavy bag hung from the ceiling. I decked the heavy bag and then shook my hand out, mouth wide in agony.

A shelf ran the width of one wall and held trophies and framed photographs of Miles from his days as a judoist and wrestler. When Miles was in the sixth grade, he had come home from school one day with a bloody lip and closed left eye, and it was the only time I'd ever seen him cry. He refused to tell my mother what had happened and he locked himself in his room until my father arrived home from work and told him to open the door. After several minutes of questioning from my father, Miles said that an Indian at school had been hassling him on the playground, pushing him around and calling him a rich kid, and Miles had taken a swing at him. A monitor had stepped in before any more punches were thrown, but the Indian and one of his friends had waited for Miles after school and beaten him up. My father told Miles to get a bag of ice for his eye and explained what they were going to do.

The following afternoon my father met Miles after school and when the Indian walked out, my father grabbed him by the back of the neck and marched him to a nearby park. He said if the Indian wanted to fight his son, he'd have to do it alone. In the park he squared them off and said, "You want to fight? Go ahead and fight." Miles returned home with a bloody nose and split lip, and there was no talk of victory or revenge. Afterward my father told him, "From now on you're on your own. I'm not going to help you again, so I suggest you either stay out of trouble or learn how to fight." Miles had asked to take judo lessons at the Y and immediately excelled at it. He'd started wrestling the following year, and the two sports resulted in a volatile mix. Through junior high Miles had a habit of using judo throws on his wrestling opponents whenever he became frustrated, launching them in high graceful arcs and slamming them to the mat. He'd be given a warning and then have points withdrawn for illegal moves. Meanwhile his opponent, unaccustomed to such crash landings, would be struggling to breathe. Miles's coaches constantly warned him about these departures from the rules. He was fine in practice, but up the ante with adrenaline, tougher competition and teammates at mat side yelling "Use your judo!" and Miles would revert to his better skill. He didn't suffer from this split personality in judo competitions. He was the state AAU champion in his weight class through junior high and placed second twice and first once at regionals.

In high school he concentrated on wrestling, confining judo to the off-season. He made varsity his junior year at 146 pounds and finished second at state. The following year he won the state title at 154. We treated Miles with special deference during wrestling season because he was so sullen and moody from constant dieting. His abstinence would have shamed Jack LaLanne: dry toast and poached egg whites for breakfast; salad and raw vegetables, no dressing, for lunch; dinner but no dessert; no alcohol, no sex with his girlfriend two days before a match, three-mile runs and hour-long stationary bike rides wearing a garbage bag, rubber pants and two sweat suits; chewing snoose and spitting into a paper cup to shed water weight. Miles would make weight and then eat as large a meal as his shrunken stomach could hold, drink a gallon of water and be eight pounds heavier then when he'd weighed in that morning. He repeated that routine for three months every year, junior high through high school.

Miles expected to get a wrestling scholarship to at least one of the state universities, but the only offer came from a community college in Idaho. He talked about trying out as a walk-on at Bozeman, but my parents thought he should concentrate on school. My mother said if he wanted to continue wrestling, he could always join an intramural team, an insult he couldn't forgive, and they battled over it the entire summer. My parents wanted Miles to go out of state to school so he'd see another part of the country and pushed for Gonzaga. He applied only to Bozeman and once there he joined a fraternity called the Farm House and began his metamorphosis into a cowboy. He returned at Christmas wearing a Stetson straw, boots and Wranglers with the white ring of a snoose can in his back pocket.

When I was in sixth grade, my father decided *I* should learn how to defend myself. I said I didn't get into fights. "At some point you may have no choice," he said. The following Saturday I was on the top floor of the Y wearing a white *gi* and belt, learning how to fall.

Within six months I was a yellow belt and had been to the principal's office three times for flipping kids on the playground. My parents found it hard to say anything. At practice one fall day, we did several sets of push-ups and sit-ups and practiced technique on one another. Then the instructor, Bill Norris (no relation to Chuck), had everyone sit at one end of the mats and called up Miles, who was seventeen. Norris was the only person willing to practice with him.

"I want a volunteer to fight Miles," Norris said.

"Feel free," someone said. Everyone laughed.

The room fell quiet. A pigeon took flight from a window sill. The group looked at the pale green mat, afraid of catching Norris's eye and being chosen to volunteer.

I sat there thinking, You pussies. You bunch of pussies. What are you so afraid of? It's only Miles. He's not even a black belt. I can't believe what a bunch of pussies you all are.

"I'll fight him." I stood up, my legs slow to react. I carefully adjusted my *gi* and wiped my palms. I'd weighed seventy-two pounds on the locker-room scale that morning.

I stood behind a short piece of white tape eight feet across from Miles, who stared flatly at me. We bowed to one another. I realized how stupid I'd been to volunteer. Norris put his right hand in the space between us, jerked it up and yelled, "*Hajime!*"

I saw Miles as though in slow motion: He had me by my *gi*, snapping me cleanly into his pivoting hip and whipping me up up up toward the tile ceiling and down down down onto the unforgiving straw mat. I felt my body hit and vibrate; my soul seemed to leave me. A guttural yell collapsed in my throat.

"*Ippon!*" Norris yelled. A clean winner.

I lay dazed and panicked at not being able to breathe. I managed to stand and found the white line. I looked into Miles's eyes, hoping for a signal that that had been a lesson in stupidity and he would now go easy on me. Nothing. Norris's hand appeared between us. It shot up, the voice yelled. Miles grabbed me, moved me left then right, an aggressive tango partner, dropped to his back, kicked his right foot into my stomach, carried me over his body and dropped me flat on my back. Then he had me in a choke hold while I arched my back to avoid being pinned. The harder I fought, the tighter Miles choked me. I was in a blind rage, jerking violently like an epileptic. Norris slapped the mat. Pinned.

I couldn't stop coughing for several minutes. I struggled up off the floor and went to the line, wanting only to knee Miles in the nuts. One good kick in the balls. We bowed and I got ready. No hand appeared.

"Who wants to be next?" Norris said to the group.

"I'm not done," I said, staring across at Miles. One kick and he could do whatever he wanted to me.

"Why don't you sit down, Dennis," Norris said.

"Up yours."

Norris snatched me by the front of my *gi* and said, "Don't you talk to me like that."

I could smell coffee on his breath and see minute black hairs on the tip of his nose. I stared back.

"You haven't had enough, huh?" Norris said, shaking me. "You want to go again? Okay. Go ahead." He let go. I adjusted my *gi*. "Ready now? *Hajime!*"

We grabbed one another, Miles leading our movements as I tried to resist his attempts to move me in one direction to set up a throw. He used a foot sweep and the world fell out from under me. He let me up. He dropped me with a simple hip throw. Let me up. A head throw. Same thing. Miles relaxed for a moment and I tried a head throw. I managed to get my left arm around his neck and lock it with my right hand. Miles lifted me off the ground and dropped us to the mat. I hung on like a pit bull, trying to strangle him. He broke my grip and slapped me in an illegal choke hold, instantly closing my windpipe. I felt as though I were trapped at the bottom of a dark pool, unable to reach the surface. Then nothing.

Walking home I stayed a half block behind him, wishing I was twice his size so I could beat him to a pulp. Two blocks from home he turned and walked back to me and it was all I could do to keep from running. I held the folded *gi* to my chest. "I'm going to tell you something for your own good," Miles said, his voice low and threatening. "If you're going to push somebody, you'd better be ready to get pushed back. Because one day you're going to realize that you can't laugh your way out of everything. Not all of us find you funny."

I refused to speak to him for a week. I felt that an unspoken rule or understanding between brothers had been violated. If he'd eased up after the first throw, I could have accepted it as a lesson in stupidity. As it was I could think of it only as viciousness. I swore I'd never trust him again.

My father came into my bedroom after two days and said, "I've talked to Miles about what happened. I told him he can't be that rough with you. That was uncalled-for. He's six years older. Sometimes he gets carried away and forgets he's not competing against an equal opponent. On the other hand, from what I understand, you *did* volunteer." Always a lawyer.

"Dennis," Anne said, standing beside me in the basement, "Miles is going out to dinner with Tammy in town. Do you want to hang out here for a while or go home?"

"You're taking off now, Miles?"

"Yeah."

"Let's hang out here for a while," I said. "Do you mind, Miles?" I was feeling somber.

"No."

We went upstairs and followed Miles out to the front porch in the fading light. Cirrus clouds floated in the west. No other neighbors were outside, and it was peaceful with the view of the lush foothills, but I couldn't help imagining some NRA lulu suffering from cabin fever going on a rifle rampage. Maybe that came with the territory.

Anne and I watched Miles drive away, losing sight of him behind a line of cottonwoods. We heard the pitch of his engine rise and fall as he shifted gears and then saw him shoot into the clear. At the same moment, we pivoted and reached for our shoes. Then laughed.

We went inside and surveyed the front room. "There are no chairs in this house," I said. "I just noticed that. Where the hell does he sit?"

"There's a couple chairs in the kitchen. The rest are in the garage."

"That's a good place for them. His stereo's in the corner so let's sit in here. Unless you want to sit in the garage."

"This is fine."

"You get the chairs and beer and I'll put on some music."

I flipped through Miles's albums. Country music was our one common interest, although we'd never discussed it. Miles had even gone to several of my Cloverleaf gigs; he was an excellent dancer. I put Loretta Lynn's "You Ain't Woman Enough" on the turntable.

Anne carried in two wooden ladder-back chairs and a six-pack of Budweiser, which she set on the floor between us. We sat at the east end of the house, clear of tools and lumber. Shafts of light angled through the west windows.

"Who's this?"

"Miss Loretta Lynn, the coalminer's daughter."

"Thinking of that, how are your former bandmates doing?"

"Haven't heard except for Montana. She's still down in Austin working as a waitress, trying to get something going, but she hasn't had much luck. She's been in a couple bands but they both sputtered out after a few months."

"Do you miss her?"

"Yeah. You'll have to meet her some time. You'd like her." I raised an index finger to the ceiling to signal for Anne's attention. "Here's today's theme song, dedicated to Miles." Loretta Lynn began singing "These Boots Are Made for Walkin'." Anne and I joined her on the chorus. "One of these days these boots are gonna walk all over you." We played it three times in a row.

"What do you think of the house?" Anne said.

"Fantastic." The beer had begun to work its way through my limbs.

"You missed half the tour. He's got some great ideas."

"I know he does. And I admire his self-sufficiency. I really do. But I always get this feeling from him that I'm somehow deficient because I have no interest in building my own house one day. If that's what he wants to do, great, but don't push it on me. Do you ever get that feeling?"

"No, but then I could never do any of this and I have no interest in doing it, so I don't care."

"Maybe it's strictly a male thing. That real-men-can-build-their-own-home kind of thing. I'd be lucky to build a goddamn lean-to, but I can give you one hell of a backbeat."

"Actually Jack has fallen prey to exactly that. I never saw this in him until we moved to the ranch. He decided the house

needed a sundeck and that he should build it. He laid it out with nails and string off the side of the house, measured everything twice and then bought all the lumber. Somehow he miscalculated and the right side was two inches lower than the left. It was like being on a sloping ship deck. I told him we'd have to put the cushions on the ground so people wouldn't get hurt when their chairs tipped over. Jack tried jacking it up, but that didn't work so I told him to call Miles. He refused to even discuss it. Finally he gave in, but when he called Miles he made it sound like he only wanted a little help. Miles showed up and slapped it together in about five hours while Jack stood around in his tool belt taking orders like a little boy helping his dad. It's a wonderful deck, but I don't think Jack will let himself really enjoy it because Miles did the work."

"He does have that effect on people, doesn't he," I said. "He's very good at making you feel like he's got it together and you don't and maybe it's time you figured out what you're doing with your pathetic little life. And this is not someone who's exactly setting the world on fire. He's making nineteen thousand dollars a year setting speed traps, for Christ's sake. Last year when I was playing with Cowboy Angst, he made me feel like I was cruising playgrounds asking little kids if they wanted a ride home. How does he get away with that?"

"I don't know," Anne said. "But you have to admit that despite the reproving tone Miles takes with you, he really does care."

"It's not the tone that bothers me. It's being held against a wall with his hand around my throat telling me I'm a smartass who will never amount to anything that bothers me. Thank God you always showed up and saved me or I would have never had my opportunity to become such a failure."

"But you proved him wrong, didn't you?" Anne said. "You're through the first year of law school, you did well the first semester and I know you did well this last semester, so who cares if Miles said you'd never amount to anything. This time you're right and he's wrong."

I couldn't look at her. I stared at the bottle in my hand, jaws tightening as the anger boiled up inside of me until I wanted to rush downstairs and punch and kick the heavy bag with all the disgust and rage I felt and keep punching and kicking until I was too tired to do it anymore.

"And besides, you egged him on a lot, too."

I shrugged, still not looking up.

"You did."

"I know."

"You knew what he'd do if you pushed him and you still did it."

"You know why I did that," I said, my tone more aggressive than I intended, particularly with Anne, who didn't deserve it. "Because whenever Miles becomes threatening, there's something challenging about it at the same time. Same with Dad. They put on that tough-guy persona and you can't help thinking, All right, fucker, let's see what you'll do if I push back."

"You'll never come out on top, Dennis," Anne said, looking closely at me now. "With either Miles or Dad. You know that."

"I should, anyway."

"You don't?"

I turned my palms up. "You know, the summer before my junior year of high school, I was running out near Mountain View by that open field on the other side of the railroad tracks. You know the one I'm talking about? It was hot and I was getting tired and I still had three miles to go. This truck drove up behind me—it had the entire street to itself—and the driver laid on the horn, so I moved over to the curb. It pulled closer and kept honking until I was running through the weeds along the fence line. I could hear whoever was in the cab swearing at me, and without looking back I gave him the finger. All of a sudden I hear this voice yell, 'We're gonna get you, you skinny fucker!' I look back and see three cowboys waving their fists at me. I hurdled the fence and started sprinting across the field toward the houses so I'd have somewhere to hide. They had to go down to the end of the street and turn right, and I could hear the truck squealing around the corner.

"Meanwhile I'm tearing past the backyards that look out onto the field, all these dogs running at the fences trying to get at me. All the cowboys had to do was follow the sound of the barking and they would have known exactly where I was. I cut down an alley and kept running. After about five minutes or so I hadn't seen or heard the pickup and I started thinking, Hey, maybe they've given up. I started jogging, twenty feet from where the alley intersected the street, listening for the pickup and trying to catch my breath. I didn't hear anything, so I picked it up to cross the street. The truck pulled in front of the alley. I thought, Oh fuck, and sprinted to the right on the sidewalk. The pickup stayed even with me while one of the cowboys jumped out. The Road Warrior meets rodeo. But the guy had boots on and couldn't catch me, so the truck pulled ahead and dumped out contestant number two, who tackled me within twenty yards. All I had on were shorts. I hit the sidewalk and scraped skin off from my chin to my knees. And these two cowboys beat the shit out of me. I don't know what you've heard about cowboy chivalry, but apparently there's no longer a stigma attached to kicking your opponent. I guess they figure if they're wearing hard pointy boots, they might as well get some use out of them. Boy, did they kick. After a while they got tired or bored, climbed in the pickup and drove away.

"The entire time these two rednecks were whaling on me, this old man was standing on his front stoop watching. I think he was going to his car when it happened. When I finally managed to get up, I saw him standing fifteen yards away, staring. I was furious. I said, 'What is this, New York City? You don't just stand there and watch somebody get beaten up. You call the cops, goddamnit!' You know what he said? 'You probably deserved it.'

"One of the neighbors let me use the phone and helped clean me up. I called Billy Smitherman for a ride. When Dad came home from work he asked if I needed to see a doctor. I told him no. He wanted to know what had happened. I said two unhappy cowboys had had a real bad day and decided to kick me instead of their dog. Dad said, 'If you'd stuck with judo, this wouldn't have happened.' Just what I wanted to hear. Then he asked if I wanted him to help find them so I could fight them one at a time. I told him no way. No fucking way was I going to fight them one at a time. Why should I get my ass kicked three more times?

"Dad looked so disappointed and ashamed, like how can my own son not insist on evening the score? It really bothered him. He asked me three or four times after that if I'd changed my mind. I wanted to say to him, Listen, if it bothers you that much, you fight them. And Mom. Mom was great, too. She wanted to know if it was my fault. Of course it was, Mom. I asked them to turn me into the human scab."

"And it still bothers you that you refused to fight them?" Anne said.

"You know what bothers me about the whole thing? What I'm ashamed of, really? That I didn't fight back. At all. I just rolled up into a ball and prayed for it to end. I didn't throw one punch in my own defense. And even though there's no way Dad could have known that, somehow I felt like he did and that when he offered to help track them down so I could fight them one at a time, he was offering me a chance to redeem myself. And I told him flat out, no way."

"So you fight them and they beat you up again. What good would that have done?"

"None, probably. But I've always had the feeling that simply being willing to face them alone, whether I got my ass kicked again or not, would have made a difference to him. Maybe not. The truth is, I didn't want to fight them. You know who I wanted to fight?

"Who?"

"Dad. I wanted to knock the piss out of him. For a long time after those cowboys beat on me, I'd be doing something and I'd suddenly see myself—feel myself—punching Dad in the side of the head, right in the temple, as hard I could. I'd go into this inner rage thinking about it. I hated him for being ashamed of me, for thinking I was a coward. I still wonder what would have happened if I'd hit him. I know he would have killed me, but sometimes I think it would have been worth it to hit him as hard as I could right there," I pressed a fist against my temple, "right in the temple, even if that were the only punch I got in."

Anne looked down at the floor, and I fell silent for a moment, ashamed that I'd told her.

"I shouldn't have told you that."

"No, I'm glad you told me," Anne said, looking up but not meeting my eyes.

"It's not that I don't love him," I said. "It's not that. I do. And I have incredible respect for him. I'm proud that he's my father. But there are times when I hate him for being so . . . I don't know. Self-contained. So fucking sure of everything in his life. Just once I'd like to see a chink in the armor. A sign of doubt or uncertainty. I've never seen that. This may sound strange, but it would actually reassure me to know that he has doubts about his own life, even if only for a moment."

"Maybe that's just it, though, Dennis. Maybe Dad feels he has to provide that certainty for us as a family. His dad didn't do that. He walked out on his wife and left her to raise three kids on her own. I think Dad wants to protect us from ever feeling that that's even a possiblity."

She stood up. "I have to use the bathroom."

When Anne returned, I said, "Why's Jack going to a computer seminar when you're going back to Boston in four months?"

"That's what I asked him. He said he thinks a computer will help make the ranch more efficient. I'm really afraid Jack's becoming attached to the ranch. I keep expecting him to tell me he doesn't want to go back to Boston, which would break my heart. I was never meant to live in the sticks."

"Maybe he's just trying to help the ranch make more money."

"I hope that's all there is to it. He says that's all there is to it. It's so damn lonely out there. I've never spent so much time at Mom and Dad's in ten years. I love them dearly, but not when I spend too much time with them. I guess that's it, isn't it? It's easy to love them as long as you don't always have to be around them. I don't have a lot to say to them and I'm bored. I want to spend time with my friends in Boston."

"Have you told Jack that?"

"He knows."

"Remind him," I said. "I think we ought to dance."

"I'd love to dance with you. Regular Patrick Swayze."

Anne cleared out the chairs and empty beer bottles while I put on Gram Parsons. I took Anne's hands in mine. I wasn't nearly as accomplished as Miles, but I knew six or seven moves and we began to swing around the floor. I snapped Anne away from me, held her at arm's length and twirled her. She let her head fall back like a figure skater and closed her eyes. Her hair fanned out around her head and she wobbled a little drunkenly. I pulled her back into me and sent her out again. We danced to several songs, then rested.

"We should call Mom and tell her we're not going to be home for dinner," Anne said.

"Why don't you do that."

"Thanks a lot."

Afterward she said, "What do you want to do? Do you want to stay here or go somewhere else or what?"

"Let's go before Miles gets back. We'll leave him some money for the beer."

"Do you think we can drive?"

"We'll go slow and take Flood Road all the way."

"What if Miles has set up a roadblock with a Breathalyzer?"

"We'll put the truck into four-wheel drive and make our escape over the hills."

"Do you know how to put it into four-wheel drive?"

"We'll ask Miles for help."

"Let's go, then."

Anne drove in the center of the road at twenty miles per hour with the exaggerated concentration of a drunk; she gripped the wheel with both hands, leaned into the windshield and squinted as if to get a closer look at the gravel road. I watched her and had grave doubts. I tested my seat belt twice. The countryside was black, broken only by the soft yellow yard lights at the end of long driveways. The crescent moon was veiled by slow-moving clouds. The truck's headlights groped thirty feet ahead, spotlighting field mice, fast-running rabbits and water-filled pot-holes that Anne now took head-on. At the crest of a hill, the lights vaporized in the night sky and I held my breath as we plunged into the pool of inky shadows below.

"Did you know most accidents on rural roads are head-on collisions?" I said. "Everyone drives down the middle."

"Tell me more fun facts," Anne said, her face green and glowing from leaning so close to the dashboard.

"My teeth are floating."

"If I pull over, you drive."

"I'll do anything."

At the highest rise on Flood Road, we could see Prairie View. It resembled an elaborately lighted circulatory system that Anne and I were being drawn toward along a dark capillary, eager to avoid the orange luminance of the main arteries. The gravel ended, the pavement began, smooth and calming. We crossed the railroad tracks at the base of Mountain View and turned north until we passed over the Sun River. Then crept along side streets and across the Missouri. I pulled up to the front of the house and left the engine running as if to make a quick getaway. I felt like we'd been gone for days. Both of us looked at the front-room window where we could see my mother's silhouette.

"You ready to call it a night yet?" I said.

"What have you got in mind?"

"Thought we might walk downtown and have a beer."

"Sounds good."

I cut the engine. We climbed out and started walking the four blocks to downtown. The air had turned brittle. Anne shivered and crossed her arms. A neighbor was standing in the alley whistling as his cocker spaniel lifted a leg on the Groseths' backyard fence. Waves and hellos. At the post office a man with muttonchops wearing a white muscle shirt sat on the loading dock smoking a cigarette. A block from Dingfelder Avenue, Anne said, "Let's run," and was suddenly out in front of me, Vibram soles flicking up behind her. I began to follow, then heard the beer sloshing in my stomach and thought it would be a real shame to have to throw up. I slowed to a walk. Anne stood waiting outside Wild Wick's Bar and Lounge. We pushed through the doors into the warm bar, our noses running, and sat on stools at the high wooden counter. Anne ordered and then raised her beer. "To a good day."

"Cheers."

Five

Early the next morning there was a violent pounding on my bedroom door. I was far away, submerged in a warm cavern of swirling dreams and alcohol, and I began the long swim to consciousness. Near the surface I heard four of Prairie View's finest using a battering ram on my door. My first thought was that Miles had tipped them off and they knew I'd dropped out of law school. Then I broke through and sat up.

"Dennis, do you want to run?"

I fell back. I knew my mother couldn't bear having me sleep late while she was in the house, even on Saturday. "Sure."

"We'll meet you in the kitchen in ten minutes."

"Uh huh." A blacksmith had set up shop behind my forehead, well into his workday, and I eased across the room to avoid irritating him.

We ran in Dingfelder Park on a mile loop of asphalt. The sun was low on the horizon, the air brisk. My mother led, shuffling along with a high arm action that came close to being a stiff uppercut to the chin. Anne followed a half-stride behind with

the easy lope of a field hockey player; she'd warned me that my
mother accelerated when anyone ran even with her, so it was
best to lag slightly behind. I felt uncoordinated and short of
breath. I blamed it on the altitude and focused on my mother's
back.

On the fourth and final lap, with Anne and I laboring behind,
my mother picked up the tempo. I noticed and thought, My own
mother's trying to dust me on a run. Anne fell back sounding like
she'd swallowed a nickel and was in need of the Heimlich
maneuver. I didn't sound any better and a painful rigidity was
creeping up the backs of my legs. I forced myself to pull even
with my mother. She accelerated. I ran abreast and glanced over
at her. Her fists pumped like pistons, inches from a knockout
blow. She looked sweaty and ruthless.

I hung on until there were only a hundred yards left, then
gathered myself and charged by with what I hoped resembled
nonchalance. When I finished it was all I could do to refrain
from thrusting my arms skyward and dropping to my knees on
the wet grass. Instead I turned to grimace at my mother: no hard
feelings? She breezed past, smiling, and continued running to
the house. I looked after her and thought, Cheater. Anne came
to a gasping halt and clutched her pink knees. When she stood
up, she looked at me and said, "Wrong finish line."

My mother served eggs Benedict for breakfast, my father's
favorite and the only eggs he was allowed for the week because
of a recent high cholesterol count. She raised her eyebrows
when he reached for the salt. He smiled at her as if to say, Oh,
that's right, I don't use that anymore, do I.

"What did you think of Miles's house?" my father said.

"I was impressed. Have you been out there lately?"

"We went out one weekend when he was putting up insulation. Somehow he roped me into helping. He had some new
system where you put a sheet of plastic over the insulation so

there's a pocket of air in between. I don't know how well it works, but it sounded good." He paused as if to consider its validity. "I lost a thumbnail that weekend, didn't I, Helen?"

"That's right, you did," she said absently.

"Smashed this one with the hammer," he said, looking at his left thumbnail. "I was a little rusty."

"I'm surprised Miles let you help," I said.

"He needed someone to hold up the plastic, otherwise I don't think he would have asked. He let me nail in one section and that's when I hit my thumb. It confirmed his worst suspicions about my abilities as a carpenter."

When we finished eating, Anne said she was driving back to the ranch. I picked up her suitcase in the hallway and walked her out to the pickup. She climbed in and rolled down her window. "Are you going to work for Dad?"

"Haven't decided yet."

"I think you should. You'd learn a lot from him."

"I probably would."

"Come out and visit us."

"I will." I slapped the side of the cab and waved as she drove off. Then I looked at the house. Once I told them, it might be years before they trusted me again. All I could do was tell them the truth and hope they could forgive me one day.

When I went inside, my father was washing the pots and pans. I grabbed a dishtowel and joined him. His sleeves were rolled up to the elbow, the hair on his thick cabled forearms almost entirely gray. He shoved a pot beneath the surface as if drowning it, then vigorously scrubbed it with a Brillo pad.

"Did you ever make it to the National Cathedral?" he said.

"What national cathedral?"

"In D.C."

"Is there one?"

"That answers that question." He handed me the clean pot.

"What are you working on?"

"You'd enjoy this one," my father said. "I'm representing a used car salesman from Chester who sold a car to a woman who stopped making payments after two months. My client drives out to her house in Whitlash to repossess it, but her husband, who's a real orangutan—he once held a forty-five to a neighbor's head and threatened to blow it off—comes out of the house with his brother carrying a tire iron and says if my client touches the car, he'll be leaving in an ambulance. And they won't be calling 911 when they're finished. Everett drives back to Chester and tells this eighteen-year-old kid who works for him, 'You get that car and I'll pay you a hundred bucks.'

"That night the kid's at a kegger with a group of friends and around two in the morning he decides to go get the car. He and a friend pick up the wrecker and drive to Whitlash. At the house they find the car wedged between two trucks and in the process of hooking it up they wake up several dogs and have to take off before the car's on right. A few miles down the road the car's swaying too much, so they dump it by a grain elevator and head for Chester. A mile later they see a truck bearing down on them and realize it's the two orangutans. The kid stays in the middle of the road so they can't get around him, but they manage to anyway, going about eighty, eighty-five, and they start throwing garbage out the windows at him. Two-by-fours, Styrofoam cups, whatever they've got. Then the brother slides open the back window of the cab and fires a sawed-off shotgun at the wrecker. The kid and his friend duck just as the truck in front slows down. The kid rams into them going about sixty mph and sends the truck sailing into the ditch. He drives straight to the sheriff's office to report what's happened, and when the sheriff gets out to the highway, he finds one brother dead and the other one a paraplegic. Now the paraplegic's asking for two point three million."

"What are his chances?" What were my own?

"He's not going to get a dime," my father said. "I could put you to work Monday morning researching how someone can lawfully repossess a vehicle from a purchaser who's defaulted. How does that sound?"

I felt weak-kneed and sick. My father had finished washing and was leaning against the counter with his arms folded across his chest. "I need to tell you something first," I said, twisting the dishtowel in my hands. "You and Mom."

"Helen?" my father called. "Come in here a minute."

My mother walked in from the entryway, flipping through the day's mail. When she glanced up at us there was a flicker of alarm in her eyes. "What's wrong?"

"Dennis has something he wants to tell us. Dennis?" His face was impassive, his eyes inscrutable. My mother was suddenly alert and attentive, missing nothing.

I looked down, unable to speak. My mouth was dry. I wanted to preface my confession with an explanation of why I hadn't told them I'd dropped out, how I hadn't wanted to disappoint them now that they were so proud of me for once, but I felt certain they wouldn't understand, that it would only appear as if I were making excuses.

I took a deep, wavering breath and looked up, focusing on the space between them. "I wanted to tell you this before, and I tried to several times. I know there's no excuse, but I was afraid to tell you."

"What are you trying to tell us?" my mother said.

"Get to the point, Dennis."

"I dropped out of law school," I said softly.

"What?"

"What are you talking about?" my mother said.

"I dropped out in January, two weeks into the second semester," I said. "I tried . . ."

"You mean you've been *lying* to us all this time?"

"Yes."

"Thomas!" my mother cried.

My father reached me before I could react, hitting me twice in the face with his open hands, then snatching the neck of my T-shirt and driving me back into the cupboards. "You bastard," he said, striking my face again, "I should knock your teeth in." The veins were standing out on his forehead and his eyes were narrow slits.

"Tom, let go of him," my mother said sternly. "Tom."

My father snapped me back against the cupboards, then abruptly let go, both of us staring at one another, breathing heavily. I lowered my chin and shoulders, preparing for him to hit me again and saying a silent prayer that he wouldn't. My face was throbbing and my lower lip felt swollen.

"How could you do this to us, Dennis?" my mother said. "How could you *lie* to us all this time and live with yourself?"

"I'm sorry I didn't tell you," I said. "I wanted . . ."

"I don't care what *you* wanted," my father said. "You came to me a year ago and said you wanted to go to law school. And even though you'd never shown *any* inclination to become a lawyer, *none* whatsoever, I said I was willing to pay your tuition. I held up my end of the agreement. You didn't. So don't come to me now and tell me what *you* wanted. Is that clear?"

"That's not what I was going to say. I wanted you to know that I didn't drop out because I didn't understand the law or was in over my head. I dropped out because I realized I didn't want to be a lawyer."

"You're the one who came to *me* and said you wanted to go to law school. *I* never said you had to be a lawyer."

"I'm not saying you did. I'm saying I thought I wanted to become a lawyer, which is why I went. I was wrong. I made a mistake and I apologize."

"That's right and you're the one who's going to have to live with it because I'm not going to help you out anymore. From now on you're on your own. Is that clear, Dennis?"

"Yes."

"How much do you expect your mother and me to give?" my father said. "You've had every advantage I can think of. When you said you wanted a drum set we went out and bought you one. We let you stay out till all hours playing in your little band. Your mother was against it, but I said, No, it'll be good for him. He'll learn some self-discipline and earn his own spending money. We sent you to the college of your choice and even let you go an extra year. Then we paid for you to go to law school. I don't know what it is you want or what else you expect from us, but I'm through supporting you while you try and figure out what it is. You can stay here for the next two weeks until you find a job, but after that I want you out of the house. As far as I'm concerned we've done more than enough for you. If you want to throw it all away, do it on your own time and money." He turned and walked through the kitchen and out the front door.

I looked at my mother, her face set, her eyes cold.

"Who else knows that you dropped out?" she said. "Does everyone else know but us? Have you told everyone else but your own parents? You have, haven't you, Dennis. You told everyone else but us. Does Anne know?"

"No."

"What have you been doing all this time that we thought you were in law school? Have you been running around spending the money your father gave you for tuition?"

"No, I have it."

"How much of it?"

"All of it."

"We expect every penny of it back."

I said nothing.

"What have you been doing all this time?"

"I worked in a record store."

"Doing what?"

"Selling records."

She slapped me sharply. "Don't you dare get sarcastic with me. I won't tolerate that from you." Her eyes were blazing. "I don't want to look at you right now, Dennis. I don't even want to hear you. I don't care where you go, but I don't want to see you for the rest of the day."

I didn't leave my room for the remainder of the morning or afternoon. I lay on my bed watching the sunlight advance across the room, then slowly retreat. In the late afternoon I slept deeply, waking up at six. I walked out to the landing and listened for my parents. When I didn't hear them, I moved downstairs like a cat burglar, ready to retreat at the first sound. In the kitchen I called Montana. She picked up on the second ring.

"I told my parents."

"*Finally,*" she said. "How'd they react?"

"About like you'd expect."

"Did they kick you out of the house?"

"Not for two weeks, but my dad made it clear he's not going to support me anymore."

"What are you going to do now?"

"I don't know."

"What about moving down here?"

"I don't know, Montana. I feel so out of it. Cowboy Angst feels like it was years ago."

"You are out of it. You're in Montana, for Christ's sake. Nothing's going to happen up there. Move down here and get back into it."

"What do you see us doing exactly? We get a band together.

Then what? Play covers at the local bars and clubs and hope someone discovers us? I don't see that happening."

"Why not?"

"You're a good singer, Montana, and you have great stage presence, but you're not a great interpretive singer. That's never going to be your thing. We need to write our own songs or we'll always be just another cover band. And to be perfectly honest, I feel like my future in music is tied to yours. If you do well, I'll do well. If you don't, I won't."

"Then we'll have to write our own songs, won't we."

"We tried that, remember?"

We'd made several attempts in college but never finished one. Within a couple hours we always began arguing about whose fault it was that we weren't getting anywhere. I complained that Montana's melodies were so clearly stolen from other songs that we were guaranteed to be sued for plagiarism the first time Cowboy Angst performed them in public. Montana snapped that if I didn't like them, why didn't I try coming up with my own instead of bitching about how unoriginal hers were? And speaking of originality, my lyrics were too clichéd and banal even for a country song, and even if I could get beyond a first verse, she'd be too embarrassed to sing them. I said maybe if I didn't have to write from a woman's point of view so Montana could sing them, I might have something to say. Montana said she should have known better than to expect me to understand anything from a woman's point of view. It was ugly and as close as we ever came to disliking one another. One of us would always walk out and a day or two would pass before we saw one another and apologized.

"We'll try again," Montana said.

"I have this vision of myself as a thirty-five-year-old in a cowboy shirt with leather fringe playing a gig in the Holiday Inn to three drunk businessmen. I don't want to end up like that."

"I don't either, but if you don't come down here and at least try, you'll always wonder what would have happened if you had."

"I know."

"Does that mean you'll do it?"

"I'll think about it."

"You'll *think* about it? You know . . . ," Montana said, annoyed. Then stopped.

Not long after she graduated from Colorado State, Montana had started to believe she was the only member of Cowboy Angst who was committed to making the band a success. She'd spent the summer in Fort Collins waiting tables and sitting in with other bands, and when I returned in August for my fifth year, she'd been excited to get Cowboy Angst going again. She'd decided we needed to rehearse at least four days a week and play gigs three times a week. The rest of us were still in school and we balked, reminding Montana that we needed to study. She pointed out that she was working eight hours a day. True, but she didn't have any reading assignments or papers to write. Montana complained that we didn't care enough about our music, that it was just a weekend hobby to us. She talked about quitting and moving to Austin or at least joining a local band that was serious about playing full-time.

We began rehearsing twice a week and playing gigs on the weekend. Montana stopped threatening to quit, but whenever a gig fell through or someone missed a rehearsal, she started talking about how rinky-dink this all was and maybe it was time to move on.

One night at Linden's in Old Town we'd played an enervating gig that dozens of people walked out on after the first set, something that hadn't happened to us since we'd first formed the band. An hour before we played, the keyboard player and other singer, Ryan Wade, had been dumped by his girlfriend of three years, and he'd started drinking as soon as he arrived, telling anyone who would listen that he didn't give a shit, he just didn't give a shit. The bass player, Chris Ostrom, was one of Ryan's close friends, and he began buying both of them shots to help Ryan feel better. By the third set Chris was so drunk, he had to sit on the floor. Soon he quit playing, rolled into a ball and went to sleep. Ryan was sagging on his stool, unable to form words, let alone sing. The rest of us tried to keep things going, but by the last set the only people left in the bar were serious drinkers who were in no shape to walk anywhere else. Afterward I apologized to the manager, who said he'd seen worse.

Outside I found Chris sleeping on the sidewalk. Ryan was on his hands and knees, retching into the gutter. Montana was standing over him, saying this was it, they were both out of the band. I told her to wait inside, then got the pedal steel player, Nick Russell, to help load Chris and Ryan into his truck bed and drive them home. I said—if they were conscious—to tell them not to worry about it, they were still in the band.

I had an apartment in Old Town above a ballet school that was only half a block away on Jefferson Street, and Montana helped me carry my drums upstairs. I got a six-pack from the fridge, but Montana said she needed something with a kick to it, so I pulled out a bottle of tequila.

We went into the living room where I sat on the couch and watched Montana pace the length of the room, complaining about Chris and Ryan's lack of professionalism. I handed her shots as she passed back and forth.

After listening to her for ten minutes, I said, "Why are you being such a pain in the ass?"

"I'm not being a pain in the ass."

"Yes, you are," I said. "I don't know what's causing it, but ever since I got back here you've been bitching about how you're the only musician in town who's committed and the rest of us are a bunch of weekend hacks. I'm tired of it."

Montana stopped pacing and sat on the floor against the wall. She was silent for a long time. We hadn't turned any lights on, and I couldn't see her face across the room.

"When I first started waitressing at the Rio Grande this summer, a couple college girls who followed the band came in for lunch, and when I walked up to take their order, they looked at me like they couldn't figure out what I was doing there. Finally one of them said, 'What are you doing here?' I said, 'I'm working.' The other girl said she thought she'd heard I'd moved to Austin. I said, 'No, I'm still here.' Was I still singing? Yes, I was still singing. Oh. Then they gave me their order. End of conversation.

"At first I thought, OK, here's two girls who don't realize that some people actually work after college. No big deal. But other people said the same thing. 'Why are you still here?' or 'Why are you waiting tables? I thought you were a singer.' Whenever that happens I feel like I have to apologize for what I'm doing. Somehow when I was playing in college, people thought of me as Montana Wildhack, lead singer of Cowboy Angst. Now that I'm waiting tables, they seem to think I must not have been as good as they thought I was. It pisses me off.

"I'm sorry I've been such a bitch lately, but I'm having a hard time adjusting to this. I feel like I'm waiting for something to happen, and it's very frustrating. Then when we have a night like tonight, I wonder what I'm doing. It feels like a waste of time. I wish you'd finished school on time so we could move to Austin or play enough gigs during the week so I didn't have to have a day job. I'm never going to be happy just playing gigs on the week-ends and making a couple hundred bucks. That may be OK for other people, but it's not enough for me. I'm going to be good at this, Dennis. I don't know how long it's going to take, but I guarantee you I'm going to be very good at this."

I could hear the heat in her voice, and I said, "I know you are, Montana."

"What?" I said now.

"Nothing."

"What? Go ahead. What were you going to say?"

"If you decide to come down here, don't do it just because you can't think of anything else to do, OK? I don't want you down here if that's the main reason. Because if it is, the first time things look grim you're going to pack up and leave again. I'd rather not have you down here if that's what's going to happen."

"That's the main reason you think I'd come down? Because I couldn't come up with anything else?"

"No, but I've wanted to tell you that in case it was a reason. I want you to be here because you need to be here, not because you don't have any other options."

"I'll keep that in mind," I said.

"Good."

"Did I tell you I miss you?"

Six

Buckaroo's was a one-story log cabin located on the west bank of the Missouri. Its name was spelled out in green shingles on the red roof and on the lighted sign covered in chicken wire showing a cowboy roping his buxom cowgirl. When I walked into the bar on Saturday night, five patrons were seated at the bar and all of them turned on their tall chrome stools to look at me. The squat bartender resembled a Rumanian weightlifter from behind and was wearing a tooled leather belt that said Vicki on the back. I considered telling him he'd grabbed his girlfriend's belt by mistake but changed my mind when he turned around.

He was a she. "Can I help you?" Vick or Vicki said, basso profundo.

"I'm with the band. Just checking to make sure the stage is clear."

"I figured you got lost and needed directions." The patrons chuckled, easily amused.

I went out to the van and began carrying in my cases. Setting up I found confetti around the rim of my snare from the New Year's Eve gig. I hung my canvas bag full of Vic Firth drumsticks on the floor tom and began to stroke each head. The Cloverleafs' bass player, Jimmy Jensen, walked in. He was wearing a toupee with thick dark bangs that swooped down and across his high forehead. I stood up and went around my kit to shake hands. We talked for a few minutes and I found myself staring at the toupee. Jimmy looked over at the bar. The bangs didn't move.

"Something wrong?" Jimmy said, patting his hair.

"No, no."

He glanced around the stage as if for eavesdroppers, then leaned into me and whispered, "Got a hairpiece eight weeks ago."

"Yeah?"

"What do you think? Is it obvious? You can tell me. I always liked your hair."

"No, it looks fine, Jimmy."

"You can't tell?"

"Only if the person knew you before."

"I need to go check it."

I watched him cross the dance floor in his polished black boots, tight Wranglers and tomato red western shirt with white piping. He'd assumed a rakish air that was in stark contrast with his normally meek demeanor. I wondered if his wife had left him.

George and Patti arrived. George's hair was grayer than at New Year's and his face was gaunt. He had pale blue eyes and whenever he was trying to intimidate someone or look highly skeptical, he would lower his eyelids and glare at his victim without blinking. He tried it on me now as if sizing me up.

"Don't give me that look, George," I said. "I know that look. It doesn't work on me."

He smiled and shook my hand. "How are ya, cowboy? You look

good." His voice sounded like it washed over a dry creek bed before heading up his cigarette-charred throat.

I hugged Patti, who had inherited Mrs. Muzzana's loose dark curls and brown eyes.

When everyone was set up, Patti kicked the band into gear with "Don't Come Home A-Drinkin' With Lovin' on Your Mind." I was happily surprised to see how energetic everyone was. It reconfirmed my belief that the Cloverleafs played best when they didn't have a gig every weekend. They were tighter as a group when they played regularly, but by the fourth successive weekend gig they'd be bored and lethargic. Patti would complain about never seeing her boyfriend (now husband), Jimmy would moan about any gig farther than forty miles away and George would care only about drinking. They'd had some awful nights.

But tonight they hadn't played in five weeks, the gig was in town at a popular bar, George was sober and their favorite drummer was home. People were streaming into the bar and three or four brave couples were out on the dance floor. By the fourth song, when George was singing "I Feel Like Hank Williams Tonight," I'd broken a sweat under the bright stage lights and the dance floor was full. I was so happy to be playing again with a band that I couldn't stop smiling. I felt strangely magnanimous, suddenly convinced the world was a good place full of kind, forgiving people where everything always worked out for the best.

We closed out the set with "My Walkin' Shoes," playing faster and faster after each chorus as I drove the band on until no one on the floor could keep up and they began laughing and clapping. "We'll be right back," George said.

George, Patti and I sat at a small corner table during the break and drank water. Jimmy had slipped off somewhere.

"We're cookin'," said George.

"Yes we are," I said.

"What are you smiling about?" Patti said. "You look like a Cheshire cat."

"Just happy to be playing."

"That's it?"

"That's it," I said. "Hey, what's with Jimmy?"

"How 'bout that?" George said.

"Did his wife leave him?"

"He's not that lucky," George said. "No, he's going to turn fifty in a couple months and he decided he was starting to act old, so he went out and bought a toupee and an entirely new wardrobe. I almost didn't recognize him the first time I saw him."

"His hair doesn't move," I said.

"That's what I said."

"Makes a hell of a helmet though, doesn't it?" George said. "Did you know he bought a motorcycle?"

"No way."

"Yeah, a real monster. He gave Patti a ride on it. He offered to give me a ride, but I wouldn't get on that thing with him. What is it again, Patti?"

"A Honda Shadow."

"Goes something like a hundred and ten."

"One thirty," Patti said.

"Fast enough that if he ever gets hit, he won't be a quadriplegic. They'll just shovel what's left of him and the bike into a box and deep-six it," George said. He clapped his hands. "Yep, it's a whole new Jimmy."

"Five minutes," Patti said, looking at her watch. "I'm going to the ladies' room."

After she left I said, "How are you doing?"

"You mean about the drinking?"

I nodded, not sure I should be asking.

"All right. A hell of a lot better than a couple weeks ago. It doesn't help being in here. Barbara and I quit smoking three days ago, too. Thought I'd tackle all my vices at once. I'm chewing nicotine gum night and day and wearing this patch on the back of my neck."

"I wondered what that was. What's it do?"

"It decreases my desire to smoke." He said it like a mantra, carefully memorized and repeated in times of doubt.

"Does it work?"

"Does it work. Well, instead of walking over to the cigarette machine and buying a pack, I *think* about walking over to the cigarette machine and buying a pack. As long as I'm not around people who smoke or drink, or I'm busy, I'm all right. It ain't easy being in here, Dennis."

"Maybe you shouldn't play for a while."

"And give up the one thing I still enjoy? No way. I know why you're smiling. I feel the same way. This is what I love. I wouldn't stop doing it for anything. Right?"

"Right."

It was a Cloverleaf tradition to start and finish every set with an up-tempo song. George believed people were more likely to resume dancing with a fast song and want to continue dancing after ending with a fast song; whereas if they ended with a ballad, couples would dance close, "get all worked up," as George said, then have to sit for twenty minutes. Meanwhile the men would be thinking of ways to get the women into bed or at least out to a pickup in the parking lot, and if successful, they'd be lost for the night. It was an empirical, hormonal theory at best, but the one I'd followed with Cowboy Angst. George began the second set with "King of the Road" and ended it fifty minutes later with the most emotional cover of "Whiskey River" I'd ever heard.

Afterward the two of us walked outside and sat on the back-steps of the bar, toweling our faces and necks. George kept spitting every five seconds as if he were chewing snoose and not gum. "So how was law school?"

"I dropped out in January."

He lowered the towel and looked at me. "No shit?"

"No shit."

"What'd your parents say?"

"I just told them this morning. They weren't real happy."

"I'll bet," George said.

"Can I ask you something? Do you think I'd be crazy to move to Austin?"

"No, I don't think you'd be crazy," George said. "It's just that there's so much luck involved. You can fall in with a talented group and take off or just as easily go nowhere."

Lately I'd been thinking how brave it had been for Montana to pack up and move to Austin alone. I didn't feel as if I'd performed one brave act since I decided to quit Cowboy Angst and go to law school. "What's the bravest thing you've ever done?"

George raised his chin and spit into the night. At the south end of the parking lot someone was spinning his tires on the gravel, and you could hear it pepper the side of a car. "Admitting to myself that I was never going to be anything but an average singer who plays local bars. That took me a long time. I never actually tried to make a career out of it, but I always imagined that someone would hear me one night and say, I'm going to get you the recognition you deserve. Kind of like what happened to Charley Pride. He opens for a couple established singers in Great Falls, they like his work and they ask him to move to Nashville where they'll help him out. Never happened to me.

"For a long time when you're growing up, which for me was until I was about forty-five, you always think you're going to be the best at something. The best pedal steel guitarist or the best singer. And then there comes a point when you realize you're not going to be the best at anything, you're just going to be like everyone else. You wonder what the hell you're supposed to do next. And you can either accept it or fuck yourself up trying to deny it. That's the way I see it, anyway, and God knows I've fucked up enough to last a lifetime." He spit to the side. "What about you, what's the bravest thing you've ever done?"

"I don't think I've done it yet."

"I know what you mean."

When we went inside, Patti and Jimmy were waiting onstage. I sat at my drums. George said into his microphone, "I'd like to dedicate this next song to our drummer, Dennis McCance, who was released from Deer Lodge last Monday after serving time for armed robbery." The crowd clapped and cheered. I laughed and played a short solo on my tom toms. George cued us into "Folsom Prison Blues." When the crowd recognized the song, they yelled louder and stomped their feet.

Following the set I got up and stood at the edge of the stage. Men returning to their tables shook my hand. "Congratulations, man!" "Armed robbery. Fuckin'-A!" "You see my old man there?"

"You're a hero," George said behind me. "Country fans love ex-cons. Merle Haggard, Johnny Paycheck. Hell, even Randy Travis was a juvenile delinquent. If you want to make it in this business, it wouldn't hurt to get thrown in jail now and then." Someone was yelling his name and waving him over like a traffic cop.

I decided to sit at the bar and began weaving through the crowd. Drunken strangers pumped my hand, clapped my back, shouted in my face. I felt as if I were going through a fraternity hazing line. A stool opened up and I slid onto it. Vicki was pacing behind the bar, rolling up on the balls of her feet like a boxer. I caught her eye and asked for water. She slammed it down in front of me. "Thanks, Vick," I said as she stormed away.

"Are you the famous felon?"

"Not if it means another slap on the back," I said, turning to see who had spoken. I saw a face I recognized but couldn't place. The woman had clear blue eyes and a plump lower lip I wanted to kiss and bite.

"No slaps," she said, smiling. "You're Dennis McCance, aren't you? I'm Renee Peterson. I went to high school with Anne."

"I knew I knew you," I said, immediately telling myself, Look up, look up. Don't look down. No. Up, up. Look her in the eyes, look her in the eyes.

"Why are you smiling like that?" she said.

"I'm just happy. I haven't played with a band in a long time."

"Anne told me you played in one."

"Two, actually. I play with these guys, the Cloverleafs, whenever I'm home, and I used to have a band down at school, but no more."

"What happened?" She squeezed in between me and the woman on my right.

"The usual country music problems. Alcoholism, car wrecks, vet school, the carpet business. Can I buy you a drink? Vicki the bartender is a close personal friend of mine. Do you know her? She's also an ex-con."

"I'll have a Bud Light."

"Vicki," I said, waving at her as she stomped past. I got her attention and yelled my order. I cringed as she slammed down the bottle and it began to foam.

"You're not drinking?" Renee said.

"I never drink on the job," I said, "which probably goes against everything you've ever heard about musicians. Truth is, I'm a lousy drummer when I'm drunk."

"Anne told me you're in law school."

I looked at her for a moment, wishing she'd said anything but that. She had thin brown hair pulled back off her face and it curled under at the nape of her neck.

"I'm sorry," she said, clearly uncomfortable. "Is that a bad subject?"

"No, no," I said, trying to pull myself together. "I was in law school."

"But you're finished now?"

"Sort of. I dropped out."

"Oh. Anne didn't tell me that."

"That's because she doesn't know. I just told my parents this morning."

"Did they pay for it?"

"Yes, they did," I said, beginning to drum on the counter. "But what about you, what are you doing now?"

"I'm a teller at First National Bank."

"That's right," I said. "I remember Anne saying that the other day. Nice bank." Renee leveled her gaze on me as if looking for any hint of reproach or irony. I leaned back on my stool and looked at the stage. I saw George walking over to it. I turned to Renee. "I have to go play our last set. Are you going to stick around?"

"Maybe."

"Well, I hope I see you again." I got up and walked back to my drums.

George said to me, "How about a polka so we can see how your hands are holding up? Play as fast you can and we'll keep up." He fixed his glare on me.

"All right," I said. I clicked my sticks together at a relaxed tempo and we began. Couples headed to the floor and began sweeping around one another as if guided by radar. I began playing faster on my hi-hat and snare. The dancers' faces became more intent as they wheeled about with increasing fervor. I went faster and faster until they were spinning about in a frenzy, careening into one another and shooting off in new directions.

A cowboy caught a flying knee in the thigh and went down. He stood up and punched the first person to ram into him. It was a woman, and her partner didn't take kindly to it. He dropped the cowboy with a punch to the throat and stooped to help up his prostrate partner. He was nailed by a thigh in the face and within seconds nearly everyone on the floor was throwing punches and lashing out with his boots. We ground to a halt.

I saw Vicki vault the counter with the grace of a gymnast, a sawed-off pool cue in hand. I began playing the opening to "Wipeout" on my floor tom, fully aware that I was throwing fat on the fire. Patti picked it up and soon we were playing an all-out country rendition of the surf tune. At the end of it, I started on my floor tom again, playing as hard and as loud as I could, loving the violent, primal rhythm of the accented sixteenth notes. The Cloverleafs joined in again. The brawl had broken down into individual fistfights. Three or four men were sprawled on the floor, kicked and tripped over by backpedaling fighters, others bent at the waist clutching their faces, stomachs, groins, the women on their hands and knees crawling over bodies, seeking shelter beneath the tables.

"Wipeout!" yelled Patti.

I was happy.

I found Renee sitting at the bar after we finished the set. She said the friend who'd driven her to Buckaroo's had left. Could I give her a ride home? Absolutely. There was a brief delay when the owner came over to pay George. He said that perhaps playing "Wipeout" during a brawl hadn't been the best in song selection. He looked at me. And maybe he should knock off a hundred bucks for damages. "It wasn't his fault and you know it," George said. "Ah hell," said the owner. He pulled a money clip from his snakeskin boot and thumbed off five hundred dollars.

In the parking lot George said, "You almost cost yourself a hundred bucks there, cowboy."

"You guys wouldn't have split it with me?"

"Not me," Patti said. "These things never happen to us when you're not around, do they, Dad?"

"Never." And to Renee: "Watch this guy."

"I will."

"Where to?" I said as I tried to start the van.

"Where do you want to go?"

"I wouldn't mind having a few beers."

"The bars are closed."

"True."

"We could always buy beer and go to my house."

"Great." I put the Angstmobile in gear and drove out of the parking lot. I was thrilled. Did I have any expectations here? Apparently so. High hopes at the very least.

We bought beer and crossed the Missouri. Streetlights on the opposite bank dropped orange obelisks of light across the black sheen of the river. We passed over two sets of railroad tracks that rattled the cymbals in back and drove east up Third Avenue where elm trees arched high overhead. Only a handful of cars were parked on every street, the houses dark and still.

"Does it seem awfully quiet to you right now?"

"It's always this quiet. You're just used to living in a city."

"I guess so. I used to live near a hospital in D.C. My first two weeks there I woke up every time I heard a siren. Later it got to where I'd be suspicious when I didn't hear one. Something had to be wrong if it was that quiet. Like the silence in a jungle just before Jim wrestles a three-hundred-pound anaconda on *Wild Kingdom*."

"Well, you're out of the jungle now, Tarzan. Nothing that exciting happens here. That's it on the corner." She pointed at a small brick house painted white.

I eased the van to a stop on the north side of the house and cut the engine. It continued to idle and shake for a few seconds, then backfired.

"Did you drive this to D.C.?" Renee said, laughing.

"You're not impressed?" I said. "No, I left it here. I don't like to get too far from home in it. That used to be a five-hundred-mile radius. Now it's about fifty."

Renee led me across the short springy lawn, both of us leaving footprints in the damp grass. The porch light was out and we stepped into a darkened foyer where she hung her jacket on an invisible peg. I aimed my coat in the same general vicinity and heard it fall to the floor. I tried again with the same result and left it there, not wanting to lose my guide. I was about to ask if the house had electricity when Renee snapped on the kitchen's track lighting. The room was white with red Formica counters, surgically clean.

"This is a clean, well-lighted kitchen," I said, smiling.

"Thanks. My ex-husband was a slob. Now I can keep everything as clean as I want with half the effort." She was rummaging in a cabinet full of glasses, the band of her sweater rising to reveal flesh. "I was thinking we could play a game," she said.

I felt my heart fibrillate. "I love games."

She turned around holding two shot glasses and I thought, We appear to be heading for a long night of power drinking. I guess this means I'm about to begin practicing my old lifestyle. Renee turned off all the kitchen lights except for the red industrial light hanging above the breakfast table. We sat across from one another and she pushed a shot glass over to me.

"What's the game?"

"You have to drink one shot of beer every sixty seconds."

"One a minute," I said, nodding. "How do you win?"

"Whoever gets drunk first wins."

"I think I'm going to be good at this." I filled our glasses and raised mine in salute. "To country music."

"Country music," Renee said and drank her shot. "I used to hate country music."

"Me too."

"No you didn't. How could you hate it when you play in a country band?"

"I wanted to join a rock band in high school but my parents wouldn't let me. They didn't want me staying out till four in the morning on weekends playing gigs and getting stoned."

"You don't do that in country bands?"

"Oh no. In a country band you stay out till four in the morning playing gigs and getting drunk." I checked my watch and filled our glasses. "To parents." *Boom*. "My parents liked the fact that George—the guy who told you to watch me—was an adult and had his daughter in the band. They figured he'd be responsible for us. They didn't know he was an alcoholic and that Patti and I took care of him. How about you?"

"That's all my ex-husband listens to. He's a basketball referee and we spent the weekends in towns like Centerville and Simms. Afterward we'd go drinking at the bars. All they played was country. It took about a year, but I started to like it."

"Do you like basketball?"

"I hate basketball," Renee said. "The first two years we were married I was the good wife and went to every game. I used to sit at the top of the bleachers and read a book. When we went out, people would ask me about the game. Most of the time I didn't even know who'd won, which is unforgivable in a small town."

We were twenty-five shots into the game, and I felt like I was winning. I wanted to lean across the table and kiss Renee, but I couldn't decide if that was a good idea. I hoped a few more shots would show the way.

"Are you home for good now?" she said, digging in her purse.

"For good?"

"Yeah. Are you just home for the summer or for good?"

I looked at her face in profile. Both her hands were below the table. She turned her face slightly away for a moment, then touched her lips and sat up. A dark fleck of tobacco on her lower lip gave her away. I reached over and brushed it off. I wondered if chewing snoose was how she'd developed such a lovely bottom lip.

"I'm embarrassed," Renee said, blushing slightly.

"No, that's fine." I knew several women, including Montana on occasion, who chewed tobacco, but I hadn't seen it in a while.

"I got in the habit from Roger. I know it's disgusting but I haven't been able to quit. I only do it when I'm drinking. Do you want a pinch?"

"No thanks." The last time I'd tried it while drinking I'd spent fifteen minutes on my hands and knees, vomiting.

"You haven't answered my question."

"I don't know the answer."

"Do you like coming home?" Renee said. "That's what I want to know. Because a lot of people who go off to college and never move back act like it kills them to visit. Last Christmas I saw a high school friend who's been living in New York City for the last seven or eight years. She told me, 'I wasn't going to fly here for Christmas but my parents insisted and said they'd pay for the ticket. Fortunately, it's only for three days.' How's that supposed to make me feel? I live here. I've lived here almost my entire life."

"I like coming home," I said. "I came home four summers in a row. I like Prairie View and I love Montana."

"But would you live here?"

"I don't know. Maybe if I could live in our house with everything in it except my parents, I would. Lots of room, comfortable furniture. Unfortunately, my parents are planning on living there a while longer."

"You don't like living with your parents?"

"I love living with my parents. I'd like to spend the rest of my life with them. I could walk to work every day with my dad, do the dishes after dinner, take out the garbage and play weekend gigs with the Cloverleafs. What a time we'd have."

"You can't always live off your parents, you know."

I felt as if I'd been slapped. I looked directly at her, my brow dropping, jaw tightening. "Is that how you see it?"

"I think your parents have done a lot for everyone in your family. They put all of you through the college of your choice, didn't they? That's more than most parents are willing to do. You said tonight that they paid for you to go to law school. Maybe you wouldn't have dropped out if you'd been paying for it yourself. Maybe you wouldn't even have started. And I remember Anne saying that your parents helped pay her rent for the first three years she lived in Boston because she wasn't making enough money to support herself. No one ever did that for me. I just don't think you guys realize how lucky you are. Try working for a while and you'll appreciate what it takes to live in a house like your parents'."

"You don't think I appreciate that?"

"I don't know," Renee said. "No, I guess not. Not when you say you'd like to live there with everything in it except your parents."

"I was being facetious."

"Fine." We sat looking at one another until Renee turned away. "I need to use the bathroom." She got up and left the kitchen.

I began pacing the floor. I don't *appreciate* what my parents have done for me? I don't have any guilt or remorse about all they've done for me and how I've screwed up? Is that how it is?

Well, fuck you. It's the goddamn guilt that got me into this mess in the first place. Wasn't I happy playing in my band? Hell yes. Did I stick to my guns? Hell no. I thought I'd show a little *appreciation* for everything my parents did for me and go to law school. Become a respected, well-paid professional. Everyone will be happy. Maybe even I'll be happy. I want everyone to be happy. Are you happy? Good. We don't want anyone around who's not happy. Do you appreciate how happy you are? You'd better, because we don't want anyone around who's happy and doesn't appreciate it. Do you realize and appreciate how lucky you are to be happy? Luck plays an enormous part in your being happy. You could just as easily been the son of parents who felt a high school education was sufficient. Where would you be then? Would you be happy? Would you be appreciative? Would you consider yourself lucky? No thinking about it, now. Say the first thing that comes to mind. Up yours.

When Renee returned, I went into the bathroom. I looked in the mirror and saw a face I was sick of. I wanted to exchange it for a more interesting one. Something along the lines of the young Chet Baker. Something with a handsome edge to it. I'd pass on the old Chet Baker face, which hadn't been served well by heroin. How do I make a graceful exit? Do I say, Thanks for a great time, Renee. Now if you don't mind I'd like to race home and fix my parents breakfast in bed? My earlier rapture had collapsed into weariness. I gave myself the finger.

When I came out of the bathroom, Renee was sitting in the front room on a love seat facing the fireplace. She was hugging her knees and holding a beer. She turned and gave me a small smile. I faked mine, trying to decide if I were in a fight or flight mode. I thought fight. "I need to get a beer."

"I got one for you," Renee said, nodding at the glass coffee table in front of her. There were two director's chairs near the love seat, and I was about to sit in one of them when she said,

"Sit here," and patted the love seat as if coaxing a small dog. I obeyed and sat next to her. "Did I piss you off?"

I laughed despite myself. "Yes, you did." I liked her for saying that.

"Do you think I was out of line?"

"No, I deserved it," I said, pausing. "My parents are in a position to help us out financially, and they enjoyed being able to. My father's father abandoned his family when my dad was fourteen, and his mother was always dependent on her relatives to stay ahead of the bill collector, so it was very important to him that he be able to help his kids. Now my parents are trying to understand why after all the economic and educational advantages we've had, none of us is making dime one." I was seeing all of this as I said it. "You don't think we appreciate it, but we do. I think all three of us feel varying degrees of guilt about how much they've done for us. Miles seemed to resent it from the beginning. He hated kids saying we were rich. Which we weren't, but they didn't know any better. In eighth grade a girl standing behind Miles in the lunch line called him a rich kid, and he turned around and dropped her. My father tried to explain to Miles that he should be proud that he did well as a lawyer. Miles said he was proud of him, but I think Miles wished he'd been born into a poor ranching family. He considers himself something of a martyr because he only accepted money for tuition, he always had a part-time job and he wouldn't accept any help once he graduated while Anne and I have always been willing to accept their help. I'm not sure what Anne's response was. Excelling in school and now work, maybe. She's always been the peacemaker."

"What about you?" Renee said. "You went to law school?"

"Yep. Worked out beautifully, huh?"

My left arm was stretched across the back of the seat, inches from her shoulder. I felt certain that if I touched her, I'd get a static electric shock. On the stereo the Judds were singing "Let Me Tell You about Love," and Renee was mouthing the words. I was confident that all I had to do was kiss her to set the wheels in motion. Don't do it, I thought, knowing exactly how it would end. I'd sleep with her, I wouldn't call, and the next time I saw her it would be awkward and uncomfortable and I'd wonder why I'd done it. There was a time when I thought I was proving something by sleeping with all these women. Look at me. I may not be able to thump anyone's melon, but I know how to pick up women. Lately I'd grown tired of it and started thinking I was as pathetic as the thug who picks fights in bars. The trick was remembering that in the morning I'd be happier I hadn't slept with her, that instead I'd gotten a good night's rest. Right now I wanted to kiss her. Maybe even touch her breasts. Then I'd go home. I leaned toward her and saw Renee turn to watch me. Just before I reached her mouth I thought: I wonder if she took out that chew? She had. Her mouth tasted faintly like salami.

Renee still had her knees drawn up to her chest and for a moment I couldn't decide where to put my right hand. I tried wrapping my arm around her legs but my hand ended at her left breast and I thought better of it. I touched her cheek and ran my fingers through her hair. After a while Renee turned her head and took my thumb in her mouth. I felt an internal clangor as emergency corpuscles with bleating sirens and throbbing blue lights raced to transport blood from insignificant areas such as the brain and feet to central headquarters. Hot moist breath in my ear raised the sirens to a higher pitch. Later a suggestion was made to move to the bedroom and we rose slowly, entwined and kissing. I had to urinate. I asked Renee not to undress without me. Then I was before the toilet with an erection, wheeling backward and forward in an attempt to guide the high arc to the target area. There was still time to leave. I could walk out the front door and be in the van before she knew I was gone. I stepped into the hall and hesitated.

"Dennis?" Renee said. "I'm in here."

She was sitting on the end of the queen-sized bed. The curtains were drawn, pale streetlight filtering through them. We stood before one another and kissed. My hands were trembling and I was afraid she'd notice. She crossed her wrists and grabbed the waistband of her black sweater. I felt as if I were at the private showing of a recently completed masterpiece, a magnificent bust seen by no one but the artist and his model. I placed my hands on her moon white stomach as the sweater rose and was tossed aside. Renee's hands moved to unclasp the front hook and free her breasts from their pink silk cups. I took an involuntary breath.

Holding them I had to agree with Anne that they were big and firm as well as stupendous and monumental. We undressed and lay on the bed. I was nervous and clumsy as a teenager. I dropped down between her legs, tongue deep in the mystery of her sex, thinking how ridiculous I'd look to anyone watching at the window. I glanced up at the pyramidal beauty of Renee's breasts and decided they were also spectacular and wondrous. Certainly not a necessity, but not a bad investment if they made you feel better and you had the cash.

Then Renee was lying on my stomach with her hands splayed flat on both sides of my head, kissing my ear and whispering, "Relax." She slipped down on top of me and began sliding above me with her eyes closed, arching back until I howled and pulled her forward to an acceptable angle.

Afterward she immediately dropped off and slept with her hands above her head like a ballerina. I watched the clock for half an hour until it said five and eased out of bed, moving around the floor on my hands and knees collecting my clothes. I was still drunk and my head hurt. Depression was already setting in. When was I going to start showng some self-restraint? I'd said I wasn't going to do this anymore and yet here I was again, crawling out of a stranger's bedroom, praying she wouldn't wake up before I made it to the van.

I let myself out and walked across the lawn. I'd been thinking that once I told my parents I'd dropped out of law school, everything would take on a sharper focus and the next step would become clear, but I was beginning to understood how mistaken I'd been.

Halfway to the van I heard a rustling in the juniper bushes on the north side of the house, and I turned to see a thickset man running at me with his head and shoulders lowered like a charging bull. My first thought was: Miles! and I felt a blood-draining panic as I turned and began to sprint. A great weight slammed into the backs of my knees, and I hit the ground with an audible thud.

There was no air in my lungs and I was suddenly back at the YMCA, jerking desperately to break loose before Miles could reach my throat and strangle me. Oh fuck oh God don't let him kill me. The grip around my knees loosened and I got to my hands and knees, kicking back like a horse and hitting something solid before scrambling up and running. I was across the street and into a small park before I looked over my shoulder. A man—not Miles—was kneeling on the grass holding his face in his hands. I stopped and turned around, hands on my knees, breathing deeply. I straightened up and began to walk back, fully prepared to resume sprinting.

I stopped at the sidewalk and noticed my hands were shaking. The man had stood up and wasn't nearly as large as I'd first imagined, maybe five foot eight and 150 pounds. His thick down parka gave him the heft of the Michelin Man. He stood with his head tilted back, plugging his nose with thumb and forefinger. He had deep sunken eyes and a week-old beard.

"Who the fuck are you?" I said, still shaking from the burst of adrenaline.

"I'm Wenee's usband."

"Who?"

He leveled his head and unplugged his nose. "I'm Renee's husband."

Oh Christ. So this was her ex, Roger. I imagined him with both hands cupped to his face at the bedroom window. Could he have seen anything? Even with the curtains closed, our silhouettes would be incriminating enough. I really had to quit sleeping with attached women. Sooner or later I was going to be killed.

"Are you Roger?"

He nodded and held his nose like a small boy about to jump into the deep end.

"What the hell are you doing here?"

"I wanted to see if my wife was sleeping with anyone."

"Ex-wife. She's your ex-wife. You're divorced now." They were, weren't they? I was trying to decide if Roger was dangerous. He looked sheepish, as if his taste for violence had evaporated with the kick to his face. "How long have you been out here?"

"I don't know. Midnight, maybe."

"See anything?"

"I saw you go into the house and drink in the kitchen, that was it," Roger said. "All the curtains were closed."

And let's be thankful for that, I thought. This guy is really a mess. There was dried blood caked around his nose and mouth and small dark streaks down the front of his parka. "Sorry about kicking you, but you scared the hell out of me tackling me like that. I thought you were somebody else."

"You know somebody who's spying on my wife?"

"No, no. Never mind. Listen, I've got some Kleenex in the van over here. Why don't we get some before you bleed to death." I guided him by the elbow over to the van. "I guess I've only got Burger King napkins, but they'll do the trick. Here, tear off a couple strips and shove it up your nose."

Roger did and stood before me with two yellow points poking out of his nostrils. He looked sad and pathetic, and I suddenly felt bad about sleeping with his ex-wife while he was lurking outside imagining the worst. There was an uncomfortable silence, as if we didn't know how to end this and go home. "Do you want to go have breakfast? I'll buy."

"Sure," Roger said.

"Get in."

We drove in silence until I blindly grabbed a cassette from a case between the two seats and put it in the tape deck. Patsy Cline was midway through "Crazy," and I hoped the song wouldn't trip some land mine in Roger's brain. I glanced over at him, staring blankly ahead with the napkins peeping out of his nose. What did this guy do for a living? Sold farm chemicals or something like that. Long hours alone in a company car with no radio. Shades of Miles.

I didn't know about Roger, but Miles had never been much of a talker. That seemed ironic with a father whose livelihood depended greatly on his eloquence, but then his father, my late grandfather, had spent the last fifteen years of his life living alone in a trailer in the Dearborn separated from his wife whose strong Catholic faith wouldn't allow her to consent to a divorce. In her mind there was no such thing. I'd heard from my uncles that my grandfather had called Mass "a lot of ritualistic horseshit," and that he'd gone every Sunday only to appease his wife. Her refusal to give him a divorce was said to have made him particularly bitter about the church. I didn't know if my grandfather had wanted to remarry. I'd never met him and my father rarely talked about him.

I wondered if people like my grandfather and Miles reached a point where they felt that the problem wasn't that people didn't talk enough, but talked too damn much. Everyone was chipping his teeth in your ear, but no one was saying anything. Still, they always ran the risk of reaching a point of silence—Grandpa McCance had no doubt been there—where they expected people to be able to read their minds. Then it all became nuance, and that got old *real* fast. A slight raising of the left eyebrow means yes, a frown no. When you misread the signals and their patience ran out, you often ran the risk of being thrashed. Maybe the only peace they could find was being alone. But when did being alone turn into being lonely?

The need for solitude ran in the family. My parents weren't much for socializing; they'd take a night at home reading over an evening with friends. Miles spent most of his free time working on his house. Even Anne, who was the most gregarious, retreated into sixty-hour work weeks at Houghton Mifflin. I could easily see myself playing gigs four nights a week and practicing on the other days just to be playing. It wasn't normal to love your work these days. No one batted an eye if you said you hated your job but did it anyway because you had great benefits and made enough money to afford things you really enjoyed. I knew there were more people than not who would tell me I was a fool for passing up the opportunity to be a lawyer in my father's firm where I could have made a healthy living *and* played in a band.

The 4-B's was full of hostile off-duty bouncers and bleary-eyed drunks trying to stave off hangovers. Roger and I were seated at a corner booth, and I told him to order whatever he wanted, within reason.

"What's that mean?" he said, peering over the menu with his dark sunken eyes.

"That means steak is out."

"OK."

I ordered blueberry pancakes and orange juice; Roger two

fried eggs with three pancakes and linked sausage, two pieces of toast, a side order of hash browns, orange juice, coffee no cream.

"Hungry?" I said. I'd come down from my adrenaline rush and wanted only to go home and sleep.

"What do you do?" Roger said.

"I'm a drummer," I said reflexively.

"Who do you play with? I'll bet I've heard you."

"The Cloverleafs." I imagined my head deep in a foam pillow.

"I've seen you play," he said with excitement. "I thought I recognized you. George Muzzana's band, right? I used to drink with George."

"Not anymore."

He pulled his head back as if from an invisible punch. "He died?"

"No, he quit drinking."

"Oh." He seemed to mull that over. "How come?"

"Probably because he's an alcoholic."

"Right," Roger said. "So you're the drummer for the Cloverleafs, huh? That's great. I've heard you play quite a few times. You're good, man."

"Thanks."

"I mean it. I listen to a lot of country music and I know what I'm talking about. You gonna go down to Nashville?"

"I don't know what I'm going to do."

"You gotta go down to Nashville. That's where it's at. Music City, man.

"I got an uncle who could've played pro hockey, but he quit at twenty-one to get married. He was playing up in Lethbridge. His wife was from Fort Benton and didn't want to live away from her relatives. She didn't like him being gone all the time, so he quit and started working at the grain elevator. When he was thirty she divorced him and moved to Denver to live with her sister.

He's still in Fort Benton, talking about how he could've played in the pros."

Roger ate as if he'd been missing meals. We discussed the country singers we liked. He was a Dolly Parton fan and owned twenty-five of her albums. I wondered if Renee's breast implants were the result of being told her own were inadequate. I got depressed thinking about it. I paid the bill and gave Roger a ride to his truck. My mother would be getting up soon, and if she saw me coming in, I'd be faced with the penance of a four-mile run.

At the truck, Roger and I shook hands. "I've got one hell of a record collection, so if you're ever interested, give me a call."

"I may do that," I said, knowing I wouldn't.

"Take my advice and go to Nashville. You're good enough to make it. If you don't go you'll end up like my uncle and never forgive yourself. I mean it." He waved and shut the door. Then opened it and stuck his head in. "One last thing." Smiling politely.

"What?"

"You sleep with Renee?"

Should I tell him? Would it help? I decided it would. "I did, yeah."

He stared at me. "Okay," he said, nodding slowly. "I needed to know."

I looked out the windshield.

"Thanks for not lying to me," Roger said and closed the door.

I drove home and parked in the carriage house. Ten after six. If I went in now, I ran the risk of bumping into my mother. I decided to sleep in back with my drums until my parents went to Mass at nine. There were two orange U-haul blankets behind the seat and I used one as a quilt and the other as a pillow. I immediately fell asleep and dreamed of Nashville, a city I'd never seen.

Seven

"What do you have planned for today?" my mother said, sitting across from me at the kitchen table. She lifted her coffee mug with both hands to her mouth and peered over it. She'd been waking me up at six-fifteen for the last three mornings to run with her, neither of us speaking, my mother always a half stride ahead. After breakfast she would hand me a list of errands to run and chores to do, as if I were still in high school and had stayed out beyond my curfew. It was understood that I would complete them before I did anything else, and that as long as I was living in their house I would observe their rules. I was expected to appear at breakfast and dinner, eating silently while my parents compared their days, not ignoring me but also not including me, then leaving me the dishes. I'd been taking my mother's daily list without resentment and offering to help without being asked, but I couldn't help thinking that I was too old for this and if I didn't leave soon, we'd be shouting at one another.

"I'm going to practice," I said. I'd been playing for five or six hours at a stretch, going downstairs for dinner before returning to the Music Room for another two or three hours. I wasn't sure if I was practicing in preparation for something, I only knew that drumming was the one thing I had to hold on to at the moment and I was unwilling to let go.

"Your father would like you to meet him at the office at twelve-fifteen."

"OK."

"And maybe you could shave and make yourself presentable for a change."

"All right," I said, holding her gaze before returning to the *Gazette*, which was reporting winds of up to sixty-seven miles an hour along the Hi-line. A Havre real estate agency was advertising "wind-front property." I glanced up and found my mother still looking at me.

"What record store did you work in while you said you were in law school?" Her voice had the brittle edge of someone who has been betrayed. Hearing it I thought it would take her longer than my father to forgive me.

"Olsson's Books and Records on Dupont Circle."

"As a salesclerk?"

"Right."

"Are you planning on applying for a job like that in town?"

"No."

"What are you planning on doing?"

"I'm not sure."

"Because we're not going to support you," my mother said. "You know that, don't you? You're on your own now. I want to make sure you understand that." She stood up and began gathering the dirty dishes. "And I won't have you sitting around the house all day just playing your drums. I won't stand for that."

She crossed over to the sink and ran the faucet. Then bowed her head for a moment as if she were crying. I wanted to be able to walk over and console her, put my arms around her and say I was sorry, I'd never meant to hurt her, but I sat rooted to my chair. When she turned to look at me, her eyes were wet and she glanced down and wiped them with a dishcloth. "Damn you, Dennis," she said quietly, her voice faltering. "I was so *proud* of you at Christmas."

The law offices of Erskine, Snortland, McCance and Bingham were in the Strain Building, and I walked downtown on streets flooded with sunlight. Clusters of men were walking to lunch together, engrossed in conversation, attorneys I knew, businessmen. Women stood on the sidewalks waiting for their lunch dates, faces tilted toward the sun. All of them employed and earning money. I wanted to ask them how they'd chosen their jobs, what other options they'd been considering. I'd been trying to think of a job I'd want in Prairie View and hadn't been able to come up with a single one. Or in any other town for that matter. I knew my father would find that incomprehensible. He'd wanted to be a lawyer before he even knew what they did.

I wanted to have his conviction about something, his absolute lack of doubt. I wanted to be able to stride into his office and tell him exactly what I planned to do, ticking off all the reasons it made sense, anticipating his objections and turning them neatly aside. Instead I would slouch into the room, hands in pockets, with no clear plans other than a half-baked idea of driving to Austin and starting another band with Montana. If I admitted that, he'd point out that I'd had over five months to think about this. What had I been doing all this time? My father conducted family discussions like depositions, hitting you with his toughest questions right away to rattle you, then firing off a volley of others while you were still reeling, never letting up, circling back to questions you ignored or evaded, asking for explanations, leading you wherever he wanted like Miles on a judo mat. The few times I'd managed to remain composed and offer a defense, he'd punched holes in my arguments and left me in tears, which only deepened his disappointment in me. I rode the elevator to the eighth floor and wondered if there would ever be a time when I wasn't afraid of him.

A paper clock on the firm's door said WE'LL BE BACK AT 1:00, and I opened it and passed through the reception area. The attorneys' offices ran along the outside walls of the building with the secretaries' cubicles inside the interior rectangle, all of them now empty, their computers humming and glowing. Sunlight fell through two domed skylights as if through a break in the clouds. It occurred to me that my father had probably chosen this hour so one else would be here to ask how I was doing in law school.

The door to his corner office was half open. I could see him sitting at his desk, swiveled slightly in his tall leather chair to look west over the city's roofs, listening to someone on the phone. His desk was covered with Montana Law Reports, legal pads, bulging accordion files. "Get to the point. No, forget it. That's a waste of my time."

He hung up and saw me in the doorway. "Sit down, Dennis," he said in the same brusque tone.

I took a seat before his broad desk, my stomach fluttering. Stay calm, I thought. Don't let him rattle you.

My father leaned toward me with his forearms on the desk. "Your mother tells me you're not looking for a job."

"Not here, no."

"You have something lined up somewhere else?"

"No."

"Then what are you planning on doing?"

I hesitated, scrambling to decide whether I should tell him I was thinking of moving to Austin. I didn't want to hear all the reasons it was a lousy idea.

"You must have some idea," my father said impatiently. "You haven't been in law school for six months now."

My throat had begun to constrict, my mouth had stiffened and my eyes were watering. I felt certain my father could see this, and I was angry with myself for being intimidated by him. I tried to calm myself, to breathe deeply. Finally I admitted, "I'm thinking of moving to Austin."

"And doing what?"

"Playing in a band with Montana."

"I thought you'd given up that idea."

"I did for a while."

"Montana is the woman who was in your band in Fort Collins?"

"Right."

"Is she in a band now?"

"No."

"So you'd be starting a new band altogether."

"Right."

"How are you going to support yourself?"

"I'll get a job somewhere."

"Doing what?"

"I don't know. Working in a record store, maybe."

"Isn't that what you did in D.C.?"

"Yes."

"What did you earn an hour there?"

"Six-fifty."

"And you lived on that?"

"I had to use some of my savings."

"I've never claimed to know anything about your music," my father said. "I figure that's your domain. But how realistic is it that you'll ever make a living at this beyond a subsistence level?

At least in Fort Collins you were established. Even then you were scratching to get by. Now you're talking about moving to Austin. You haven't played in a year, you don't have a band, and the city is probably filled with capable musicians trying to get a break. Have you thought about any of these things?"

"Yes."

"What if it doesn't pan out? Let's say you move to Austin and find you can't cut it. For whatever reason. What are you going to do then?"

"I'll find something else."

"Name one other option you've come up with in the last six months."

I was silent, a white heat rising up the back of my skull.

"You don't have any, do you?"

I wanted to say something cruel, something cutting that would put him on the defensive for once.

"You know, this doesn't help anything. I'm not some hostile witness you need to browbeat into submission. I don't need to hear all the reasons this is a bad idea. I can do that myself. What were *you* going to do if you couldn't cut it as an attorney? What if you'd moved here after law school and couldn't find any clients?"

"I never had any doubts that I'd make it."

"Well, good for you," I said. "You were lucky."

"Luck had nothing to do with it," my father said. "How are you going to get down there?"

"I thought I'd drive," I said, retreating to sarcasm.

"You think your van will make it?"

"Maybe, maybe not."

"When would you leave?"

"Why, do you want me out of the house?"

"No, I told you you could stay two weeks and I'll stand by that." Now he sounded judicious and fair while I sounded petty and sullen.

"I'm going to leave a week from Sunday," I said, feeling like I was being boxed into this decision. "That way I can play a gig here next Saturday and have enough money to get to Austin."

My father sat back in his chair and looked at me very deliberately, like a judge making his final appraisal before delivering the verdict.

"I'm not going to help you," he said. "If you don't make it or you run out of money, you're on your own. I'm not going to bail you out."

"I understand that." When I saw he was finished, I rose halfway out of my seat, then sat down. "I want you to know that I understood the law. I was scared to death that I wouldn't, but I did. And I understood what we talked about on the phone most of the time. I wasn't faking that. I just realized one day that I'd be very unhappy practicing law for the rest of my life."

"But you couldn't tell me the truth," my father said.

"No, I couldn't," I said. "I apologize for that."

When I got home there was a postcard from Susan Hall in San Francisco saying she'd received my letter and would be in Prairie View on Friday for a week. She'd call me on Saturday. It failed to improve my mood.

I retreated to the Music Room for the rest of the afternoon, trying to drum my way out of the feeling that everything was pointless, that in the end it wouldn't matter whether I moved to Austin, stayed in Prairie View, or took a flying fuck at the moon. Whatever I chose to do my parents would give me a half-dozen reasons why it wasn't a wise decision. As my father had pointed out, I probably wouldn't be able to cut it in Austin, and then where would I be? Why not save myself the drive across west Texas and start looking for a job in town. After all, the musicians in Austin were much better than what I was accustomed to, and there were more of them. Hundreds, maybe even thousands. All of them looking for gigs and million-dollar contracts. And what would I be doing? I'd be stocking bins at the local Sam Goody, apologizing to customers for not having all of Kenny Rogers's CDs in stock. And if I thought I could survive on those hourly wages, I was wrong. Not unless I lived in the Angstmobile.

The truth was I didn't want to be some country-and-western wanker living in fantasyland, telling myself I was going to hit the big time when it was clear to everyone else that at best I'd spend my nights playing "Orange Blossom Special" at the local Ramada Inn. Maybe I'd already reached that point and only my parents could recognize it. No, I didn't believe that. They'd thought it was time for me to quit when I left for college, afraid that I'd call home and announce I was dropping out to play full-time in a band. The fact that I graduated and then played full-time didn't make them any happier. And now they were telling me again that it was time to quit. To face up to things.

Part of me couldn't blame them. It didn't take any musical knowledge to see there wasn't going to be much interest in a drummer who couldn't sing. If anything happened, it would be because of Montana. She would be the person to attract interest and attention. If Montana wasn't there and looking to start a band, I wouldn't be considering moving to Austin. At the same time I had some trepidation about being so dependent on her. I felt as if she'd moved ahead of me in the last year simply by her willingness to move to Austin alone. I wasn't sure we were on equal footing anymore, and that made me nervous. Bands broke up all the time when the lead singer quit, but they continued to roll along when the drummer left. We were anonymous, re-placeable. Good lead singers like Montana weren't. I didn't mind being anonymous behind my tiers of cymbals and drums, but I didn't want to be replaceable. You wouldn't ever replace me, would you, Montana?

Around six o'clock the kitchen light flicked on and off three times, and I thought either Anne was home or it was time for dinner and my mother was irritated that I was still playing. I headed downstairs, pausing on the first-floor landing to see if I could tell who was here. I heard Anne and Jack, and then my mother asking Miles something. I realized she must have called and invited them to come over to the house so I could tell them the news myself. My impulse was to walk out the front door and keep going, but I checked it and walked toward the kitchen, my movements as heavy and slow as a deep-sea diver's. The entire family was standing at the far end of the cooking island eating cheese and crackers, laughing and talking. My mother looked up and saw me, her eyes cool and direct, and it was clear that no one had broken the news. I thought there would be no end to these scenes of confession and contrition.

Anne and Jack said hello and offered me a cracker. I shook my head.

"How was your gig last weekend?" Anne said.

"It was fine," I said. Then I panicked at the thought that she'd talked to Renee. "Why, did you hear about it?"

"No, I was just asking. Did something happen?"

"No."

My father had leaned against the sink counter, arms folded across his chest, sunlight streaming through the window behind him and making it difficult to see his face. He looked removed, a detached observer at a family gathering. Miles, on the other hand, appeared to be studying me, looking for signs that would betray my guilt.

"I believe Dennis has something to tell you," my mother finally said.

I felt strangely weightless, disembodied.

"You got your grades," Anne said, looking at me, then my mother. "Is that it? Your grades showed up?"

I could tell Anne but I didn't want to tell Miles. Anne would understand, but Miles would tell me he'd known all along I wouldn't last.

"Dennis," my mother said.

"I dropped out of law school," I said, unable to focus on anything.

"What?" Anne said.

"I dropped out."

"I *knew* it," Miles said. "I knew it the minute I saw you at the airport."

"I don't understand," Anne said. "You mean you're not going back?"

"He *quit*," Miles said.

Anne glanced at him, then turned to me for an explanation. Jack slipped out the back door.

"I dropped out in January, two weeks into the second semester."

"You mean you haven't been in law school all this time?"

"No."

"I knew you'd never make it," Miles said with disgust.

"At least I could get in," I said, suddenly angry. "You couldn't even get past the LSAT, let alone law school. You couldn't even get a job as a goddamn shop teacher."

"At least I don't quit everything I do."

"Oh yeah? Well maybe you have a different word for what you do, Miles. Because it sure looked to me like you quit looking for a teaching job. Then if I remember correctly you quit working as a framer before quitting as a ranch hand. Come to think of it, what job haven't you quit? The only reason you even have a job as a deputy is because the sheriff is one of Dad's clients and he wanted to do Dad a favor."

Miles had slipped around the corner of the island and was walking toward me, head lowered, shoulders rolled in, hands at his sides. His face was clouded with anger and I watched him approach me, aware of nothing but his minatory presence. I felt reckless. "What are you going to do, Miles? Kick my ass? Is that the only thing you know how to do? Someone pisses you off so you kick his ass?"

"Don't touch him, Miles," Anne said.

He was before me, inches away, the smell of beer and cheese on his breath. "Keep pushing," he said. "Just keep pushing."

He drove his shoulder into mine and spun me sideways. I watched him leave and immediately regretted saying anything, knowing he was going to make me pay for this.

When I turned back to the room, Anne walked by without looking at me. My father hadn't moved. I wondered if he would have stepped in if Miles had started hitting me. My mother looked distraught, as if she'd somehow believed this would turn out differently. I wanted to ask if she were happy now.

I walked upstairs and found Anne waiting for me in the Music Room. She said, "I'm pissed at you."

I stood in the doorway, head down like a chastened schoolboy.

"How could you do that, Dennis?"

I looked up at her. "I didn't want to be a lawyer."

"I'm not talking about *that*," Anne said. "I don't care about *that*. How could you *lie* to me all this time? I thought you told me everything. Haven't you always told me everything? Who are you going to tell in the family if you don't tell me? Who are you going to tell, Den?" Her cheeks shone with tears.

"Oh Anne," I whispered, crossing the room and putting my arms around her. I could feel her trembling as she tried to catch her breath.

She looked away from me and wiped her eyes. "Why didn't you tell me?"

"I don't know," I said. "I don't know why I didn't tell Mom and Dad either. Fear mostly. They were so pleased with me for once."

"You weren't afraid to tell me, were you?"

"I don't know. I guess not. Maybe I was afraid you'd force me to tell Mom and Dad before I was ready."

"I wouldn't have done that."

"It's a lousy secret to lug around," I said. "God, what a relief not to have to carry that around anymore."

We sat on the floor as I told Anne the entire story. Afterward, as if on cue, the Municipal Band began playing "The Star Spangled Banner" at the Dingfelder Park band shell to open its summer season. When the song ended, dozens of car horns blared in lieu of applause.

"What are you going to do now?"

"I'm thinking of driving down to Austin and starting another band with Montana. As you can imagine, Mom and Dad aren't very enthusiastic about the idea." I waved it all away. "Let's not talk about it right now. I've spent the entire day talking about it. What else is going on these days?"

"I ran into Renee Peterson downtown today."

"Yeah? What'd she have to say?"

"Just that she bumped into you at Buckaroo's. Did you recognize her?"

"I did, yeah."

"What'd you think?" Anne said.

"Of?"

"Her breasts."

"Her breasts?" I said, grinning. "I thought they looked lovely."

Anne backhanded me in the chest.

"You asked."

"I don't know why."

On Friday I was standing in line at City Drug to pick up a prescription for my mother. The store smelled like boxed chocolates and chloroform. Six people were ahead of me and the morose pharmacist kept saying he was supposed to be on his lunch break. The woman directly in front of me glanced back and said, "Can you *believe* this wait?" I couldn't.

An enormous pair of callused hands slipped around my throat from behind. When I tried to turn my head, the grip tightened enough to discourage me. "I've been hearing rumors about you around town, McCance," a voice whispered to the top of my head. I stiffened. I could feel the heat of the man's breath on my skull. "Ugly fucking rumors that a man of my size and character hates to believe before he's checked them out himself." The thumbs were readjusted across my spine. "The first rumor I heard was that you're back in town. For how long, nobody seems to know. Here you are, so I guess it's true. The second rumor, the one that makes me crazy until I want to crush someone"—the grip tightened again, making it impossible for me to swallow. Panic had almost taken over and I was getting ready to stomp on the man's feet and jab with my elbows—"is that you're in law school." I relaxed. "My own mother started this rumor. Said she heard you were going to school somewhere back East. Delaware or D.C., what's the difference? I told her it couldn't be true. Dennis McMenace in law school? Never happen. He's going to be on the Nashville Network any day now. Say it ain't so, McCance."

"It ain't so," I whispered. The hands dropped from my neck and twirled me around.

"How are you, Dennis?" Billy Smitherman said. "Did I scare you? I could feel you tense up. What are you waiting in line for? Let's walk down to Weckworth's and you can tell me what you're doing home."

Billy was already guiding me toward the door, people turning to stare at this six-foot-six, 230-pound behemoth in the tan suit.

"You've gotten huge," I said out on the street.

"Been pressing the weights," Billy said, curling an invisible barbell toward his forehead. "So fill me in. What are you doing here?"

"It's a long and sordid story, which in a nutshell is that I dropped out of law school in January and just told my parents last week."

"So you did go."

"One semester."

"Really enjoyed it, huh?"

"Loved it."

"I wondered why I didn't see you on *Hee Haw*," Billy said. "I couldn't believe it when my mom said that's what she'd heard you were doing."

"I couldn't either after the first semester," I said. "What are you doing?"

"Working for my dad,"

"How'd that happen?" I said. Billy's father owned Smitherman Inc., a beer distributorship.

"So I was in my sixth year at Arizona State—five years and a semester, actually—and I got this call from my dad asking when I thought I might be planning on graduating. I said I had two classes I had to repeat due to inattentiveness the first times through. Dad said, 'Billy, do whatever you have to do to get out.' I asked what he meant. Bribe someone? Because that's what it sounded like. 'Whatever it takes, just get out.' So I buckled down and finished. Dad wanted me to come home and start working for him, but I had a part-time job as a spotter for the cheerleading squad—I must have told you about this—and the girls really wanted me to stay through basketball season. It's not easy to find someone who's six-six and can press women over his head. I had to choose between staying in Tempe for the winter lifting blonde cheerleaders or going home and working in a refrigerated warehouse. I ended up staying until last March when Dad finally said

I had to come home or he wasn't letting me in the business. By then my parents had moved to a place on Flathead Lake. Dad trained me for eight weeks and put me in charge. Now he flies down twice a month to make sure I'm not running it into the ground."

He opened the door to Weckworth's and I passed under his arm without ducking. "Let me ask you something," I said, handing the prescription slip to the pharmacist and turning to look up at Billy. His sandy blond hair was receding at the temples, making a peninsula of his bangs, darker eyebrows intersecting at the bridge of his nose above deep green eyes. Over the years I'd heard several girls say that Billy had beautiful long eyelashes that made him look vulnerable. It baffled me how a man who was six-six could even begin to look vulnerable. "You've been living here for what, three and a half months? How is it?"

"You mean am I going to stay?" Billy said, following me to the checkout counter. "Probably. My dad's letting me make most of the decisions, and he says he's not interested in selling as long as I want to run the business, so there's no reason to go anywhere else. It would take me years to do what I'm doing now. I've discovered I enjoy telling people what to do."

"That's good," I said, paying the cashier and going outside. We stood on Dingfelder Avenue. "But how are you handling living here?"

"I fly to Tempe every chance I get to see my girlfriend. She's a cheerleader. I think I've flown there six times since I've been home. Fly out Friday night and back late Sunday night. When I first got here I was going out all the time with people I hadn't seen since high school, crawling into bed at three in the morning and getting up at six to go to work. That lasted about two months and then one of my dad's friends called him at the lake and said he thought I had a drinking problem. Dad asked me if it was true. I said no and pretty much quit going out altogether. Bought a VCR and started staying home.

"If you stick around here, Dennis, you'll discover that Prairie View is small enough that if people want to find out what you're doing, they will, but it's big enough that when they do, it'll be exaggerated. So if you get out of hand one night and are staggering around, by the time word gets out, you'll be a raving lunatic who spent the night in the drunk tank for smashing a toilet at the Barking Dog. That's actually how I heard you were home. I mentioned your name at work yesterday and one of the guys in the warehouse said he thought he saw you at Buckaroo's. He said, 'Long-haired dude who plays the drums? I heard he just got outta prison.' So you see what I mean?"

"Well, I'm glad you found me. I would've never thought you were home. We should go out tonight."

"I'm flying to Tempe at six-thirty. Get back on Sunday at midnight. I'll call you on Monday."

"Good."

"Your parents miss me?" Billy said.

"Terribly. They keep waiting to read in the *Gazette* that you've been picked up for offering candy and rides to junior high school girls. How about yours?"

"They've still got you pegged for stag films."

"*The Return of Johnny Wadd?*"

"Exactly."

"Give them my love."

Our parents, connected only by our friendship, had had a falling-out seven years ago involving Billy and me and didn't talk to one another again for two years and then only to be civil. The incident occurred during a seventeen-hour bus ride from Portland, Oregon, to Prairie View, after the symphonic band had performed for nine minutes at the Sixteenth Annual Northwest High School Music Festival. Billy was the last chair trombonist, and we were sitting near the back of one of the two Greyhound buses where a third of the horn section was on mescaline and several others were devouring Indian River oranges they'd injected the night before with vodka-filled syringes. Billy and I hadn't planned that well and were playing paper-scissors-rock to amuse ourselves, with the winner of each round earning the right to slap the loser's wrist.

In the unending Columbia Gorge, a drunken tuba player sitting behind us mooned a passing motorist, which started Billy and me discussing the risk involved in performing that act on a bus with tinted windows; it seemed negligible. Billy challenged me to a game of his own invention called dick tag, in which you had to touch people with your member without getting caught. Points were awarded on the basis of risk and difficulty. Since he'd invented it on the spot, a point system had to be drawn up and two friends recruited to act as impartial judges.

We began tentatively: I scored first with a tag to the back of the pant leg of a girl standing in the aisle. Since she had her back to me, the judges awarded only two points. Billy tagged a girl's shoulder but earned only three points because she was asleep and wearing a Walkman. I complained it was like earning points for tagging a coma patient. I knelt next to Janet Crumley in the aisle and, while talking to her, touched her bare calf. Four points. Billy answered this with a tag to the back of the head of Linda Rooter, fully attentive and seated in front of him; he did so without having to stand on his seat, which greatly impressed the judges. Six points. I decided a thirty-seven-inch inseam was a real advantage. By the time the bus neared Umatilla, the two judges had me trailing by eleven points. They told me I was going to have to do something spectacular to win before we stopped for lunch in Kennewick. I tried to imagine what that might be.

I saw my opportunity when the two buses slowed in tandem behind a line of cars swinging out to pass a loaded-down station wagon with a flat tire parked on the side of the road. There was some kind of disturbance, and everyone crossed to the south side of the bus to gawk. As we watched, a man very calmly snatched a pink Samsonite suitcase out of the back of the car, did two complete revolutions with the handle clasped in both hands and launched it into the alfalfa field; then he reached for the next one. Three or four suitcases had already landed at various spots in the field, and the man seemed to be getting better distance with each throw. A young woman stood by the hood of the car with a hand on her hip and her head cocked to one side, smoking a cigarette, watching.

I moved quickly down the aisle past kids kneeling on the armrests to get a better look. Billy and the two judges followed. I picked out two clarinet players, Joberta Hoof and Libby Pro-tulis, who were leaning toward the green window. I decided to attempt the never-before-attempted across-the-body tag, which would involve leaning across Libby on the aisle seat, right leg in front to hide my intentions, and touching Joberta's arm.

I slipped in front of Libby, who was craning her neck back at the luggage toss. Member in hand, I leaned forward to touch Joberta's wrist, which was resting on her thigh and now pain-fully close. I was perspiring heavily, praying that someone was witnessing this. Afterward I would learn that Billy had seen what I was up to and decided to use me as a diversion to tag Libby's left earlobe and ensure his victory. At the same time that I was inching toward Joberta's wrist, Billy was moving toward Libby's ear. The bus suddenly accelerated to resume cruising speed. I caught myself but Billy lost his balance and bumped into Libby, who turned her head and found herself eye to eye with a snake. She recoiled and screamed with palpable terror. Joberta swiveled her head like a gun turret to see what had happened and spotted my member an inch from her wrist. She screamed in near-perfect pitch with Libby. Then Joberta did something very strange; she grabbed hold of me with one hand and began tugging with terrifying vigor. Later she would claim this was to prevent me from slipping myself back in my pants and denying everything. I howled and slapped wildly at her hand and wrist, frantic to break loose. People were standing up in their seats to see what was going on. The bus ground to a shuddering halt, air brakes hissing. I was thrown to the floor and freed from Joberta's pernicious grip.

I was wedged between a seat and seatback when the band director, Mr. Loomis, appeared above me and asked what the hell was going on.

"He touched me with his . . . *penis*," Joberta breathed.

"*Who* did?"

"Are we already home?" a drugged voice asked from the back of the bus.

"Dennis did," Joberta said. "Look!"

I had just pulled myself up and now found a circle of faces staring at my crotch where Joberta was pointing. I looked down at my fully zippered pants and then up at Mr. Loomis. "I don't know what she's talking about," I said.

"*I had it right here in my hand!*" Joberta cried, waving a clenched fist.

Libby kept pointing at her ear.

Billy and I were suspended for thirteen days for lewd and unbecoming behavior. The principal said he had considered not letting us graduate and wanted to know what we thought of that. Not too much, we mumbled. Apparently it wasn't the answer the principal was looking for because he pounded his desk and yelled, "You're goddamn lucky is what you are." We weren't sure how, but decided not to ask.

My father, in the low, tight voice usually reserved for hostile witnesses, told me to quit playing games and straighten up. My mother wanted to know where I thought this kind of perverted behavior was leading. I said I really didn't know. "Well, I do," my mother said, "and I refuse to spend sleepless nights waiting for a late-night call from the police saying you've been picked up for indecent exposure or some other depravity. I just won't, Dennis. Get it together for once in your life."

In my mind now, I saw my parents spinning like hammer throwers, a pink suitcase with my belongings clutched in their hands, then letting go and sending it rocketing alone into the future.

Eight

I was cruising alongside the Missouri in the Angstmobile. A motorboat was slightly ahead of me on the river, pulling a beginning water-skier who stood with petrified rigidity in the center of the boat's fat wake. Two passengers in the boat had their arms raised as if signaling a touchdown while a third gave the thumbs up. The skier began to lean dangerously backward, jerked the orange rope into his chest to recover and was snapped face first into the water. On board all arms dropped. The road curved away from the river and began to climb toward Moccasin Heights, which rose above the south side of Prairie View and was popular among the city's upper middle class. I passed a towheaded boy under a birch tree who pointed a green machine gun at me and made loud choking noises. "You're dead, mister!" he hollered. The warm wind in my face held the promise of summer, and I wanted to be out on the highway with the windows rolled down and the reflective markers ticking by at seventy-five miles an hour while I sang through my nose with Dylan.

I parked in front of the Halls' house and sat in the van for a moment preparing myself. Susan had called at noon and said she was sorry she hadn't written or called sooner, but she figured she'd see me in a few days anyway. She invited me over for dinner with her parents, telling me just before hanging up that she had exciting news. I asked what it was. "It's a surprise." I tried to imagine what it might be and couldn't resist hoping that her boyfriend had finally shown himself to be a soulless misogynist whose primary goal in life was to make truckloads of money performing cataract surgery on the elderly. I had to admit I enjoyed thinking the worst of Tim or Jim. It would be a real shame to meet him and discover he was strictly run-of-the-mill.

The house was a one-story wooden A-frame with two rectangles on either side. Parked in front of the garage was a gray Mercedes sedan with MIDDLEBURY and SMITH stickers on the back window and one taped to the bumper that said: MY CHILD MADE THE HONOR ROLL AT PRAIRIE VIEW WEST H.S. This was the first time I'd been invited to the Hall's, and it made me nervous. I rang the doorbell and thought, Be a gentleman.

The front door opened and I looked at Dr. Hall, whom I'd seen several times before—usually on the golf course lagging thirty yards behind his wife—but never met. He was taller than me, a handsome man with cropped gray hair and the gauntness of a fitness fanatic.

"You must be Dennis," he said, sticking out a large pale hand. "Dr. Hall."

"Nice to meet you, sir," I said, thinking Dr. Hall's handshake was awfully soft in comparison with my father's.

"Gloria's busy in the kitchen and Susan's not ready yet," he said, leading me down a hallway that opened out into a sunken living room. "Would you like something to drink? Beer, mineral water?" I asked for a beer and Dr. Hall told me to go out onto the deck. The outside wall of the living room was glass with a single wooden beam running across its center. The blinds were pulled back and gave a clear view of the city. The room was done in mauve with a wine-colored carpet and stiff, formal chairs. On a low glass table, copies of *Architectural Digest* were arranged like a fan. The large stone fireplace shone with lacquer. I had the feeling the room was never used, the blinds drawn at sunrise so the colors wouldn't fade. I went out onto the deck, shaped like the bow of a ship, and looked out over the tiers of houses below. Smoke from a barbecue floated up toward me and I could hear someone mowing. "Hello there," someone called. I looked at the deck next door and saw a woman in a white bathrobe holding a martini glass in one hand and waving at me with the other. I waved tentatively back. "Do I know you?" she said, steadying herself on the railing. "I don't think so," I said. "Thas OK," she said. "Whyn't you come over for a drink. I could use some comp'ny." "Maybe later," I said. "Later," she said bitterly. "That's what all you bastards say." She gave me a Bronx cheer and weaved her way back indoors.

"What do you think?" Dr. Hall said, coming up behind me and handing me a glass of beer.

"I think she's lonely," I said.

"I meant the view."

The eastern skyline was crystalline blue, the Highwoods lit by the sinking sun so that they looked within a half hour's brisk walk. "Beautiful."

"It is, isn't it," Dr. Hall said, taking a seat at the glass table. "I understand you're going to be a lawyer like your father."

"Well . . . ," I said, hoping to avoid that topic and happy to be wearing my sunglasses so I wouldn't have to make eye contact.

"Plenty of lawyers these days," he said, nodding.

"Too many."

"Plenty of lawyers."

"Yes, sir."

Dr. Hall looked at me as if he'd just thought of something he'd been trying to remember and said, "Do you exercise regularly, Dennis?"

"I've been running every morning lately."

"Never stop."

"Okay."

"Never stop taking care of yourself. If there's one thing I've learned in my twenty-six years as a doctor, it's to never stop taking care of yourself. Did you know I had a serious heart attack three years ago this July?"

"I didn't know that, Dr. Hall."

"A cardiologist who has a serious heart attack," he said. "What do you think of that, Dennis?"

"I think it's ironic, sir."

"Well, it is ironic, and it changed my life, I can tell you that. You know why it happened? I'd quit taking care of myself. Afterward no one had to tell me that if I didn't make some lifestyle changes I was going to die. So I did it. I went on a vegetarian diet and drastically reduced the fat and cholesterol I ate. Plenty of pasta, plain salads and exercise. I get up every morning at five and go down to the Y. I do a series of stretching exercises, a series of lifting exercises, and then ride the station-ary bike for forty-five minutes. By that point I'm really sweating. I love to sweat, Dennis. Then I do another series of lifting exercises, followed by more stretching and finally fifteen min-utes in the sauna when I'm completely soaked in sweat. I don't know what it is, but I love to sweat."

"How long are you down there?"

"Ninety minutes."

"That's a lot of sweating."

"Every morning, seven days a week. I find I don't function as well during the day without it. Do you lift weights?"

"I'm afraid I don't, no. But I play my drums, which is pretty good for your arms. Or at least your wrists. My wrists are strong."

"Never stop taking care of yourself, Dennis. That's my advice."

"Well, thank you, Dr. Hall. I'll remember that."

The glass door slid back and Mrs. Hall stepped onto the deck carrying a tray of hors d'oeuvres. She was tall, with wide strong shoulders developed from a lifetime of golf and tennis. I'd seen her playing both at the country club, and she hit the ball with well-heeled ferocity. On the tennis courts she had the reputation of aiming at the head of anyone who rushed the net and certain people refused to play with her.

"Hello, Dennis," she said, drawing out the *o*. Her dramatic elocution always formed a picture in my mind of Mrs. Hall sitting in front of her vanity mirror shortly before bed, stroking her hair and saying, "The rain in Spain stays mainly in the plain," one hundred times before retiring. Susan had once told me that her mother had seen Billy and me at the club pool; she thought we were uncouth.

"Hello, Mrs. Hall," I said, standing as she set the tray on the table between us. The hors d'oeuvre was melba rounds spread with pâté and a sprig of parsley held down by a sliced black olive.

"Would you like another beer?" Dr. Hall said.

"Please," I said, realizing too late this meant being left alone with Mrs. Hall. She had on a white pantsuit with a wide blue collar that made her look like a sailor. One who would have crushed Fletcher Christian in a second.

"Susan will be out in a moment," Mrs. Hall said. "She's speaking on the telephone."

I nodded.

"Are you working for Weed Control again this summer?" She made it sound as though I'd been there since birth.

"No, not this summer."

"That's right, you're in law school now. I suppose your father has you working at the firm."

"Actually I'm not working right now. I'm just playing a few gigs around town."

"Oh. How interesting."

My father had once told me that when I decided to marry, I should first meet my future mother-in-law to get a sense of what my wife would be like in thirty years. I wondered if Susan would be as snobbish as her mother in five years, let alone thirty, always telling me my friends were uncouth. Would she insist on a living room that looked as natural and inviting as those featured in *Architectural Digest* and would I be allowed to use it other than when we had important guests? When I was sixty-four would she let my dixieland jazz band, the Crocodile Daddies, rehearse in the garage once a week? And would she aim at my head when I tottered to the net as a bald seventy-two-year-old with Coke-bottle glasses?

The glass door slid back once again, and Dr. Hall and Susan walked out. I looked up at her and felt my doubts slip away. She was tall and broad shouldered, and her long dark hair was damp and tousled as though she had stepped out of the shower into a stiff crosswind. She had a wide smooth face with her mother's green eyes and large mouth. She was smiling at me as if amused to see me alone with her mother. I stood and found myself moving across the deck to hug her. Halfway there I saw Dr. and Mrs. Hall staring at me, but it was too late to turn back.

"Did you survive?" she whispered. Her breath in my ear gave me goose bumps.

"Barely."

"Maybe someone would like a drink, Peter," Mrs. Hall said.

Dr. Hall asked if anyone would like a drink. His wife said she'd have a vodka and tonic, and Susan said she would too, but when her husband was at the door, Mrs. Hall changed her mind and said what she'd really like was a Tanqueray and tonic. Susan decided she'd rather have white wine if they had any. I thought I saw Dr. Hall cross his eyes before going inside. Mrs. Hall waved at a neighbor watering her garden and said the woman's son was in the class she taught preparing high school students for their college entrance exams; his vocabulary skills were appalling. Dr. Hall returned and asked how I liked D.C. Without waiting for a reply he said he'd recently attended a medical conference in Alexandria, Virginia, and spent all his free time at the Smithsonian. He wondered how many years it would take to see all of it, and would I excuse him for a moment while he went to get more ice for his wife? I listened to Mrs. Hall and Susan discussing Jeremy Hall, Susan's younger brother, who was at a computer camp in Vermont and had called the night before to say the camp director had told him that . . . Dr. Hall sat down and asked me what the percentage of black people was in D.C., and was it difficult to find a safe neighborhood to live in . . . the seven years of the camp's history. I felt I was going insane.

"Why don't you tell Dennis the news?" Mrs. Hall said, bringing a halt to the babbling.

Thank you. I looked at Susan, who crossed her legs and glanced at her mother. "What's up?" I said, feeling as if I were about to open a birthday present that everyone insisted I'd love and they were crowded around to watch me weep with joy. I raised my glass to hide my face.

"I got a new job last week."

"That's great," I said. My interior pressure dropped so fast my limbs felt dull and shaky. "Still with San Francisco State?"

Susan had been the Director of Annual Funds at the university, handling small contributions that went toward the school's operating budget.

"No, this is with UC, Berkeley. I'm going to be the Director of Major Gifts."

"I'm impressed," I said. "What constitutes a major gift?"

"Anything over five hundred dollars. It involves a small pool of people contributing large sums of money."

"Congratulations."

"There's more," Mrs. Hall said brightly.

"More money?"

"Well yes, that too," Mrs. Hall said, "but more news."

"What's that?" I've been set up here. These people have set me up, and I don't like it.

"I'm getting married August fifth."

I closed my eyes behind my sunglasses. I saw myself swinging a five iron across a tabletop covered with martini glasses, shattering all of them. I did one complete revolution and smashed the club head into a wall mirror before turning to survey the rest of the room, full of glass cabinets and porcelain figurines, and racing toward them with the iron held over my head like a machete. I opened my eyes.

"You're getting married," I said quietly. "Who to?"

"Come on, Dennis, you know who I'm marrying," Susan said, forcing a smile.

"No, I don't. I don't know who you're marrying. What's his name?"

"Tim Waterwick."

"That's his name? Tim Waterwick?" I said. Susan nodded. She's going to marry Tim Waterpick. That's terrific. Isn't that terrific? I don't think it can get any more terrific than this. What other terrific things could possibly happen to me? Maybe she'll ask the Cloverleafs to play at the wedding reception. Wouldn't that be terrific? A little cowboy-hat music at the wedding reception of Tim and Susan Waterpick. "Could I have another beer, Dr. Hall?"

"Certainly," he said, looking happy to escape.

"Will you two excuse me for a minute," I said. "I need to use the lavatory."

In the bathroom I locked the door and jabbed at my reflection in the mirror. You walked right into this. Right into it. I swung at the mirror again. You are the dumbest sonofabitch I know. When are you going to learn? What did you think she invited you over for? To tell you she missed you? You fall for a woman with a serious boyfriend and then you're surprised when she says she's getting married. Wake up, goddamnit. I had to sit on the padded toilet seat cover for a moment. I just wanted something to work out, that's all, I thought. I just wanted something to work out.

When I returned everyone had moved to the dining room. I was seated next to Susan. While her parents were in the kitchen, she asked if I was all right. "Terrific," I said. Dinner began with what Mrs. Hall called a Celebration Salad. I told her it was terrific. She explained that it would be included in the cookbook she was currently writing. This in addition to her weekly food column in the *Gazette*. The entrée was Tagliatelle with Asparagus, also included in the book, which would be on sale next fall. $14.95. I smiled across the table at Mrs. Hall with a full mouth while her husband replenished my beer. I had a feeling the good doctor was trying to get me drunk. If so, he was succeeding. I continued to ignore Susan. Dr. Hall asked if I were an Alpine skier, and when I said yes, we discussed the merits of various mountains. I said for my money Bridger Bowl couldn't be beaten. Dr. Hall agreed and filled my glass. Mrs. Hall said she preferred Big Sky. Dessert was Mocha Alaska Pie. Susan said she'd pass, thank you. I could tell she was angry, and although I knew it was childish, it made me feel much better. I helped clear the dishes, thanked the Halls for a terrific evening and said I really should get home. Dr. Hall said I'd had quite a bit to drink and suggested Susan drive me, but I said no, I wanted to walk. Good exercise. I said good night to Mrs. Hall, shook Dr. Hall's hand, softly, and walked down the front hallway to the door. Stalked closely by Susan.

"Why are you acting like this?" she said when we were outside.

"Like what?"

"Like an *ass*."

"I'm sorry. I didn't realize I was acting like an *ass*. I thought I was being very polite."

"To my parents."

"I wanted to make a good impression since this was the first time I've ever been invited to meet them. And it really couldn't have been a more pleasant situation. I think we really hit it off, don't you? I'm going to the Y tomorrow morning with your dad to do a series of sweating exercises and then meeting your mom on the driving range at the club. I'm going to stand at the hundred-and-fifty yard marker and see if she can hit me with her three wood."

"What are you trying to punish me for?" Susan said.

"Punish you for? Nothing. I was just trying to thank you in my own inimitable way for inviting me to your parents' house so I could meet them, have a few drinks on the back deck and then when I was starting to feel at ease have you tell me you're getting married. I thought that was very courteous of you, Susan. It's too bad your brothers couldn't have been here and maybe a few of your closest friends. They probably would have enjoyed it even more than I did. Next time send a postcard."

I left her standing at the top of the driveway and began walking home. A block away I looked back at the house, but I couldn't see Susan and knew she wasn't the type to linger. I guessed she was standing in the kitchen telling her mother about her plans as Director of Major Gifts. I crossed through an empty lot, knee-high with weeds, and flushed two cats who scrambled up an eight-foot fence and disappeared. I walked on the left side of the street, climbing a short, steep hill and leaning back as I headed down the other side. Someone's electric garage door was open, the overhead light shining brightly in the night; it looked like a set waiting for its actors to enter stage left. A Camaro barreled around a corner and flashed its brights at me. All I could think about was how the hills and my boots were giving me blisters and how good it would feel to slip my feet into a tub of hot water.

"I want to see you," Susan said over the telephone the next morning.

"Okay," I said, a glutton for punishment.

"Today."

"All right. I'll pick you up in an hour. We can go for a drive."

"Good. I'll see you at noon."

I hung up and thought, Now that's an assertive woman. Berkeley will be a much richer place for having hired her.

Earlier that morning I'd run to her house and picked up the Angstmobile. I made lunch, packed it in a cooler and left a note for my parents, who were at church, and drove to the Halls' again. Susan walked out as soon as I pulled up. I reached over and opened the passenger door and she climbed in. She had on sunglasses, making it difficult to judge her mood.

"Where are we going?"

"I don't know."

The windows were down and the sun shone hot on our thighs through the windshield. I headed east on Eleventh Avenue South and had the good fortune to hit every green light until the town dropped behind us in the rearview mirror and was replaced by the interlocking panels of wheat, barley and soil that rose and fell on both sides of the highway. There was still snow on the Highwoods and Little Belts and the sky yawned far beyond the horizon.

For a few miles I forgot my fears and was content to be in the country where there was enough space for everyone to breathe easier and deeper and where I'd be happy to do nothing for the next few hours but sit silently and watch the land sweep past at sixty miles an hour. Soon we were dropping quickly past Belt. Foothills ran tight to both sides of the road, pale green and flat on top, then nothing but vaulted sky. It wasn't hard to imagine an Indian on horseback sternly watching the matchbox cars from up there, or a river centuries ago coursing through the winding ravine that was now Big Otter creek. Traces of both were still there if you were willing to look and knew what to look for. Since I'd returned I'd been feeling as though I didn't belong, and I wasn't sure when I'd lost the connection to Prairie View and Montana as home.

Was it living in a city that eroded the connection—soaking up all that hustle and hostility until you couldn't feel at ease in your home town—or was it something more? My parents had lived in Montana their entire lives except when my father went to Korea and both of them went to Gonzaga. As far as I knew, they'd never considered living anywhere else. Miles definitely had the connection, but then he'd never left. Anne had never had it and still didn't. I'd always thought I'd come back to live here one day, but now I was beginning to think I'd end up returning only for Christmas holidays and summer car trips to Glacier to show my kids the state where their dad had grown up. At the same time, whenever people asked where I was from, I always said Montana, even though I hadn't lived here in seven years. I'd met people in D.C. who hadn't lived in the state in twenty years but still considered themselves Montanans. These same people would say of a non-native who had lived in the state for twenty years, "Well, he's not *from* Montana."

"What are you thinking about?" Susan said. She was leaning back against the headrest with her face turned toward me.

"I was wondering if I'll ever live in Montana. Do you ever think about that?"

"Occasionally I think how convenient it is that my dad can bike to work in five minutes, but that's where it ends. Do you still feel attached to it?"

"In some ways. I always thought I'd marry someone from Montana so if I ever decided to come back, my wife would understand why."

"I'd understand but I still wouldn't do it."

"Well, you're not going to be my wife, so it really doesn't matter, does it." This had more of an edge than I intended.

Susan turned and looked out the windshield. On the south side of the road a billboard announced: WORLD FAMOUS TESTICLE FESTIVAL. JULY 7-9. RAYNESFORD.

"Once you're married, what name are you going to go by?"

"I thought I'd continue going by Susan."

"What about your last name? Are you going to go for the hyphen, Hall-Waterpick. . ."

"Wick."

"Wick, right. Are you going to go with that, Hall or straight Wick? Water. Wickwater. Now there's an interesting last name. Maybe you could both change your last names. Tim and Susan Wickwater."

"You're being evasive," Susan said.

"Am I?"

"Yes. Why don't you come out and say it. You're mad at me because I'm getting married. I know it and you know it, so why don't you stop trying to punish me and admit that you're upset.

I'm getting married, Dennis. I'm marrying Timothy Jerome Waterwick at eleven o'clock on August fifth at the First Presbyterian Church. I'm home for a week to make sure everything's in order for the wedding before I begin my new job at Berkeley. I'd like to have a good time while I'm here and that doesn't include having you mad at me. All right?"

"All right," I said.

"All right what?"

"All right, I understand."

"I'm not asking you to understand, I'm asking you to explain. I'm the one who doesn't understand. It hurts me to know you're angry that I'm getting married. I didn't expect you to be elated, and I realize it was unfair to tell you like I did, but I was afraid. I didn't know how you'd react. I decided the easiest way would be to invite you over for dinner with my parents. You're right, it was a lousy idea. I put you in an awkward position and I apologize."

Susan pushed her sunglasses on top of her head. "I want to know what you think about all of this, Den. Because I really don't know. When I came home last Christmas, I decided I wasn't going to call you. I'd been with Tim for a year and a half, I was happy, and I know what happens when you and I get together. I didn't want to risk that. Even when I saw you at the bar and you gave me a ride home I thought, Nothing's going to happen. I almost made it, too. If that stupid door on your van hadn't frozen shut, I would have said good night and slipped out. But then I had to climb out your side and you had to kiss me, and I blew it. I knew better and I still blew it. Every time we're together, I get in trouble.

"I was confused. I couldn't rationally explain to myself how I could feel that strongly about you when I was already in love with Tim. That's not supposed to happen to me. And why then? Why not before? I never felt like that any of the other times we've been together. I always had a great time, but it wasn't anything like at Christmas.

"When I flew back to San Francisco, I didn't see Tim for three days because, naturally, he was on call and didn't have any free time. When I finally did see him and he kissed me, I thought of you and pulled away. He wanted to know what was wrong. I said nothing was wrong, everything was fine, but I know he didn't believe me. I've told him about you, so I'm sure he suspected what had happened. He once told me, jokingly, that he thought I'd end up marrying you one day. Anyway, it took me a week before I felt normal around him. Then you called from D.C. and sounded so distant I didn't know what to think. I wanted you to tell me you felt as strongly as I did. When you didn't, I was furious with you. And myself for letting it happen. Then I decided I was crazy to have ever thought anything could come of it. I was in San Francisco, I had a serious boyfriend, and you were in D.C., going to law school. It was ridiculous. Then I got a letter from you saying you were having trouble studying and wondered if you really wanted to be a lawyer and that you missed me. That was as personal as it got. That's as personal as you ever get. I assumed it hadn't meant as much to you as it did to me. Did it?"

"Yes."

"I didn't know that," Susan said. "You never told me that."

The land had flattened out before us in long stretches of prairie. Small towns appeared and vanished: Raynesford, Geyser, Stanford, each one visible on the horizon as a pocket of trees, houses, a silver water tower.

"You know what bothers me about you, Dennis?"

Here it comes, I thought.

"Even more than the fact that you rarely tell me what you're thinking? At least half the time I'm with you, you're not there. Physically you're there, but mentally you're a thousand miles away. And I never have any idea where you are. None. I can see it happen. What's worse is you even used to do it when we slept together. Not all the time, but sometimes, and every time it happened I'd wonder, Is it me? Am I boring him? I could actually feel your spirit leaving. The first time I felt you were completely there was last Christmas when we didn't sleep together. That was the first time. And the most exciting time, too, I thought. Maybe that's why I felt so strongly about you. You were entirely there for me. I don't know why or what caused it. I'd like to know, but I don't. Do you?"

"No."

"Tell me what you're thinking," Susan said.

The question rendered me blank. Ahead and above I saw a hawk bank in a thermal, glide, then bank again. A hundred yards to the south was the second missle silo I'd noticed today, a square of chain-link fencing and barbed wire surrounding a single white death spire pointing at the sky. Susan turned in her seat to face me.

"I need a minute to organize my thoughts."

"I don't care if they're organized, Dennis. I'm not asking for a cohesive statement. I want to know what you think. I don't even care if it makes sense. Just start talking."

"Start talking."

"Right."

"Okay," I said. "You're right, I was pissed when you said you were getting married. I was ready for mayhem."

"I could tell."

"Even with my sunglasses on?"

Susan smiled. "When you get angry your entire face compresses toward your nose."

"That's my Cro-Magnon ancestry showing through," I said.

"On whose side?"

"My dad's."

"Have you evolved at all?"

"From my dad or my ancestors?" I said.

"Both."

"I don't know about my ancestors. From my dad, less than I thought. I used to think I was night and day from him and Miles, but lately I'm not so sure. I may not be as prone to violence, but I certainly share their tendency for reticence at the wrong times."

"Like when?" Susan said.

"Oh, you know, you get to that point where you know you have to say something but for some reason you're not able to." I felt like the hawk circling in the sky and knew I could stay up where it was safe or tuck my wings and dive.

"Give me an example."

She wanted me to dive. "Like at Christmas. That first night I had the bloody nose and you came into the bathroom. It was so passionate, it scared me. I couldn't get close enough to you, and I wasn't sure where that had come from. By the time you left I thought that, uh. . . I thought. . . I was in love with you. It was that powerful for me. I'd never felt like that with anyone else." I glanced at Susan, who avoided meeting my eyes.

"I wanted to tell you that then, but I couldn't quite pull it off. Do you realize I've never known you when you haven't had a boyfriend? Falling for women with boyfriends or women who live far away is a problem of mine, so a part of me doesn't trust myself when I'm around you. Part of me can't help wondering if the attraction is because I know I shouldn't be doing this. Maybe I need that illicit quality to give it an edge. It's always exciting, but I wonder what it would be like if there weren't anyone else, if it were only the two of us. And I don't even know where that would be. Somehow I can never see us being together anywhere outside Prairie View. When you're in San Francisco, I think of you leading a very different life. You've got your work, your fiancé, your friends. I never see myself in that picture. Do you? Do you see me fitting in with your friends?"

"It's not that you couldn't fit in with them," Susan said.

"But it's hard to imagine, isn't it?"

We were silent until Susan asked me to stop at Eddie's Corner for a minute. I pulled into the parking lot and watched her walk inside. She had her mother's athletic stride, long and graceful like a tennis champion walking to the net to shake the hand of her vanquished opponent. She disappeared and then could be seen through the plate glass window walking behind several men slumped on stools at the counter, all of whom turned to watch her pass. She smiled and waved at me and I waved back, embarrassed to admit how much it thrilled me.

Half an hour later we were descending into Lewistown, cast in shadows by cumulus clouds that had collided to form an island. The surrounding foothills, lush and looking as well tended as a municipal golf course, were brightly lit by bands of sunlight breaking through the soft edges of the clouds. I drove slowly along Main Street, past couples sitting in the shade of front porches, past Woolworth's, the state liquor store and the Snow White Café with a sign in its window that said: I'M A SHRINE CIRCUS MAMA. Past the YoGo Inn, which welcomed the class of 1940, and two miles later, on the edge of town, the Pamida Discount store, having a sale on athletic tube socks. Then climbing through the the thickly wooded Judith Mountains, the smell of pine flowing sweetly through the open windows, hitting prairie again on the other side.

A sign indicated Grass Range and I turned onto a road where waist-high weeds had broken through the asphalt on the shoulders. The foothills were densely covered with blue-green sagebrush that called to mind coral. I parked on the edge of town and gathered the cooler and a U-haul blanket. We crossed a creek and climbed a steep hill overlooking the town.

"This was a good idea," Susan said, taking the blanket from me and spreading it on the ground. She tried to sit down but kept moving, looking for a spot clear of sagebrush. "Too bad we didn't bring any folding chairs."

I sat down and realized what she was talking about. "Kind of like sitting on a dead porcupine, isn't it?"

I handed Susan a sandwich and took one myself. I counted seven cross streets in Grass Range. Only Main Street was paved. Three-quarters of the homes were double-wide trailers, neatly aligned with electrical hookups and anchored with cement and expensive additions. At the north end of town was an abandoned grain elevator, its wood red and rotting, and across from it was an overgrown rodeo corral. Along the highway to Roundup was a café and a motel. The latter looked to be ancient car trailers whose hitches had been cut off and run nose to bung in the shape of an L. "Anne lives around here somewhere," I said.

"I remember you saying that at Christmas. How's she doing?"

"Can't wait to leave. It's funny, Miles would have loved to have inherited a ranch but Anne feels like she's being punished." I looked at her. "I need to tell you something."

"What?"

"Remember when I wrote you after Christmas and said I was having a difficult time getting into the rhythm of law school again?" Susan nodded. "Well, I never did get back into it."

"You flunked out." She almost whispered it.

"No, I didn't flunk out," I said, irritated. "I dropped out. I just told my parents last Saturday. I have to be out of the house in a week."

Susan hugged her knees and began rocking back and forth. "Are you shocked?"

"No, I'm not shocked," she said. "I don't know what to say. What are you going to do?"

"I'm thinking of moving to Austin and starting a band with a friend of mine who used to be the lead singer of Cowboy Angst."

"Is this Montana. . . what's her last name?"

"Wildhack."

"Are you interested in her?"

"Interested in the sense that she's one of my closest friends," I said.

The sun had slipped behind low-hanging clouds and the air smelled of an impending storm. The northern sky had darkened and long veils of clouds brushed the ground where it was raining. "Do you mind if we go visit Anne and Jack?"

"Do you know where they live?"

"Sort of."

On the way down the hill, Susan said over her shoulder, "Did you ever think about moving to San Francisco?"

"Not seriously. Why?"

"Just curious."

At the south end of town we crossed a small wooden bridge over the creek. A post with twenty white arrows, all pointing west and bearing last names and mileage, indicated the way to the Siegrist ranch. We followed the gravel road through a small valley, which soon gave way to low rolling hills in the south while the north side of the road was bordered by sparsely wooded hills. Triangular outcrops of shale, their tops worn smooth by centuries of unforgiving weather, jutted out from their sloping sides. Around the next corner I saw a white house with a large red barn and outbuildings down by the creek, checked the odometer and said, "This should be it."

I parked next to the ranch pickup in the dirt turnaround rutted with tire tracks. The house was a simple two-story rectangle with tall narrow windows and a small addition off the south side. Jack and Anne were reclining on the deck in lounge chairs, reading. Susan and I were halfway to the deck before they noticed us.

"What are you doing here?" Jack said, standing up and smiling.

"We were having a picnic nearby and thought we'd come visit," I said.

I introduced Susan to Jack, and the two women said hello, having met before. Anne caught my eye and arched one eyebrow: I want to hear about this.

"I was telling Jack this morning that we had to get you out here before we go to Boston," Anne said from her lounge chair.

"Have you decided when you're going?" I said, pulling up a metal deck chair for Susan before sitting down.

"A week from Tuesday," Jack said.

"Permanently?" Susan said.

"If I can help it," Anne laughed, looking over at Jack. "No, we're just going back for two weeks to visit friends and inquire about jobs. I took a leave of absence from Houghton Mifflin, but the whole publishing industry's been shaken up so badly that I need to find out if there's anything to return to. I don't know what Jack's going to do. What are you going to do, Jack?"

"Let friends take me to lunch and hope you land a good-enough job so I won't have to work."

"A herder has the sheep up on a pasture in the Big Snowy Mountains, so it's very slow around here," Anne said. "We've forgotten how to work, haven't we?"

"We've become giant amoebas," Jack said. "Can't get out of bed in the morning unless we've slept nine hours and even then it's a struggle. I can't remember the last time I averaged nine hours of sleep a night before we came back. Can you, Anne?"

"Junior high."

"Junior high? Even then I didn't get nine hours a night."

"That's because you were a junior whiz kid trying to win a scholarship out of here."

"That's right, I was, wasn't I? And look where it got me."

"How would you like to make dinner tonight, Dennis? I can't think of anything to make and Jack claims there's nothing in the fridge. We shopped yesterday so there has to be something."

"How about manicotti?" I said.

"Jack?"

"There's nothing in there. We spent a hundred dollars on groceries, and I swear there's nothing but cold cereal and lettuce. I don't understand it."

"I'll go look," I said. I went through the sliding glass doors into the kitchen and checked the refrigerator. I was pulling out what I needed when Susan walked in and stood on the opposite side of the open door.

"Do you need to get back to town?" I said. We were staring at one another, inches apart. I was glad there was a refrigerator door between us or I might have tried something stupid like kissing her.

"No."

"You don't have any plans with your parents?"

"No."

"Okay," I said. "I'm going to cook now."

Susan continued to look at me, then walked out to the deck, small squares imprinted on the backs of her thighs from the deck chair.

After dinner she and Jack volunteered to do the dishes. I was wiping down the dinner table when Anne came over to me and said quietly, "What's going on here, Dennis?"

"She's getting married August fifth."

"So what are you doing?"

"Out having a picnic with an old friend."

"It's me. Anne. Your only sister. I can tell by the way you're looking at one another that something's going on."

"How's that?"

"Like you've both had your bells rung."

"I swear to God, Anne, I have no intention of laying a hand on her."

"It's not your hand I'm concerned about," she said. "I'm glad you came out today, whatever the reason. You should probably spend the night. The road into town's probably a mess by now."

It had been raining for the last hour and a half. I walked over to one of the living room windows. The night was deeply black, and it was only in the orange glow of the yard light near the barn that I could see how hard the rain was falling.

Anne came back from the kitchen and said she'd told Susan we were going to have to spend the night because of the roads. She was calling her parents to tell them where she was.

"They're going to love that," I said.

"What time is it, honey?" Anne said to Jack, who'd wandered in.

"Quarter to ten."

"Are you ready for bed?"

"Not at all."

"Let's go upstairs, Jack," Anne said. "Dennis, there's one bedroom off the kitchen and two upstairs. See you in the morning."

"I guess I'm going to bed now, Dennis," Jack said.

"Night, Jack."

I went over and flipped through David Siegrist's record collection, which filled half a dozen wooden apple crates. I put on Merle Haggard's *Big City* and took a seat at the end of a long deep couch covered with a Hudson Bay blanket. Behind me I heard Susan's footsteps on the hardwood floor. She sat in a Windsor chair across from me.

"My mom wanted to know if I thought this was a wise idea," Susan said.

"What'd you say?"

"I said it hadn't been planned. She didn't seem to think that mattered. It wasn't planned, was it?"

"The weather's beyond my control," I said. We were sitting in the dark with ambient light from the kitchen.

"Did you plan on coming here today, though?"

"No. I could have just as easily turned south and gone to Neihart."

"I don't want anything to happen, Dennis," Susan said. I could barely hear her voice above the record and rain. "I don't even know why I said I wanted to see you. Every time I'm around you I only get in trouble. I can't let that happen this time, which is why I shouldn't be here."

"I know."

"What do you think we should do?"

"I think you should go to bed."

"What are you going to do?"

"Call my parents and then listen to the stereo for a while."

Susan stood up and I also moved to stand. "Don't get up. I don't want you to hug me good night."

I sunk back into the couch. "You can sleep upstairs or there's a bedroom off the kitchen."

"I think I'll sleep upstairs."

"Okay."

"Good night, Dennis."

"Good night." I watched her walk up the stairs and thought, That's the first honorable thing I've done in months.

Nine

Miles was a page-five hero. The Tuesday *Gazette* reported that Deputy Sheriff Miles McCance was at the home of his girlfriend, Tammy Wyland, around 11:30 P.M. when he heard her car start in the garage. McCance walked to the front door and saw someone backing out Wyland's Honda Accord. He ran to the car but couldn't get in the front seat because the driver had locked the door, so he jumped into the rear seat as the car continued to back out the driveway. McCance and the driver wrestled as the Honda drove down the street at forty miles per hour before he was able to stop the car and arrest Rufus Other Medicine, twenty-two, of 617 Seventh Avenue South.

Other Medicine was taken to Saint Ignatius Hospital where he was treated for minor head and neck injuries suffered in the arrest. He was now in the county jail awaiting his pretrial hearing on charges of burglary, felony theft, driving under the influence, and reckless driving.

McCance was not injured, authorities said.

. . .

When Billy Smitherman dropped me off after dinner, I found a
note taped to the first floor bannister saying Montana had called
at seven-fifteen. My parents were about to leave for Whitefish
on Monday for a two-week vacation.

One of Montana's roommates answered and insisted on knowing who was calling, then said in a bright Texas accent, "Well, hey,
Dennis, hang *own*," and yelled for Montana with her mouth so
close to the receiver that I yanked the phone away from my head.

"Hello?"

"I heard you called."

"Dennis," she said. "I spoke with your lovely mother. Whenever I give her my name, she always repeats it with a question
mark as if she's never heard of me. *'Montana?'*"

"She probably thinks it's some sort of prank call," I said.
"What's going on in Austin?"

"You're not going to believe this," Montana said. "Remember
Chuck, the guy I've been seeing?"

"Oh yeah. What'd he do, shoot someone in a bar who spilled
his drink?"

"No. He asked me to marry him last night."

My knees sank as if I'd been hit by a great weight in the chest.
"What'd you say?"

"I told him no."

I closed my eyes and let my head fall back against the wall.
Thank you for that. I don't deserve it, but thank you for that. My
hands were shaking and my heart was pounding. "What happened? Are you all right?"

"I'm all right, I guess," Montana said. There was silence on
her end for a moment, and I could hear someone holler, "See
y'all," and a screen door slap shut. "Do you ever think I'm a
bitch, Dennis?"

"No. Why? Did Chuck call you a bitch?"

"No, I was just wondering. I think I've been a bitch this time. It made me think maybe I was with the other men I've been with too. I started to laugh when he asked me to marry him, Dennis. Can you believe that? I thought he was joking. I really did. When I realized he was serious, I turned bright red, I was so ashamed. I started babbling that I wasn't laughing at him or the idea of marrying him, it was just so unexpected, he'd caught me so off guard.

"We were driving out to his parents' place. I think he had it planned out that he'd ask me on the drive, I'd say yes and we'd walk into his parents' house and announce we were getting married. He waited until I stopped babbling and asked me again if I'd marry him. He was so earnest. I started crying. I think he thought that was a good sign. I finally told him, 'I can't marry you, Chuck.' I thought he was going to make me get out and walk, but he made a U-turn and drove me home without saying another word."

I didn't say anything for a moment, picturing the two of them in the pickup silently returning to Austin. "You were honest with him. I don't think that necessarily makes you a bitch."

"I don't think I was honest with him. If I had been, he would have known I wasn't interested in getting married. I must have done something to make him think I'd say yes. He'd never even told me he loved me, that's how unexpected it was. How can you ask someone to marry you before you've even said you're in love? Doesn't that seem crazy?"

"Oh, I don't know," I said. "Some people have a tough time saying that. Chuck might have assumed that if he asked you to marry him, you'd know he was in love with you."

"Maybe," Montana said. "But that's why I feel so bad. I wanted to have a good time. I told him that all along. And we did have a good time. We had a great time. I think I knew how much he cared but I didn't want to admit it because I didn't feel the same way. I liked him a lot, but I was never going to fall in *love* with him. That's why I feel like such a bitch. He wanted to marry me, and I wanted to have fun. I don't want to do that to anyone again."

"Hmm." I'd slid down the wall and was sitting on the floor with my elbows propped on my knees.

"Hmm?" Montana said. "What does that mean? Hmm that's interesting or hmm I need to go clip my toenails?"

"It means I'm thinking. I'm not sure what to say."

"Well, listen," she said. "I was thinking of getting out of town for a few days. I've got some vacation coming and my dad gave me a frequent-flier ticket awhile ago that I haven't used. I was thinking maybe I'd fly out there and drive back with you."

"Fly out *here?*"

"Yeah. I'm not trying to put any pressure on you, I just need to get out of Austin for a few days. I thought we could stop in Laramie and see my parents, maybe spend a night in Fort Collins. That is, if you're still thinking of moving down here."

"I told my parents I was leaving for Austin on Sunday," I said, sounding more assured than I felt.

"Seriously?"

"Seriously," I said. "And I'd love to see you and drive back with you, but I'm not sure you want to stay here right now. The tension's running a little high. "

"I don't have to stay there. I could get a cheap motel room."

"No, you don't have to do that," I said, feeling guilty, as if I didn't want her to visit. "I know. You could stay with my friend Billy Smitherman. He'd be happy to put you up for a few days."

"You're sure?"

"Positive. I'd love to see you. You could sit in with the Cloverleafs on Saturday."

"I just need to get out of town for a few days."

"When would you get here?"

"I'll have to fly standby so either tomorrow or Thursday, depending on what's available. I'll call you right before I leave."

"Great," I said. "And Montana?"

"Yeah?"

"I'm glad you're not getting married."

"So am I."

"I mean really glad," I said. "That's the best news I've heard in a long time. Seriously. That's great. Not for Chuck. That's too bad for Chuck, but I'm really happy to hear it."

The Prairie View Bar and Grill had an ornate pressed-tin ceiling painted ocher. In the center of it was a deep vaulted skylight painted the same color, and the sun filtering through it turned my mother's skin a soft red. She looked up from her menu toward the entrance and said, "Susan Hall just walked in with her mother."

I turned slowly and found myself looking directly at Susan. Smiles and small waves. Nice to see you. Off they went behind the hostess.

"Have you talked to Miles?" my mother said.

"About what?"

"Since he was in the paper yesterday."

"No. Have you?"

"I talked to him last night. He said Tammy couldn't believe how lucky she was that he was there. She didn't hear the car start or back out of the garage, so she didn't know why Miles suddenly jumped up and ran out the front door."

"I'll bet that Indian couldn't believe how *unlucky* he was to have chosen the one house where Miles was sleeping."

"I don't think he was asleep."

The waitress arrived. I ordered and looked for Susan. She was sitting diagonally across the restaurant from me, directly beneath a wandering Jew, listening intently to her mother.

"It would mean a lot to me if you two could make an effort to get along this summer."

"We're getting along fine," I said.

"You've hardly seen one another."

"That's when we get along best," I said, laughing.

"I don't think that's funny, Dennis."

"I do."

"He's your only brother."

"I'm aware of that."

"Then why can't you make an effort?"

"Mom, we have this conversation every time I'm home. Nothing ever changes."

"And it never will if you don't make some sort of effort," my mother said. "Don't roll your eyes at me. It tears me up inside knowing that you don't get along."

"I know it does," I said. "And I'm sorry we don't, but I wouldn't even know where to begin."

"Just *talk* to him, Dennis."

"About what? We have nothing to say to each other. Whenever I try and talk to him, he looks like he can't wait for me to shut up so he can leave. And he doesn't talk to me unless he has to. So I can't see us having an extended conversation."

"You have to try."

"I have tried."

"I don't believe that."

Our meal was delivered and we ate in silence for several minutes. My mother dabbed the corners of her mouth with her napkin and gave me a small, tight smile as if to say, I'm trying, Dennis. I'm really trying.

"My friend Montana Wildhack is flying into town tomorrow.

She's going to stay here till Sunday and then drive down to Austin with me."

"Where's she going to stay?"

"Billy Smitherman's apartment."

"Does she know him?"

"No, but he said she could sleep on his couch."

"What does she do in Austin?"

"She's a waitress."

"How do her parents feel about her singing career?"

"They're supportive. They think she's talented and they know she's working hard, so they're optimistic. They used to drive down to Fort Collins occasionally to see us play."

My mother arched her eyebrows, trying to fathom driving sixty miles to watch a country band. She and my father had attended one of my Cloverleaf gigs when I was seventeen, sticking it out for the first set before bolting. Afterward my mother complained about the smoke and told me the music had been "a little too twangy for our taste."

"What do her parents do?"

"Her dad's an anthropology professor at the University of Wyoming and her mom teaches high school science. Chemistry and physics. They're a very academic family. Her brother, Marshall, is working on his doctorate in physics at the University of Chicago and her sister, Rachel, is planning on getting hers in Romance languages. Montana's the only one in the family who's not on that track, which I think her parents find refreshing."

"Do you have a place to stay in Austin?"

"I'm going to stay with Montana."

"Does she live alone?"

"No, she has a couple roommates."

"I never thought this is what you'd end up doing," my mother said. "Maybe I was being obtuse all these years, but I always thought of music as your hobby, not something you'd pursue as a career. Then again, I never thought Miles would become a deputy sheriff."

"Is it that disappointing?"

"Mothers have high expectations for their children," she said.

"Maybe you could have high expectations for my music career."

She titled her head slightly, doubtful. When the waitress brought the check, I went to use the bathroom. I took a route that avoided Susan and her mother, but when I walked out, Susan was waiting by the pay phone in the alcove.

"How are you?" she said.

"I'm fine. How are you?"

"OK." She glanced over her shoulder and moved closer to me. "My mom has me booked up today and tomorrow, but I thought maybe you could come to dinner with us on Friday."

"With your parents? No, I don't think that's a good idea."

"How about afterward?"

"We can't get together, Susan. We both know that. Besides, I have a friend flying into town tomorrow."

"Who?"

"Montana."

"Oh," she said, surprised. It occurred to me that this was the first time our positions had been reversed, even if Montana wasn't my girlfriend. There had never been a question of whether *I* was available, only whether Susan would betray her boyfriend. I found myself enjoying the reversal.

"Well," she said briskly, trying to recover, "I guess we probably won't see each other again while I'm home then."

"I guess not."

A woman came out of the bathroom and excused herself as she passed between us. I wanted to say good-bye with a measure of grace, but I wasn't sure I could do it outside the bathrooms. I saw Mrs. Hall crossing the restaurant with her long arrogant stride, her chin raised to a regal level, the other patrons invisible to her. Then she spotted us and hesitated, clearly debating whether to approach us, before walking over.

"Hello, Dennis," she said, gliding to a halt alongside Susan.

"Hi, Mrs. Hall."

A businessman asked to get by us, and we drew back from one another and stood on opposite sides of the alcove. The door to the men's bathroom swung open, and a man could be heard hawking up phlegm from his throat and spitting violently. Susan looked at her feet and brushed a strand of hair from her face.

"I hope I wasn't interrupting anything," Mrs. Hall said.

"Not at all. We were just saying good-bye," I said. Across the restaurant I saw my mother point toward the entrance to indicate that she'd wait outside for me.

"Our appointment is at two," Mrs. Hall said to Susan. Then to me, "We're meeting with the caterer today to select the menu for the wedding reception." She made no move to leave.

"Great," I said flatly, running out of patience with Mrs. Hall and with Susan for not asking her mother to excuse us for a moment. Looking at them together, I knew there had never been any hope for Susan and me. Her mother never would have allowed it, and Susan never would have defied her.

"Well, if you'll excuse me, I need to get going. My mother's waiting for me. Susan, congratulations on your upcoming wedding. I'm sure you'll be very happy. Nice to see you again, Mrs. Hall. Take care."

Susan made no move to speak or hug me good-bye, and I nodded at them and passed through the restaurant. I walked outside into brilliant sunlight, shielding my eyes with my hand. I expected to feel a sense of loss, but I was only irritated.

My mother was waiting for me down the block, peering into the plate glass window of a furniture store. When I walked up, she continued looking inside and said, "Did you say good-bye to Susan?"

"I tried. Her mother wouldn't leave us alone."

"I understand she's getting married."

"August fifth."

"I never thought she was your type," my mother said. "A little too snooty for you. Of course, what else would you expect with her mother. "

"Mrs. Hall never cared for me," I said, enjoying this rare moment of agreement.

"I wouldn't consider that a loss."

I walked my mother to her wood-paneled Wagoneer and thanked her for lunch, then headed home. Just before I reached the corner, a gray Mercedes sedan swept through the intersection, and I caught a glimpse of Susan and her mother, both of them wearing sunglasses and looking straight ahead, paying no attention to pedestrians.

Ten

I was an hour early. My mother had told me to call the airline before I left, but I'd ignored her and the flight was forty-five minutes late. She'd also asked if I were going to pick up flowers for Montana, which struck me as a curious question. I said no, I hadn't been planning on it. "It might be a nice idea," my mother said. I'd ignored that suggestion as well. I'd never bought flowers before and wasn't sure this was the best time to start. For one thing, the flower shops were closed, and I didn't know where to get flowers at this hour. Then there was the question of which flowers to buy. You couldn't buy just anything, I knew that much. Different flowers had different meanings. Roses, for example, meant something that say, tulips, didn't, although I had no idea what that was. Love versus camaraderie, maybe. Ditto the colors. Red versus yellow, pink versus purple. Get either one wrong and you were in trouble. Instead of looking like a thoughtful guy welcoming a friend to town, you might come across as an unwelcome suitor about to drop to one knee. And then there was the act of presenting them, which seemed as important as buying them. It had to be done smoothly, urbanely, as if you bought flowers all the time. I saw myself being self-conscious and awkward, afraid that I'd bought the wrong flowers and was sending the wrong signal, cruelly misled by the florist. Besides, giving Montana flowers might make her nervous as well, unsure what I was saying. Was I just happy to see her or was I interested in being her boyfriend? Or both? I *was* happy about seeing her, and I *was* interested in being her boyfriend, but I thought it was too soon to say that. Maybe she'd changed her mind since our last night together in Fort Collins. Maybe she'd forgotten about it. Maybe that had been my only chance.

When the flight arrived, I stood on the edge of the crowd so I could watch her for a moment before she saw me. Passengers began streaming into the terminal, and I was suddenly keyed up. I pushed my hair behind my ears and straightened my shirt. A group of people separated, and I saw Montana walking up the ramp carrying her battered guitar case that was held together by silver duct tape. Her hair was cut close to her head, no more than an inch long, and it made her face look younger and more open. The bridge of her nose and cheekbones were sunburned and shiny. In her cowboy boots and faded Levi's she was as tall and slender as I'd remembered. She saw me and smiled broadly, her eyes bright.

"God, it's nice to see you," I said, hugging her tightly.

"You, too," Montana said, holding me around the waist with her free arm.

I leaned back to look at her, touching her hair.

"What do you think?"

"It looks great. When did you get it cut?"

"About a month ago. I got tired of all these country singers with big hair and decided I'd do something different."

We took the escalator to the luggage carousel and waited with the other passengers and their families. Montana was telling me about her attempts to get a flight, and I kept looking at her and smiling.

Finally she said, "What are you laughing about?"

"I'm not laughing."

"Yes, you are."

"I'm just happy to see you. I can't believe you're actually here."

I said hello to people I knew and shook hands with an attorney whose name I'd forgotten. I felt radiant, buoyant. He said he'd heard I was in law school. I smiled and said no, I'd dropped out. Nothing could deflate me. He said I'd made a wise choice, that personally he couldn't wait to retire, then shook my hand warmly and wished me good luck as I left to grab Montana's suitcase.

Climbing in the van I said, "Are you tired?"

"God no, it's only ten o'clock. Let's go do something. Is there any place to hear music around here? Or should we go by and see your friend first? I don't want to show up on his doorstep at midnight and say, Here I am."

"Billy gave me a key today and said to let you in. He goes to bed around ten, so he said he'd either meet you in the morning or after work."

I drove to Buckaroo's and parked near the river. We stood on the bank and I pointed across the Missouri toward Dingfelder Park, my parents' house and the courthouse rotunda. Behind us I could hear pickup trucks pulling into the gravel parking lot, doors slamming, Randy Travis floating from an open window.

Inside the Prairie Dogs were well into their second set but only a handful of couples were on the dance floor. My favorite bartender, Vicki, was prowling behind the bar. I ordered two beers and she delivered them with her customary vigor, barking the price at me. I paid and said to Montana, "Old friend of mine."

"I can see that."

The lead singer was warbling his way through "I'm So Lonesome I Could Cry," and Montana winced whenever he reached for a high note. The drummer was having difficulty finding the beat, but no one seemed to notice. "Are the Cloverleafs better than this?"

"They're studio musicians compared to these guys."

We sat on the tall chrome stools at the end of the bar until the band launched into "Fire on the Mountain." I finished my beer and held out a hand to Montana, who guzzled hers. I led her to the floor, took her other hand and said, "Ready?" A sly smile. I flicked my wrists to send her pulling away from me. At the point of resistance I snapped my wrists to draw her in again, then out, then in; now raising my left hand over Montana as an axis for her to turn on while letting go with my left hand to push on the small of her back and send her spinning. Then flicking her out again and feeling Montana's grip tighten as she swept toward me. She had strong hands with callused fingertips from playing guitar, and she could follow wherever I led.

We danced until the end of the set, stood drinking at the corner of the bar during the break and danced throughout most of the third set. Then found an empty table near the wall. A cowboy came over and asked if he could borrow a chair. I waved him on. He swung one over his head and knocked off another man's black Resistol without realizing it. The man jumped up swinging, clipping the obtuse cowboy in the back of the head and knocking him down. The chair clobbered a woman on its way to the floor, and her date pivoted and clocked the first person he saw. Soon four or five men were punching and gouging one another, chairs, tables, bottles and glasses tipping over as people jumped clear. Montana and I were pressed against the log wall. Two meaty bouncers shoved through the crowd and grabbed for people, sucking up two men in their arms and carrying them out the door yelling, "Get outta the way!"

"This is an exciting town you live in," Montana said.
"Isn't it?"

We sat down. A waitress approached balancing a tray full of beers, and I waved at her to place an order. She set two Budweisers on the table. I reached for my wallet and said, "You're a mind reader."

"Guy at the bar bought it. Said it's nice to see you out on a date. Feel free to tip me."

I handed her a dollar and scanned the bar. No familiar faces until a man with dark hair and deep-set eyes raised his glass. Roger, I thought, nodding hello. Must be relieved to see me out with someone besides his ex-wife.

"Another old friend?" Montana said.

"Fellow country music fan."

"What do your parents think about this move to Austin?"

"They're not happy. It's bad enough that I dropped out of law school and lied to them for five months, but now I have to make things worse by telling them I want to start another band. To them it's a giant step backward. They sort of view my entire musical career as a phase I should have outgrown by now. They think it's time I start pursuing some sort of career. If I do this, they see me working at a string of dead-end jobs. Basically they think I'm being unrealistic. They think I can't recognize that it's time to quit and grow up. And I understand that. I don't want to be working in a record store when I'm thirty-five, telling myself that the big break is right around the corner and then calling my parents and saying, 'Guess what? I've got a shot at becoming store manager.' That scares me.

"How do you know when it's time to quit and do something else? I don't know. You're lucky, at least your parents know what's involved and they enjoy what you do."

"Yeah, but they still worry about how I'm going to end up if nothing happens. My dad would love to see me quit waiting tables and do something else. He has this fear that I'm going to become a professional waitress. At Christmas he made me promise I wouldn't wait tables after I turned thirty. He's always encouraging me to look for a job at the University of Texas as a lab assistant where I can put my biology degree to use. I keep telling him I don't want to hang out in a lab all day. And besides, the pay's lousy and you don't get tips. My dad says at least I wouldn't have to take orders from people all day. So they're supportive and they want to see me succeed, but they still worry. Especially after this last year when I'd join a band and we'd rehearse for a couple months and then someone would quit and the entire band would fall apart. They found it even more frustrating than I did. I had to tell them, 'Relax. This happens all the time.' They're excited that you're coming down. I talked to my mom last night, and when I told her you were moving to Austin, she said, 'Now you can finally get going.' They have great faith in you."

"Really?"

"My mom said she felt like I was waiting all year for you to get down there before I really got serious and that's why it didn't bother me so much that the other two bands didn't work out. "

"That's nice to hear."

I'd gotten to know Montana's family after spending every Thanksgiving holiday and several weekends with them while I was living in Fort Collins. The first time she'd invited me home for Thanksgiving was shortly after we'd formed Cowboy Angst as freshmen, and we'd driven up to Laramie after class on Wednesday. All she'd told me about her parents was that both of them were teachers.

Montana's mother, Margaret Bowman, had just returned from the grocery store when we pulled up to the family's ranch house on the edge of town. Montana and I helped carry the groceries into the kitchen where Mrs. Bowman shook my hand and said, "Dennis, I have no idea what we're having for dinner tonight, so be patient with me." She was a tall, comely woman in her forties with an open, friendly face and long hair that had turned prematurely gray. She called down a hallway to let the other two kids know that Janey was home, but they didn't respond. Montana went to look for them just as her father, Warren Bowman, walked in the front door. Mrs. Bowman introduced us and suggested we go into the living room while she got dinner ready. Instead Mr. Bowman led me downstairs to the family den and got me a beer. He asked how long I'd been playing the drums and whether I'd been in a band before Cowboy Angst. I gave brief answers, assuming he was only being polite and not wanting to bore him. But then Mr. Bowman put a Bill Monroe album on the stereo, and I realized he might be sincerely interested. Mr. Bowman said he played mandolin in a local bluegrass band called the Chugwater Ramblers that rehearsed every Thursday night and played gigs once a month around town. I told him about the Cloverleafs and the songs we were rehearsing in Cowboy Angst. Soon we were going through his record collection, which stretched the length of one wall, pulling out albums and playing cuts for one another, saying, "What about this? Have you ever played this song?"

Mr. Bowman said he'd been teaching himself to play the dulcimer, and he set it up in the center of the room to show me what he'd learned. He was a tall, angular man with a gleaming pate and a corona of dark wiry hair that was turning gray. His bony knees jutted out from beneath the dulcimer, and he hunched over it like a miser, lightly striking the strings with the hammers. He played a song I either didn't know or couldn't recognize, then looked up at me and said, "What do you think?"

"Is that a song you've been practicing?" I didn't know what else to say.

"It's taken me weeks to learn that," Mr. Bowman said, laughing. He picked up the dulcimer and set it in a corner. He wanted to know how Janey was doing as the lead singer of Cowboy Angst. I told him how she'd frozen up at our first gig and then confessed that she'd never sung in public before. We'd played two gigs since then, and she'd tried not to look out at the audience. When she did she forgot lines or dropped entire verses, but for her first three gigs she was doing fine.

"I'm surprised she never sat in with your band," I said.

"She did," Mr. Bowman said. "She used to come with me to rehearsals even before she started playing guitar. She'd watch and never say a word. Even when she'd learned all the songs, she wouldn't go onstage with us. She said she wasn't good enough yet. And you could never get her to sing in front of anyone. We'd hear her singing in her bedroom all the time, but the second anyone opened the door, she'd stop. At the time she was more interested in sports than anything else. She'd start basketball practice in August, then switch to volleyball in the winter and track in the spring. She was always either going to practice or returning from practice."

We ate dinner in the kitchen with her parents and younger brother and sister, Marshall and Rachel. During the meal I asked Montana to hand me the salad, but she didn't seem to hear me and I said, "Montana?"

There was a moment of silence and confusion as everyone else eyed one another. I thought I'd missed something.

"Why did you call her Montana?" Rachel said. She had a remarkably direct gaze for a fourteen-year-old.

I looked at Montana, who was now paying close attention to the food on her plate. "You haven't told them about this?" I said.

"Told us what?" her mother said.

"Her stage name."

"Stage name?" Mrs. Bowman said.

"What stage name?" Mr. Bowman said.

Montana was sinking in her chair.

"When we started the band, Montana—Janey—said she wanted to be called by her stage name, Montana Wildhack. You never told them about this, Montana?"

They laughed. They thought it was hilarious. Montana Wildhack. They kept repeating it to one another and laughing even harder. Montana tried to say something, embarrassed and upset, but they drowned her out and it was impossible to sustain any sort of anger in the face of that much laughter.

"Wasn't Montana Wildhack a porno star?" Marshall said.

"That's right," Mr. Bowman said. "On the planet Tralfamadore."

"My oldest child's named herself after an alien porno star," her mother said.

Montana balled up her napkin and threw it at her.

Afterward she gave me a tour of the house and its comfortable, lived-in rooms. Most of the walls were lined with bookcases that were crammed with books, stacked and wedged into every available space. Encyclopedias, cookbooks, novels. Magazines were piled in baskets and strewn across coffee tables. The rest of the family had parked themselves throughout the house with something to read, oblivious to us as we passed by.

In Montana's bedroom the built-in bookcases were lined with trophies, medals, silk ribbons, framed certificates and photographs: Montana neatly flicking a jump shot over an opponent's outstretched fingertips. Diving for a blurred volleyball on a gym floor, her body parallel to the ground. Sailing into a long-jump pit, knees drawn into her chest, arms thrown back.

"I used to be a jock," she said, leaning against the doorframe, watching me examine everything. She looked embarrassed by all of it.

"So when did you decide to become a singer?"

"When I was about fourteen. I'd been going with my dad to his band rehearsals for a long time and I'd been playing guitar for a couple years, but I never really thought about starting my own band. It was just this thing I enjoyed doing on my own. Then I saw Emmylou Harris at the state fair when I was in ninth grade and I thought, That's what I want to do. The problem was I didn't know anyone else my age who wanted to play country music. All the guys I knew with guitars wanted to play "Free-bird" or "Stairway to Heaven," and there was no way I was going to play that shit. So I just practiced alone in my room. I'd listen to my dad's records and try to copy them.

"I was already really into sports by that point—I'm sort of the jock in the family—and I decided I'd keep doing that until I went to college. I got an offer to play volleyball at the University of Idaho, but I was ready to do something else. I always knew, once I got to college, I'd find people who wanted to start the kind of band I wanted to play in."

"Do you miss it?" I said, pointing at the bookcase.

"The only thing I miss is the confidence I had. I'd get nervous before games, but I never had any doubt that I'd do well. I don't have that assurance yet as a singer. I'm still afraid of screwing up in front of people. When you're playing basketball or volleyball, you're too busy concentrating to pay much attention to whoever's watching. On stage you're standing in front of all these people and they're all looking up at you, waiting. I look out at them and think, Now what?"

"You'll get there."

"I know, but I wish I didn't have to learn in front of fifty strangers."

. . .

"Care to dance, ma'am?" I said.

"Love to, cowboy."

The Prairie Dogs finished playing "Truck Driving Man" and led into "Six Days on the Road" and "White Line Fever" before downshifting to "Georgia on My Mind." I stepped into Montana and slipped my hands around her waist. Couples had flocked to the dance floor and held one another in varying degrees of ardor, one man leaning on his partner, both hands clamped to her ass while an older couple held one another with ramrod formality. I moved my hands across Montana's back and felt her hold me tighter. At the end of the song, we looked at each other a little shyly and I said, "Should we go?"

In the parking lot a soothing breeze came off the Missouri and the clear night sky was stretched tight to the horizons. We drove across Dingfelder Bridge. To the north the river's glazed surface shone with pylons of rainbow-colored light.

"Have you heard anything from Chuck?" I said.

"He called last night and talked to one of my housemates, but I wasn't home. Emily said he sounded drunk and he kept telling her to put me on the phone. He wouldn't believe I wasn't there. He started calling every ten minutes and asking for me until Emily finally unplugged the phone. I feel really bad about it and I thought about calling him, but I knew if I did, it would only make things worse. He'd want to know *why* I wouldn't marry him and there would be nothing I could say. It's better to stay away for a while."

I pulled up to Billy's apartment complex and carried Montana's suitcase to the front steps. We both hesitated and fell silent. I was suddenly nervous, not sure what to do. I tried the key Billy had given me and said, "Well, the key works." I felt like Montana was waiting for me to guide us through this, but I wasn't sure how to begin. Maybe it was too soon to do this. Maybe she was still getting over Chuck.

"I had a really nice time tonight," she said, deadpan.

"So did I."

"I don't usually go on blind dates, but that was nice."

"I'm glad you enjoyed it," I said. "You know, it's funny, my friend told me you were a blonde."

"Really? My friend told me you had a crew cut."

"That was back when I was in the service."

"I'd invite you in for a drink, but I have to work in the morning."

"Maybe next time."

"Call me."

"I will."

"You have my number, don't you?"

"I think so."

Montana laughed. "'Night, Dennis."

Late the next morning we walked around town. I gave Montana a tour of my parents' house, the neighborhood and downtown. Earlier my mother had asked when they were going to meet her and suggested we all go out to dinner. I said we already had plans with Billy. What about Saturday night? I said I had a gig but promised to bring Montana over on Sunday before we left for Austin.

We ate lunch downtown and then drove along the Missouri beneath scudding clouds. A windsurfer in a wet suit raced parallel to the road, then veered sharply away. We ended up in the parking lot of the Lewis and Clark State Park and Fish Hatchery. It began to rain and we dropped the idea of walking down to look at the fish. A black Trans Am swung into the lot and parked two spots away. A heavy metal band was blasting over the car's stereo, and it was so loud I could feel the vibrations in my chest. Soon smoke began to leak from the car's windows. I looked over and saw the driver and a woman passing a bong back and forth as casually as if they were in their own basement.

"Remember that gig in Albuquerque?" I said.

"That was the best gig we ever played."

"Are you kidding me? That was a horrible gig."

"That was the best one we ever played," Montana insisted. "We were never more energetic than that night."

"*You* were never more energetic. You were a fucking lunatic. The rest of us were terrified."

"I loved that gig," Montana said. "It was my one chance to be a rock star."

Cowboy Angst had been invited to play at a three-day country music festival in Tucson, Arizona, during my last quarter of college, but as much as we wanted to play there, the pay wasn't nearly enough to cover our travel expenses and I was going to decline.

Around that time our bass player, Chris Ostrom, had missed several rehearsals and showed up late a couple of times, and Montana was pressing me to replace him. I'd already saved him once after the gig at Linden's when he'd fallen asleep, and I told Chris, the next time he missed a rehearsal he was gone. He swore it wouldn't happen again, that he'd been busy with school, and he'd make it up to us.

When we received the festival invitation, Chris said he had a friend, Spike, who worked at a club in Albuquerque, New Mexico, and he might be able to line up a gig for us on our way to Tucson to help pay for gas. I usually handled all the band's bookings, but since this was his friend I told him to take care of it. At the next rehearsal Chris said it was all set, we could go to

Tucson. He'd arranged for us to play a two-hour gig for three hundred dollars, sharing the bill with two other bands. I shook his hand and welcomed him back into my good graces.

A month later we drove to Albuquerque in two vans. For the last few weeks, Chris had been telling us what a great guy Spike was and how we were going to love this club, but now that we were on our way, he was subdued, and he seemed to be avoiding me whenever we stopped for gas. He bought a six-pack of beer in Pueblo and finished it before we reached Raton. I said if he fell asleep at this gig, I would personally strip him naked and leave him on the sidewalk.

At a gas station outside Santa Fe, Chris sidled up to me and said there was something I should know before we got to Albuquerque. He knew he should have told me earlier, but he'd only just found out himself: Spike had been fired last week.

"But the gig is still on," I said.

"Definitely," Chris said. "Definitely."

We reached Albuquerque around ten o'clock. The Poison Club was a one-story metal building located outside town at the end of a strip mall. The name had made me uneasy when Chris first mentioned it, but the parking lot was filled with pickup trucks and all-terrain vehicles, and I felt reassured.

We parked behind the building and climbed out, stretching and yawning. Montana and I walked around to the front entrance. A dull, heavy sound was coming through the walls. We looked at one another.

"That sound like pedal steel to you?" I said.

"I didn't want to say anything, but I've had doubts about this ever since Chris told us the name. I've yet to hear of a country bar called the Poison Club. Maybe this will be a first."

We stepped into a short hallway and were hit by a wall of buzzing guitars, crashing drums and rasping howls. A bouncer with a shaved head sat slumped on a stool behind a podium covered in sheet metal. Tattooed serpents were coiled around his beefy forearms and biceps. He held up five blunt fingers to indicate the cover charge. A flier taped to the podium listed tonight's featured bands: THRASHING VIRGINS, RAPE & PILLAGE, and COWBOY ANGST.

I yelled over the din that we were Cowboy Angst and needed to see the manager. The bouncer plucked a yellow earplug from his head. I yelled again next to his ear. He jerked his thumb back over his shoulder. I smiled and nodded.

The hallway led into a large open space with a bar in the center and openings on either side. The floor and walls were painted metallic silver. The tables stood chest-high and were also covered in sheet metal. There were no stools or chairs and men were standing around drinking, using hand signals to order from the bartenders. Most of the patrons had shaved heads or military buzz cuts. A number of them wore camouflage pants tucked into their combat boots like paratroopers. I wondered if they were stationed at a nearby military base or simply admired paramilitary fashions.

Montana put her mouth to my ear and yelled, "Is this a gay bar?"

I looked at her, confused. She nodded. I shook my head and mouthed, No way. She pointed toward the opposite room, and we slowly worked our way through the men crowded around the opening. As we got closer, I smelled beer, sweat and urine.

A heavy metal band was onstage, the lead singer screaming into his mike. The dance floor was a drunken mass of sweaty bodies ramming into one another, moving wherever they were pushed or shoved. Two floor-to-ceiling sections of chain-link fence had been installed on either side of the large room, and every few minutes two men would grab someone's arms and hurl him into the fence; he would hit the chain-link and be catapulted back into the crowd. A wiry guy with no shirt hit the fence and was knocked down on the rebound. Half a dozen men immediately began kicking him before he struggled up and raised his arms above his head, signaling that he was still alive.

I imagined playing "Stand by Your Man" to this crowd and thought, They'll kill us. I touched Montana's arm and led her back toward the manager's office. I was trying to calculate how much money we could save by sleeping in our vans or staying at a KOA campground. Hell, I was even willing to shell out three hundred dollars from my own pocket. Anything was better than being stomped by this crowd and having my drums trashed.

The manager's office was built into a corner. A lighted door-bell said: MANAGER. I pressed it and waited. After a moment a small metal hatch slid back. An eye shone in the opening, then a mouth yelled, "What?"

"Cowboy Angst. Here to play a gig."

The hatch was shut and the door swung open. A pleasant-looking man with thinning blond hair held it for us and nodded hello. Montana and I stepped past him into the tall narrow office. The walls had been covered with gray soundproof foam used in recording studios, and when the door closed behind us the din was replaced by a Beethoven piano concerto.

"I'm the owner, Harry Packer," the man said, shaking our hands. Montana and I stood against the wall so he could get by us to his desk. He sat down and swiveled in our direction. He was in his late thirties, early forties, dressed in an expensive sport coat and white polo shirt. He was tan and wasn't wearing socks with his soft leather loafers. "I was beginning to think you were going to be a no-show. Most of the bands we book are from the area."

"I think there's been a mistake, actually," I said. "I don't know what you were told, but we're not a heavy metal band. We're a country band."

"A country band," Mr. Packer said. "Hank Williams, Willie Nelson. That kind of thing."

"Exactly."

"I was told you were strictly metal. Why else would I have booked you?"

"Normally I arrange all our gigs, but our bass player arranged this with a friend who worked here, Spike."

"Spike is no longer with us," Mr. Packer said.

"That's what I understand. Now I don't know what Chris told Spike or what Spike told you, but we don't play heavy metal."

"Let me explain something to you," Mr. Packer said. "This is not a country crowd. This is a Megadeath, Judas Priest kind of crowd. Skinheads and rednecks. They like to get drunk and hit each other. That's their idea of a good time. This is not a crowd that wants to hear "Blue Eyes Crying in the Rain." So unless you know two hours' worth of heavy metal or speed metal, I wouldn't suggest getting on stage."

"But you're not going to pay us if we don't play," I said.

"Absolutely not."

"We'll play," Montana said.

"Montana, we're not going to play. They'll kill us." I turned to Mr. Packer. "I apologize for any misunderstanding, but we're not going to be able to play."

"We'll play," Montana said.

"The lady says you'll play," Mr. Packer said.

I turned to Montana. Her eyes were set, and I knew it was pointless to argue. "Fine," I said. "Fine. We'll play."

"In that case I'm going to need you to sign a waiver releasing the Poison Club from any damages or injuries you might incur during your performance," Mr. Packer said, swiveling back to his desk and searching for the form. He produced it and handed me a pen. "All very standard."

I signed.

"You go on at midnight. Good luck." He stood up and shook our hands.

Outside I said, "Why the hell did you say that? Did you see those guys? They're neo-Nazis from hell. They'll stomp us before we get through the first song."

"We need the money," Montana said. "That's the only reason we're here. And I refuse to let Chris get out of this."

"Oh, that's great, Montana. That's just great. What about the rest of us?"

"It'll be fine. Trust me."

Nick and Ryan were tossing a football behind the club. Chris was lying in the back of Ryan's van drinking from a pint bottle. He looked up at me and said, "Am I out of the band?"

"Not yet. But you're going to wish you were when you see this place."

I told the three of them to go inside and check out the crowd. When they came back, they drove to a grocery store, bought a case of beer and began drinking. We drew up a set list we thought might appeal to them and decided to play everything as fast and loud as possible.

Rape & Pillage ended their set promptly at eleven-thirty. We watched them pack up and reluctantly carried our equipment inside. When we were almost ready, I went outside and found Montana walking back and forth behind the club, rolling her neck and shoulders, shaking her arms and talking quietly to herself. She passed by me and said, "Tell Ryan I'll do all the singing."

We were out of time. All of us except Montana walked inside and took our places. The stage stood five feet high, with another tier for the drummer, and Nick, Ryan and Chris had set up as far back from the edge of the stage as they could; they looked frightened and timid, ready to run for the back door the moment anyone climbed onstage. The crowd stared dully at us. Their drunken faces looked bleached under the black lights. A handful of them were bleeding, dabbing at their cuts with their shirt sleeves. A couple others had black eyes and missing teeth.

I yelled out the tempo and we launched into "Cocaine Blues," playing double-time and sounding like an aberrant country-punk band. The crowd looked sullen and confused. Halfway through the song Montana still hadn't appeared. Nick and Ryan were glancing back at me with palpable fear: Where the hell is she?

Then the crowd's attention shifted to the left, and Montana was striding across the stage in a black leather vest, Levi's and black cowboy boots. We came around for her intro. She snatched the microphone off the stand and began singing about how she'd taken a shot of cocaine and shot her woman down, spitting out the lyrics with venom. She strutted across the stage, twisting low to sneer at the crowd. She whipped her long hair, ran in place, shook her ass. The rest of us in the band were glancing at one another, startled that she knew how to do this. I realized she was going to get us through this, and I loved her for it.

We jumped into "Folsom Prison Blues," tearing along so quickly that it was hardly recognizable. Parts of the crowd had started moving again, lowering their shoulders and driving them into one another. A body was flung into the fence; it bounced off and was knocked down. Montana marched across the stage, snarling about shooting a man in Reno just to watch him die. She was becoming more and more confident by the minute. She shook her fist, pumped her hips. She grabbed a bottle from someone in the crowd and took a swig. Then she turned and spit it over the crowd. They stopped slam-dancing and swung toward her. Montana froze. There was a dangerous lull, as if everyone were trying to decide how to react. A man in front drank from his bottle, spun around and spit over the heads behind him. Soon everyone on the floor was spitting. Beer, saliva, whiskey, no one cared. Spitting and slamming into one another.

Montana led us into "Take This Job and Shove It." The crowd sang along with her. She goose-stepped to the far end of the stage as they cheered. She pivoted, dropped her mike and ran toward the center of the crowd, doing a swan dive into them. They passed her overhead, clutching and grabbing her. She disappeared from sight for a moment, and I was suddenly terrified that they would drop her on the floor and begin kicking, but she resurfaced and was handed back up to the stage.

At a quarter to two, we closed with "Up against the Wall, Redneck." Montana held out the microphone to the crowd for the chorus. As we finished, she bowed deeply to them and yelled, "Good night, you redneck mothers!"

The rest of us were breaking down our equipment before the crowd had stopped cheering. As we carried everything outside, Ryan kept saying, "She almost got us killed. She almost got us killed." We loaded up the vans. Montana was standing with a group of men at the side of the stage, drinking from the bottles they offered her.

I walked through the club to the manager's office. The dance floor was covered with puddles of alcohol and shards of broken glass. I rang Mr. Packer's doorbell. One of the bartenders said Mr. Packer had already left, that he'd settle up with me. He counted out three hundred dollars and I walked back outside. Nick, Ryan and Chris were sitting in their van with the doors locked and the engine running. We agreed to meet at a motel we'd spotted earlier. Montana was talking to a couple men in camouflage pants. I started the Angstmobile and pulled up next to her. She climbed in and waved to the two men.

"I have to tell you this," I said, pulling out onto the strip mall. "You were fantastic."

"Thank you." She was grinning.

"I really thought they were going to kill us, but you pulled it off."

"I told you it would be all right. You just have to trust me."

. . .

Sitting in the van now, I thought my problem wasn't that I hadn't trusted Montana—I'd always trusted her—but that I hadn't trusted myself. I'd been filled with self-doubt for the last year and a half, unsure about everything I was doing. When Montana had asked me to join her in Austin after I'd dropped out, I'd been afraid that she'd shot ahead of me and I wouldn't be able to catch up. I'd imagined arriving in Austin and discovering that I couldn't cut it and having Montana tell me she was sorry, but she was going to have to find another drummer.

But now that she was here I was no longer afraid that would happen. I knew she wouldn't have flown to Prairie View if she didn't want me to join her or doubted that I was good enough. Since she'd arrived, I'd realized just how much I'd missed her. Missed being with her, talking to her, seeing what she would do next onstage. I didn't want to be apart from her again. I suddenly believed that going to Austin with Montana would be the smartest thing I would ever do, a decision I would never question or regret. I was filled with hope and light.

"I know you've had some doubts about this," I said, "but I'm ready to go now."

"Where?"

"To Austin."

Montana turned to look at me. "You're serious."

"I'm serious," I said. "I'd go right now if I didn't have a gig tomorrow night."

"You really mean it."

"I really mean it."

"That's great!" Montana said. "You really mean it. " She drummed her fists on the dashboard, pounded her feet on the floor. She leaned over and pressed on the the horn, alarming the stoned couple in the Trans Am. "He really means it!"

Eleven

I was driving the Angstmobile into the sun on my way to Simms. Montana was supposed to be with me, but when I'd called to say I was on my way to pick her up, Billy said she was taking a nap. The three of us had stayed up till three in the morning the night before drinking and talking, and I knew Montana was probably suffering from jet lag as well, but it irritated me more than it should have that she wasn't ready. Billy said they'd meet me later, and I reluctantly agreed and gave him directions.

In Fort Shaw I slowed for a cat in the crosswalk that moved so languidly as to be suicidal. Several pickups were nosed in to a building marked simply BAR, shaded by the long shadows of cottonwoods that stood guard over the town. Far ahead, the dark serrated outline of the Rockies connected the high-running foothills on either side of the highway. Wheat fields on the south side ran at the hills and banked halfway up their concave sides.

A few miles later I turned into Simms, marked by hundreds of high cottonwoods. Three horses grazed on someone's front lawn. In the front-room window of the house were dozens of gold rodeo trophies. I drove down Main Street looking for the Sun River Valley Lions Club. George had said it was across from the Volunteer Fire Department and a barber shop called Head Hunters. There were no sidewalks and most of the buildings were in need of paint, windows, a bulldozer. I spotted the Lions Club, a corrugated metal building with a tin roof, and pulled around to the rear. I climbed out and knocked on the locked back door. I was about to knock again when the door opened a few inches, revealing the wizened face of a little man wearing horn-rimmed glasses and a egg-yolk yellow vest. "Yes?"

"I'm with the band."

"Who?" An elephantine ear was turned to the opening.

"The Cloverleafs. I'd . . ."

"You must have the wrong address." The door closed.

Okay, I thought, walking around to the front of the building through a vacant lot of tall grass and empty beer cans. Inside the front door I found a terrifically fat man, also in a yellow vest, sitting behind a card table counting money in a strongbox. I could hear him breathing heavily through his nose. He looked up at me and said, "You're not from here, are you?"

"No, I'm not."

The Sun River Valley Lions Club was sponsoring tonight's dance in order to raise money to send eight Simms High School cheerleaders to a regional competition in Lincoln, Nebraska. They'd finished second at the state meet in Billings and were hoping to advance to the national championship in Orlando, Florida. If the Cloverleafs wouldn't mind, the round man, Bill General, told me, the girls would perform during the second break. His voice was rich with lascivious anticipation. I said it sounded like a fine idea.

I set up and was sitting in the Angstmobile listening to the Flying Burrito Brothers when George and Patti parked alongside me. Patti climbed out and slammed her door. She glared at me, said, "Men suck," and went to the back of the Suburban to unload. George came over and rested his forearms on my open window. "Vince forgot their first anniversary last night. Poor son of a bitch. He'll be in the doghouse for the next year. Fortunately, Barbara writes me notes reminding me when ours is coming up, so I've never missed one. You ready to play, cowboy?"

"I'm ready."

When I went back inside, the club had rapidly filled up. Young men and boys in cowboy hats and boots were leaning against the outside walls, plastic beer cups in hand, keeping an eye on the door for any female prospects. The older men and two or three women were standing at the bar or sitting at tables. From the looks of it, the bartenders were serving anyone tall enough to peer over the counter; it was for a worthy cause.

We completed our sound check and started the set with "Whiskey Bent and Hell Bound." No one moved to dance. I looked out at the crowd and realized there was an appalling lack of women. The ratio of men to women was roughly eight to one. I hadn't seen the cheerleaders but thought they could finance the trip to Orlando by charging a dollar a dance. Patti sang "Your Good Girl's Gonna Go Bad," and George turned to roll his eyes at me. Halfway through the set there was still no one dancing and between songs George swiveled on his stool and said to us, "What's wrong with these fuckers?"

"No women," I said.

"I wonder why," Patti said bitterly.

"Jimmy?"

"No idea, George." He was decked out in a freshly blocked white Resistol, green silk shirt and tight black jeans. I looked at him and thought, What's going on in your life, Jimmy? Are you working up the nerve to cheat?

I suggested "I Can't Dance" and we played it as if challenging everyone in the place to resist dancing, which they did without difficulty. We tore into "Cash on the Barrelhead," and finally two couples rose from their tables and moved to the linoleum dance floor. Three girls in summer dresses waltzed through the front door, and five boys pushed away from their places along the wall to ask them to dance. Several other boys took this as a cue and began moving among the tables in search of partners.

At the end of the set, George got up from behind his pedal steel guitar and said, "Gonna be a long night."

I checked my watch and wondered where Billy and Montana were. I felt a creeping anger I didn't immediately identify. I made my way to the bar, asked for a glass of water and stood in the breeze of the front door looking out at the street. Behind me I heard someone say, "What do you think, Tom? Sure looks like a girl to me. Think we should take her outside and give her a real haircut?" "Yeah, we should."

I turned slowly and found two high school kids, their hair cropped, faces sunburned, thumbs hooked into the top of their jeans. "Is there a problem, boys?" I said.

"You a queer?" the taller one said.

"As a matter of fact, I am," I said. "So you better stand against the wall so I don't try and bugger you. Now fuck off." I saw them glance above my left shoulder and thought, Oh shit, the rest of their friends are here.

"Good to see you making friends, Dennis," Billy said, placing a large hand on the back of my neck. "Everything OK, guys?"

They continued staring up at him, vastly diminished. "Yep."

"Good. Go away now." And to me: "That's worth a beer. I'll find us a table and you can get the beer." He smiled at Montana, and I was murderously jealous, unable to speak for a moment.

"You want a beer?" I said curtly to Montana.

"Sure."

"What happened, Billy get lost?"

"No." She was watching me, trying to understand what was happening. "I woke up from a nap around seven-thirty and then we went to dinner."

"Great."

"What's wrong?"

"Nothing's wrong. I was just under the impression that you wanted to sit in with us."

"I do want to sit in with you, but I thought I'd wait till the last set. I don't want anyone in the Cloverleafs to think I'm muscling in on their gig." She touched my arm. "I'm sorry we were late, Dennis. I fell asleep on the couch, that's all."

I nodded, feeling petty and mean and wanting to be able to rise above it. You asked him to let her stay there, so don't get bent out of shape that they're getting along, I told myself.

The bartender served us and we sat at the table.

"How's the crowd?" Billy said.

"Big dance fans," I said. "The Simms High School cheerleaders are supposed to perform after the next set, so maybe things will pick up. I thought you might be able to give them a few pointers."

"Were you a cheerleader?" Montana said.

"A spotter."

"How was that?"

"It had its advantages."

"Like what?"

"There are worse ways to spend your afternoons than lifting Arizona State cheerleaders over your head. It's as close as I've come to being good at a sport. Plus they paid me, which really wasn't necessary."

Inertia had set in again during the break, and in an attempt to get anyone out on the floor, we put aside all slow songs and began to play with an almost desperate fervor. Billy danced with Montana and as soon as it became clear to the men in the crowd that this six-six giant with size-fifteen Top-Siders wasn't much of a dancer and his partner was, they perked up. A cowboy cut in during the next song, "Act Naturally." Other men and boys led partners to the floor and swapped for Montana whenever possible and at a rate that soon became comical. Billy's own attempt to cut in was rebuffed by a boy who stood slightly higher than his navel. I saw Billy wave from the bar and shrug.

We closed with "My Shoes Keep Walking Back to You." As we left the stage, Bill General lumbered up the stairs to announce the moment you've all been waiting for, the reason we're all here tonight, the Simms High School cheerleaders! Someone in the audience belched. Several people clapped. I told Montana I needed to go out to the van and change my shirt. She said she'd go with me. Billy said he had to stay and appraise the squad. Montana and I headed outside as eight girls in cardinal red and black skipped and yipped through the back door, trailing in their wake the heavy scent of hair spray and perfume. I climbed into the van and changed my shirt.

When I finished, Montana was standing in the tall grass with her arms folded, looking up at the night sky. Her face and throat were lit by a silver ambient light, and her white blouse was glowing.

I stepped out of the van and walked toward her. Montana watched me approach, letting her arms fall at her sides. I raised my hands to her face, touching her lightly and running my fingers through her hair.

"I don't want to do this just for fun," Montana said softly.

"I don't either."

She tilted her head a few degrees to the west and closed her eyes. I kissed her, dropping my hands down her back and drawing her to me. Both of us were trembling. I kissed her mouth, eyes, throat. Her skin tasted damp and salty. We held one another so tightly that it was difficult to breathe. After a while I pulled Montana down into the tall grass, wanting to feel her weight on top of me. She arched her back, and I pulled her toward me . . .

"It's that time, cowboy!" George yelled from the back door.

Montana went limp, resting her forehead on my shoulder and breathing heavily. "God, that was a short break."

During the third set, I kept rushing until George finally wheeled around on his stool and glared at me. I nodded, I know, I know. The cheerleaders were dancing in the arms of their boyfriends or boys who hoped to be their boyfriends soon, preferably by the end of the next song. Billy was two-stepping with a long-legged brunette in Wranglers and boots, a red corsage pinned to her shirt. Montana danced with a bald man in his fifties who held her at arm's length and kept his eyes closed as though imagining himself as a twenty-five-year-old full of possibility and a thick head of hair.

At the break George put his arm around my shoulders and said, "Are we in a hurry?"

"No hurry."

"Liar."

Billy waved me over to a table and introduced me to the young woman he'd been dancing with, Eryn Tunnicliff. She had a fresh-scrubbed faced with high shiny cheekbones and large white teeth that looked like they'd been cut on a thousand ears of corn. It turned out Eryn had grown up on a wheat farm in Kansas and been a cheerleader at the University of Michigan for two years. After graduating last spring, she'd accepted a job teaching English and history and coaching the cheerleaders at Simms High School before even seeing the town because she'd wanted to live in Montana as long as she could remember.

"Don't you just love it out here?" Eryn said.

"I wouldn't live anywhere else," Billy said.

I laughed. No shame, Smitherman.

Eryn said she had to talk to her cheerleaders about practice on Monday and would meet Billy out front.

"She needs a ride home," Billy said in way of explanation.

"Where does she live?"

"She's house-sitting for a couple in Fort Shaw." He clapped his hands once. "So she's applied for a teaching job in Prairie View next fall. Said Simms was too small." Billy grinned down at me. "Montana, do you need to get your guitar before I leave?"

She took his keys and headed to the car.

"By the way," Billy said, "are you interested in Montana? Because that would be a very smart move, in my opinion."

"You think so?" I said, smiling.

"Very smart. Trust me on this one." He went to find Eryn.

I introduced Montana to the Cloverleafs. Patti apologized for the crowd and George said he hoped she could help generate some energy. The largest Lion, Bill General, came over to the edge of the stage as we were about to start the last set and asked if we'd mind quitting half an hour early. A number of the older Lions were sleepy and wanted to go home. George said it wouldn't be a problem.

The crowd wanted nothing but slow songs and we obliged them. Couples clutched one another and shuffled in slow lazy circles. Boys moved their hands down girls' backsides until being stopped and forced to start over again at mid-torso.

Before the last song, George told us he refused to play an entire set of slow songs and said to play "Stay All Night." Couples immediately began to leave the floor, anxious not to break the spell of romance they'd enjoyed for the last half an hour.

"You've been a great crowd," George said as we played. "I know we sure wish we could stay all night." By now no one was actively listening. The Lions were loudly folding and stacking metal chairs and sweeping plastic cups off tabletops into garbage bags. We continued playing, George signaling us to go around once more.

"On my right, ladies and gentlemen," George said, "the best-dressed bass player in the United States, Jimmy Jensen!" Jimmy stepped forward, played a twelve-bar solo and bowed stiffly to the emptying hall. "On keyboards and vocals, my lovely daughter, Patti Anderson." A pounding, two-minute Jerry Lee Lewis–style solo complete with backhanded glissandi. "On acoustic guitar, all the way from Austin, Texas, Montana Wildhack." She held her guitar high on her chest, rising up on her toes and strumming furiously. "On drums, the longhaired felon with the fattest backbeat in country music today, Dennis McCance!" I began playing pianissimo on the metal rims of my drums like a tap dancer starting his warmup routine, eighth notes on the bass drum his heartbeat, gradually moving faster and louder until the dancer's feet were a machine-gun flurry of rhythmic metal clicks. Then bringing it down again so Patti could say, "And finally, on pedal steel guitar, the man in black, George Muzzana!"

All of the Lions had stopped cleaning and stood watching, metal chairs and plastic bags still in hand, bewildered and transfixed by this band that could have stopped playing twenty minutes ago but instead had erupted with pent-up energy. Only we realized that none of us wanted it to stop or even knew how to go about stopping as we played through the song for the fourth time until George raised his hand over his head, jumped up from his stool and slashed downward with his fist.

"Good-night, Simms, Montana!"

"I'm ready to drive. I'm ready to dance. I'm ready to drink a six-pack of Bud and smoke a big Bob Marley reefer," I said, dancing in place like a Zulu beside the loaded Angstmobile. Montana was sitting sideways in the driver's seat with the door open, laughing at me.

"Go park somewhere and watch the sun rise," Patti said. "Vince and I used to do that all the time in high school."

"Where the hell was I when you were out that late?" George said from the back of the Suburban.

"Out doing the same thing, probably."

"Oh." George shut the double doors and came around to the side. "It wasn't much of a gig until that last song but this should help." He handed me $150. "Well, cowboy, I guess this is it. Good luck in Austin. Be patient and give it a chance to happen. Anytime you're in town be sure to give me a ring so you can sit in with us. You, too, Montana. You're always welcome to play."

"Thanks, George," Montana said.

I thanked him, shook his hand and kissed Patti on the cheek. He climbed into the driver's seat and I waved as they drove off. Then turned toward Montana.

"Come here, you," she said, jumping down from her seat.

"Me?"

I walked over to her, wrapping my hands around her waist. A powerful ache went through me as we kissed.

After a while Montana put her mouth next to my ear and said, "Where can we go?"

I thought of and eliminated Billy's apartment and my parents' house and said, "We can get a room in town."

"OK."

Thirty miles, I thought. It's thirty miles. We tried to move to the driver's door while kissing one another. Montana broke away and climbed over the seat. "It's gonna be a long thirty miles."

"Speed."

"I most certainly will." I started the van and patted the dashboard, whispering, "Don't let me down, baby."

The countryside was now black outlines and looming trees

except where yard lights threw orange disks of light. Two yellow eyes glowed in the borrow pit grass, blinked and were gone. On the stereo the Dave Brubeck Quartet was playing "Blue Ronda à la Turk," its headlong insistence inching my impatience one notch higher and compelling me to drive faster. Through Fort Shaw where a crosswalk sign on a wire over the road bounced in the wind. Very possibly Billy was asleep somewhere in this town, his white paddle feet dangling far beyond the end of a strange woman's bed. Then out of Fort Shaw and into darkness again.

Montana slipped her tongue in my ear, causing my foot to drop heavily on the gas pedal and the Angstmobile to shudder until I eased off. I turned my head to kiss her, left eye on the road, right thumb on the inside of a warm tapered thigh. Two miles to Sun River, too damn far to Prairie View. Headlights appeared in the rearview mirror, a quarter mile back. I wondered what someone else was doing up at two-fifteen in the morning. The lights were rushing up behind us at a startling rate. Now *this* son of a bitch was in a hurry. I moved my hand farther up Montana's thigh and wondered where the nearest motel was. The car was right up behind us when there was an explosion of blue flashing lights. Montana jumped back from me and yelled, "What?"

"Busted," I said, easing the van over to the shoulder. I killed the lights and quickly grabbed what I needed, thankful that I'd taken care of my tags and insurance. "Be right back." I got out, checking to make sure I had everything, blue light washing over my body. I looked up. It was Miles. I closed my eyes for a second, the paper in my hands beginning to tremble, and thought, Oh sweet mother of God.

"What's up, Miles?" I said. My blood had turned to sand in my limbs and I could barely move forward. I stopped at the back of the van as Miles kept coming toward me.

"What did I tell you, Dennis?" he said, his voice low and ominous.

"I'm leaving tomorrow, I swear."

"I warned you, you little *fuck!*" Miles's right hand shot up from his hip and caught me by the throat, slamming my head into the window. My stomach heaved and blood pounded its way to the back of my skull. Miles had his hand right up under my jaw, lifting me up to the balls of my feet. The nausea passed and I was furious, gasping for air and struggling to pull his hands away from my throat so I could cave his forehead in with a bat or metal pipe.

"Fuck you, Miles." It was hardly above a whisper.

Miles yanked me away from the van with both hands, shifted me to the left and slammed my head into the window again. It cracked and gave under the force of my head. He put his face so close to mine I could smell his stale breath. "You don't know when to stop, do you? You always have to see how much you can get away with." Miles snatched me away from the van and snapped me back into it. "When are you going to learn, Dennis? Huh? They're through taking care of you. When are you going to figure that out? I've supported myself since I was twenty-one, but you're twenty-five and still got your hand out. You're a lazy shitheel, Dennis. You know that? You have been as long as I can remember. You think you're so much smarter than the rest of us, but you're not. Where do you think you're going to end up? Huh? Where do you think you're going to end up? Nowhere! Because you've never done anything by yourself. Everything's always been given to you."

"Stop it!" Montana yelled from the side of the van. "Stop it! You're going to kill him."

Miles loosened his grip enough that I dropped to the heels of my feet and sucked wildly for air before he could close my windpipe again. He looked over at Montana and said quietly, "Get back in the van."

"Let him go. Please let him go."

"GET BACK IN THE VAN!"

The back of my head was about to split. I squeezed my eyes shut and gritted my teeth. Then butted my forehead into the side of Miles's head. There was the crack of bone on bone and a red flare burst inside my skull. I heard Miles yell "Fuck!" as if far away and felt myself falling to the pavement. Miles was above me, kicking wildy with the pointed tips of his boots as I struggled in vain to roll into a ball. I saw a blurred tip skimming the ground before arcing up toward my face and thought, Please stop. Please stop. And suddenly it did.

Twelve

was dead, but I could still hear the tunnel echoes of jangling keys and slamming doors. I was being buried in catacombs and no one would ever be able to find me except the men who were carrying me.

Sometime later a sweet clear thought like the first draw of air after swimming up from the deep: I can't be dead. I'm in too much pain to be dead. My head felt as if all the blood in my body had been trapped in my brain where the cells were rapidly expanding and pounding against the walls of my skull to be set free. It hurt to breathe deeply or move and I guessed Miles must have cracked at least one of my ribs kicking me. I tried opening my eyes but couldn't do it before everything began slipping away from me again.

This time I was weeping. I didn't know why, but I was completely unhinged and unable to help myself. It hurt to weep that hard and I wanted so badly to stop but I couldn't do anything about it. Then I realized I really was weeping and that my shaking was making my ribs hurt. I slowly opened my eyes, the left eyelid not cooperating, and wiped them with the sleeve of the orange jumpsuit I was wearing. I was looking up at the metal slats of a bunk bed.

"How you doin' there?"

I wasn't sure who was being addressed, and I didn't want to turn my head for fear of increasing the clangor inside it, but when no one else answered I said, "I'd really like to piss."

"Can you move?"

I tried to sit up and gasped. I lay back. "Not too well."

"Ron, why don't you help him out."

A large pair of hands slipped under my shoulders, grabbed me beneath the armpits and lifted me under and up from the bed. I steadied myself on the upper bunk where a pockmarked Indian with long black hair turned his head to stare at me. I nodded at him and clutched my sides with one arm. I hobbled around the end of the bunk and stepped up into the dim narrow bathroom. There was a chipped sink with no mirror and a severely battered toilet with no seat. Gray paint was flaking off the walls and fallen chips covered the wet cement floor. The ceiling tiles had creeping brown water stains and the narrow barred window allowed only a band of dull jaundiced light. I stood before the toilet. I'm in jail, I thought. I'm actually in jail. And it's a dive. I laughed and was immediately bent over holding my sides. Then I was suddenly near tears and I had to tell myself, No, you're not going to let this get to you. He can kick the shit out of you and throw you in here, but you're not going to let this get to you. You're not going to give him that satisfaction. If this was one of his goals, then fine, he's done it, but you're not going to let this get to you.

I stood in the bathroom doorway and looked into the cell. It was a small, high-ceilinged room with two metal bunk beds bolted to the walls on either side. A massive young man, at least six foot four, 240 pounds, was jutting out perpendicularly from the north bunk beds, doing push-ups with both feet on the lower bunk. His neckless head narrowly missed hitting the opposite bed as he bobbed up and down with alarming ease.

"Impressive, isn't it?" said the man sitting on the top north bunk with his back against the wall. He was in his early forties, with short graying hair and a clipped red mustache, looking over the top of his reading glasses. He stuck out a hand. "Gerry Richardson."

I walked over to the bunk, skirting the twenty-four-inch color TV where two spotted hyenas were tearing at the intestines of a prostrate zebra. "Dennis McCance."

"Any relation to Tom?"

"Son."

"No kidding. Tom McCance can't get his own son out of jail?"

"I don't think he knows I'm in here."

Gerry Richardson took off his glasses. "I happen to be a student of your father as a litigator. He's the master as far as I'm concerned. Beautiful to watch in court. Always impeccably prepared and completely ruthless. I've been a lawyer for fifteen years now and I still go watch him whenever I get a chance to see what I can learn. Little things. For example, did you ever notice how he always takes the table nearest the jury? I asked him about it once. He told me he goes in early the first day of every trial to claim it because he wants to be as close to the jury as possible. I do the same thing now." He jumped down from the bunk. "You know how to play hearts, Dennis?"

I said I did.

"Good, we need a fourth. You ready to play, Clyde?"

The Indian lying on the opposite bunk said, "I'm ready."

"Ron, you about finished there?"

"Thirty more," Ron grunted.

"He does four sets a day of three hundred," Gerry Richardson said to me, "but he's still lost at least fifteen pounds since being in here. For a noseguard that's the kiss of death."

Ron finished and sat on the floor, his face flushed with blood. The Indian slipped off his bed and joined him on the floor. Gerry brought out a deck of cards from his orange jumpsuit and began to shuffle. He introduced me to the others: Ron Vandenboss and Clyde Standing Rock. The three men had been playing a running game of hearts since Friday night, and it was decided I should be given one more point than Gerry, who was in last place. I cut the deck. Gerry dealt and began a running monologue of what each of them was doing in jail.

Ron Vandenboss was a starting noseguard at Montana State and had been First Team All-Big Sky last year. He was now serving a month-long sentence for an incident involving his pit bull terrier. This spring Ron had been taking his usual blend of anabolic steroids and horse amino acids while lifting weights six days a week when he decided to see what the same chemistry would do for his pit bull, Alzado. At first the dog only became fat and lethargic until Ron realized what was happening and began to run the dog every day. The combination of drugs and training mixed with Alzado's natural aggressiveness had the wallop of a moon shot; it launched his testosterone level into the stratosphere and sent him on a neighborhood rampage that left four dogs and two cats dead and came within twenty yards of mangling the police officer who pumped the full chamber of his .38 into Alzado's shorthaired brainpan. It had briefly looked like Ron would be let off with a warning until the Humane Society got involved and went to the *Gazette*. "You can't believe how fit Alzado was," Ron said to me. "This dog was cut." He shook his head, the pit bull flexing before his eyes. "It was a fuckin' tragedy what that cop did."

Clyde Standing Rock was serving ten days for indecent exposure. He'd actually been urinating out the back window of a station wagon going eighty miles per hour on the highway. The driver refused to pull over and Clyde couldn't hold off any longer. It was unlucky that two cars back was a deputy sheriff who saw things differently.

As for himself, Gerry Richardson was a third-time DUI offender who'd had his license revoked and was serving a two-month sentence on the weekends. Gerry said he really didn't mind because he was allowed to bring his work and he could get more done here over the weekends without the constant interruption of phone calls than he ever could in the office.

"What about you, Dennis?"

"My brother, Miles, who's a deputy, put me in here."

The others looked up from their cards. "Your own brother threw you in here?" Ron said, frowning.

I nodded.

"Why?"

"We don't get along too well."

"Obviously," Gerry said.

Lunch was delivered on metal trays: one hot dog without condiments, carrot sticks, applesauce and an eight-ounce carton of milk. I pushed my tray across the floor to Ron, who'd been eyeing it, and briefly explained the events leading up to my arrest last night: Miles had me by the throat when I realized I had no idea what I'd actually been arrested for. It was as though I'd assumed Miles had the right to do this to me.

When I finished my story, Ron shook his head at the wonder of a world where a cop could shoot a well-muscled, well-trained dog and a deputy could throw his own brother in jail.

"Did he read you your *Miranda* rights?" Gerry said.

"Not while I was conscious."

"And you've got a witness, right?"

"Yeah."

"We'll kill 'em, Dennis. False arrest, police brutality. We'll have a field day in court. And I'm reasonably priced. Eighty-five an hour."

"This is my brother," I said.

"The same guy who shitcanned you and tossed you in here."

"I'm not interested."

"Don't rule it out," Gerry said. "Clyde, are you cheating? Because I haven't seen you take a trick yet. Either you're a card sharp or you're cheating."

"We have a word for people like you," said Clyde. "*Equiopa.*"

"Yeah, what's that?"

"Lawyer or bigmouth." Clyde was grinning.

"*Equiopa,*" Gerry said. "I like it, Clyde."

The game ended when Gerry said he had work to do and climbed back up to his bunk. I lay on my bunk and drifted off for a few minutes before my left eye began to itch and woke me. I thought of Miles and my head was immediately filled with scenes of violence: I was battering him in the head with a metal pipe, feeling his skull go soft beneath the blows. When he finally fell I began kicking him with both feet, cursing and crying. It took me awhile to clear my head, and when I did I thought, I'll never forgive you.

Later I wondered if my parents knew I was in jail or if they were doing anything about it. They probably thought this would be a good lesson for me. Or maybe this was my father's way of showing me that he wasn't going to help me out anymore. Then I had a moment of fright wondering where Montana was and whether she was okay. Would Miles have left her out on the highway without the keys to the van or would he have taken her home in the patrol car? I felt better thinking about her, and I thought that when I got out of jail I was going to get as far away from here as possible.

There was a thin red line painted on the hallway floor of the jail, and when a deputy came for me at nine-thirty in the morning to handcuff and march me across the street to the county court-house he told me to walk the line.

"Johnny Cash fan?" I said.

"Shut up and walk." The deputy had a Fu Manchu like Miles, and I wondered if cops grew them to look forlorn and mean, even when they smiled. I followed the deputy and two other prisoners in orange jumpsuits along the red line, passing one door marked BEHAVIOR MODIFICATION ROOM and another with a pair of eyes peering out from behind the barred hatch.

We went down the stairs and were halted at the door of the main holding pen where five more prisoners were added to the group. We were moved slowly through three clanging metal doors before we were outside and two other deputies had appeared to accompany us on the fifty-yard walk to the court-house. A car stopped to let us cross. On the sidewalk a woman was pushing a stroller, and two blue-haired ladies were walking arm in arm, and the three of them stared so blatantly that I felt myself growing angry.

But when I caught the first glimpse of myself since Saturday night in the reflection of the double glass doors, I understood why they'd stared. There were reddish purple hand marks around my throat and my left eye was purple and swollen as if a plum were trapped beneath it and had stained the lower half of my forehead. I was a fright.

Justice Court was on the first floor of the courthouse in a small, book-lined room with two large support beams on the east side that made it necessary for anyone sitting on that side of the gallery to lean to the left in order to see anything. Presiding this morning was Justice of the Peace Claudia Bright, whose previous law experience before becoming one of the city's two JPs had been as a playground monitor at Sacajawea Elementary School.

We were seated in the gallery and called one by one before

Judge Bright to be formally charged. I was next to last and sat listening as three people were charged with driving under the influence, two with disorderly conduct, and one with passing a bad check and criminal mischief. Then my name was called and I stood before her.

Judge Bright glanced at the file on her desk and looked up at me with solemn concern. She had heavy jowls and broad shoulders, a beehive and tortoiseshell reading glasses on a long gold chain. "Does your father know about this?"

"I don't know."

She looked down at the file. "You are charged with three counts. On Count One, a felony, you are charged with felony assault upon a police officer. If you are convicted of that charge, the maximum sentence is ten years in the state prison, or a maximum fine of five thousand, or both. On Count Two, a misdemeanor, you are charged with resisting arrest. If you are convicted of that charge, the maximum sentence is six months in the county jail, or a maximum fine of five hundred, or both. On Count Three, also a misdemeanor, you are charged with exceeding the speed limit, driving sixty-four in a fifty-five zone after dusk." She glanced up. "I see the arresting officer is your own brother."

I was finding it difficult to breathe and my legs were about to buckle. It was all I could do to stay upright. A felony? Why didn't anyone tell me this was a felony? I didn't know this was a felony.

"Deputy McCance *is* your brother, isn't he?"

I nodded dumbly, not sure what was being asked.

"You are entitled to an attorney. If you cannot afford one, the court will appoint one for you. Do you have an attorney?"

Did I have an attorney? "I have an attorney, yes."

"Your father?"

"My father? No, uh, Hugh Erskine," I said, naming the one attorney I knew well in my father's firm.

"Really? I thought for sure your father would represent you. If I were you, I'd hire your father," Judge Bright said, peering over the top of her glasses and pausing as if to give me time to change my mind. She shook her head. "Well, that's your prerogative. Normally for the felony charge, particularly this one, bail would be five to ten thousand dollars, but because I know your father, I'm going to release you on your own recognizance."

I nodded.

"You can plead to the driving offense at this time but this court has no jurisdiction over the first two counts. For those you will be bound over to the District Court and the county attorney will file an information. How do you plead to the speeding charge?"

"Guilty."

"Good. Thirty-five bucks," Judge Bright said. "Next!"

At the jail the deputy with the Fu Manchu handed me my clothes in a plastic bag and checked off each personal belonging as he pulled it from a manila envelope. When he finished, he said, "Hey, are you really Miles's brother?"

I was struggling to put on my T-shirt without raising my arms. "Yeah."

"I didn't know he even had a brother."

"Can I go now?"

"Follow me." We went into the hallway and onto the red line, silent cameras in high corners sweeping over us, through the metal doors, past the bored jailer staring vacantly at the wall of black and white TVs, and through the final door. "By the way, your van's still out on 200," the deputy said.

Montana was waiting for me at the bottom of the stairs, and she took them two at a time to help me, draping my right arm over her shoulders and putting her arm around my waist. At the corner we stopped and held one another, neither of us speaking for a moment.

"Are you OK?" I said.

Montana nodded.

"How'd you get home?"

"Your brother made me ride in the patrol car," she said as we turned and began walking toward my parents' house. "He went crazy after you hit him. He kept kicking you as if he couldn't stop himself. I was yelling at him to stop, but I don't think he even heard me. It was like he was all alone. I tried to push him away from you, but he just brushed me off. The second time I pushed him, he seemed to remember where he was and he finally stopped. He was sweating and shaking, and when I tried to help you he said, 'Don't fucking touch him.' Then he seemed to get hold of himself and he told me to lock the van and get in the car. He picked you up and put you in the backseat, but he wouldn't let me sit with you. You didn't move or make a sound for a long time, and I was crying and telling him that he'd killed you. After a while you started moaning, and I said we had to get you to a hospital, but he wouldn't answer.

"At the jail he and another deputy carried you inside and I kept telling anyone who would listen that they couldn't leave you here, they had to get you to a hospital. Then I thought maybe I could bail you out and I started asking what I needed to do, how much money did I need? The only deputy who would listen told me to forget it, you weren't going anywhere until Monday. I tried to call Billy, but he wasn't home and I couldn't get a cab, so I ended up walking to his apartment. By the time I got there, Billy was home and I told him what had happened and we decided to wait until seven and call your parents. By the time we called, your dad told Billy he already knew and there was nothing anyone could do until Monday morning. I got down here just as they were walking you over to the courthouse."

"So you heard what he charged me with?"

Montana nodded.

"A fucking felony. For assault. *He* assaulted *me*, but it's okay because he's in uniform."

"You have to get a good lawyer."

"I'll tell you what I'm going to do. I'm going to get a gun and shoot him, that's what I'm going to do."

"Don't say that."

"I'm sorry. But you don't do that to your own brother. I don't care how much you hate him, you don't do that to your own brother."

We had arrived at the house. My mother's Wagoneer was parked in the driveway, not yet loaded. I found myself reluctant to face them, as if I was to blame for this. In jail I'd been thinking they might believe I deserved this, that Miles had administered the kind of physical punishment my father would have have given me if he hadn't felt restrained by a sense of decency. As far as I knew they hadn't checked on me at the jail or been present at the courthouse. Maybe this was what it was going to be like from now on.

"Listen," I said. "I have to go in and talk to my parents. You don't want to meet them like this. Why don't you walk over to the park and I'll come get you when I'm through. Is that OK?"

"Sure."

"I'll meet you by the band shell in half an hour."

My parents' suitcases were sitting in the entryway. Obviously nothing was going to get in the way of their vacation. I stood slouched in the hallway with my left arm pressed against my ribs and listened for them. I heard the dishwasher changing cycles and my mother striding across the kitchen and yelling upstairs to my father, "Tom, did you grab our . . ." She saw me and raised a hand to her face. "Oh my God," she whispered. "Tom!"

"What?"

"Come down here," my mother said, not taking her eyes off my face. "*Now*, please."

She'd stopped five feet away and seemed unable to move any closer. My father came around the landing in a pair of tennis shorts carrying a pillow under each arm. He stopped at the bottom of the stairs. "Are you all right?"

Do I look all right? I thought, my temper flaring. "No, I'm not all right."

"What exactly happened?" he said.

"What did Miles tell you?" I said, guessing he'd been the person who'd told them I was in jail.

"Right now we're not concerned with what Miles told us. I want you to tell us what happened."

I was suddenly too weary to argue. "It doesn't matter," I said. "Just let me grab my stuff and I'll leave."

"Damnit," my mother cried, "it matters to us. You don't come home on Saturday night so that I'm worried sick thinking you've been in a car wreck, and then we get a call from Miles early Sunday morning saying the two of you have had an altercation on the highway and that you're in jail for resisting arrest and assaulting a police officer."

"An altercation? That's what Miles called it? An altercation? You call this an altercation?" I pointed at my face, furious. "Let me tell you about our altercation. First Miles grabbed me by the throat and slammed the back of my head into the window, then he choked me until I almost passed out, and finally, when I was down on the ground, he kicked the shit out of me until . . ."

"You don't need to speak like that," my father said tersely.

"That's what he did, Dad. He kicked the shit out of me . . ."

"That's enough."

"I'm sorry I don't have your lawyerly control, but that's what happened. The honorable judo star who'd never hit somebody when he was down kicked me with his boots when I was lying on the ground. And I couldn't do anything about it. That's all. Just a minor altercation out on the highway. And now I'm the one charged with a felony for assault." I pushed my hands out before myself as if shoving it all away, disgusted. "It doesn't matter."

"Let us decide what matters," said my father.

"How can you possibly say that, Dennis?" my mother said, voice wavering, her face red and contorted.

"It doesn't, Mom. It really doesn't." I felt myself caving in so that I was close to crying. "I knew he was going to do it. I've known for a long time he was going to do it."

"But *why?*"

"Why don't you ask him?"

My mother turned and went upstairs. In a moment the bathroom door shut. My father handed me the two pillows, picked up the suitcases and carried them out to the Wagoneer. I stood behind him as he loaded the two bags in the back and took the pillows from me. He closed the tailgate and faced me. "You're going to need a lawyer."

"I'm going to call Hugh Erskine."

"And you may not be able to leave the state for a while."

"I'm not staying here," I said. "I'll go to Anne's."

"Did you assault him?"

"What do you think?"

"I'm wondering how you got the bruise on your forehead."

"I gave him a head butt in self-defense."

"Do you need to see a doctor?"

"No."

We walked up the front steps. At the door my father said, "I don't condone what Miles did, Dennis, and I'm going to tell him that."

I went into the kitchen and called Hugh Erskine at the office. His secretary wasn't sure if he was in yet, then said hold on, he'd just walked in the door.

"What can I do for you, McCance?" Hugh said.

I explained to him in detail what had happened, then said it was hard to believe.

"What?"

"That Miles would actually charge me with a felony. The rest of it doesn't surprise me, but charging me with a felony . . . This is serious, Hugh."

"If you hit him as hard as you think you did and left a mark on him that the other deputies would have seen, he might have felt like he had to charge you."

"I could go to jail for ten years for this."

"That's why you called me," Hugh said. "Let me make a few calls. You going to be at your parents' house?"

"No, I'm going to be at my sister's in Grass Range."

"Give me the number there and I'll call you in a couple days."

I called Anne and asked if I could drive out and stay for a few days. She said of course. Then I left a message with Billy's secretary asking him to stop by after work. When I hung up, my parents had left.

I walked across the street to the band shell. Montana was sitting on the front of the stage, her long legs dangling over the side, and I sat next to her.

"How'd it go?"

"I want to get out of here."

"Where can we go?"

"We can stay with my sister and brother-in-law in Grass Range."

We walked back to the house and began packing. My duffel bags were too painful to lift and I dragged them downstairs while Montana carried my stereo boxes. We were sitting on the front porch swing around five o'clock when Billy arrived. He walked up the front steps apologizing for not making it earlier, then halted when he saw me. "Christ, he really did a number on you."

"He's very thorough," I said. "I need to ask you a favor. My van's out on 200, and I need to pick it up so Montana and I can drive to Anne's for a few days. I'll tell you what's happened on the way."

The van was still parked on the narrow shoulder where I'd left it. The three of us circled it, looking for any damage. The left side of the rear window was a silver cobweb. "My head," I said, pointing.

"Nice."

"By the way, how did things turn out for you?"

"Well, I drove Eryn to where she was house-sitting, and she invited me in for a beer. We sat on the couch with two over-weight cats and listened to Bob Seger, who seems to be required listening in the Midwest. Eryn said she'd been seeing some guy in Ann Arbor but had broken up with him at Christmas and hadn't seen anyone since, which is a long time to be single in Simms. Then she said there was something vulnerable about my eyes that she'd immediately liked when I asked her to dance. I took that as my cue and kissed her."

I was bent over, clutching my sides.

"Go ahead and laugh, Dennis, but you know you'd give up that mop for these eyelashes."

I had to sit down on the bumper. When I could breathe again, I looked up at Billy and said, "What about your girlfriend in Tempe?"

"That was a problem. Just when things began to really heat up, I started feeling guilty and thought, What if Margot's doing this right now with someone? I'd be pissed. So I waited a while, twenty, thirty minutes—I didn't want Eryn to think anything was wrong, right?—and then said I had to go home. And about an hour and a half later I did."

"Are you going to see her again?" A semi rolled close by, followed seconds later by its sucking tailwind.

"We're going out to dinner tonight at six, so this is actually convenient for me," Billy said, checking his watch. "You going to be at Anne's for a while?"

I said we were.

"I'll come visit and bring some beer."

He loaded my stereo and duffel bags into the Angstmobile, and Montana drove as we headed back toward town. I was wearing sunglasses to hide my swollen eye and when I glanced at myself in the vanity mirror I looked like a middleweight boxer whose manager had committed a gross error in choosing my last opponent. I remembered when I was a child going with my parents to watch Miles at his judo and wrestling matches. I'd thought there was something romantic about the black eyes, cracked ribs and taped limbs that most of the athletes had more often than not. Afterward at home, my mother would fix ice packs for Miles, plug in the heating pad, and wrap his ribs tightly with an ACE bandage, all while Miles said he was fine, it really didn't hurt that much. I couldn't wait to earn my share of injuries. I sensed that being injured was as important as winning, and that the greatest accomplishment was being injured and then winning, after which teammates, friends and family could offer a mixture of sympathy and praise. But the first time I took a severe beating—at the hands of the two rednecks in the pickup—all the romance went out of it. Every close call after that only reinforced my desire to avoid another one at all costs. Right now it hurt to breathe, sneeze, laugh, move my arms or my bowels.

By the time we were halfway to Belt, dark scudding clouds were clipping the tops of the Highwoods and Little Belts. A few raindrops appeared on the windshield. The temperature had dropped dramatically, and I reached behind the seat to grab jackets for both of us. Hank Williams was singing "Ramblin' Man" and I thought it would be nice to simply drive for the next eight hours feeling the hum of the road up through my seat and not have to explain to anyone who I was or what I was about or why I was wearing sunglasses on a cloudy day or why oh why I would drop out of law school without telling my family.

For the next hundred miles it was only Montana and me and the country, foothills now hugging the curves of the road past Raynesford and Geyser, now giving way to the plains, the heavily wooded mountains rising up in the south, the sky growing darker until shortly before Lewistown it began to rain in sheets so that the windshield wipers couldn't keep up and Montana had to park on the side of the road for a few minutes with the hazards on until it let up and she could see well enough to drive. Ten miles past Lewistown the rain abruptly ended, and I cracked the window vent to smell the sweet air. Montana made the turn into Grass Range, drove through town, across the bridge made of railroad ties over the creek and rattled along the gravel road toward Anne and Jack's.

It was nearly eight o'clock by the time we pulled into the muddy turnaround and parked next to the pickup. I stood by the van for a moment, looking south at the dim undulating fields, thankful that Anne was letting us stay here.

I knocked on the sliding glass door and stepped into the small, dark kitchen, calling Anne's name.

"Dennis?" she said, walking in from the living room. "Are you all right? Mom called from Clearwater Junction and said you and Miles had a fight on the highway." She turned on the lights and saw me. "Oh my God."

"That's what Mom said. Nice, huh?"

"Did Miles do that to you?"

"Part of it. The forehead's my own fault. I tried to head-butt him and wound up on the ground." I placed my hand on the small of Montana's back and said, "Anne, this is my friend Montana Wildhack. Montana, this is Anne."

They said hello, Anne still looking stunned. She touched my arm and seemed to realize where she was. She went to the freezer and began taking out ice cube trays and rapping them on the counter top. "There's Tylenol in that end cabinet. Take two and go sit down in the other room. This'll be ready in a minute. Have you iced it at all? No? Dennis, you should have iced it right away."

"The county jail's a little short on the amenities of home."

"How bad was it?" She was dropping ice cubes into a plastic pleated bag.

"Not that bad. It's not a gulag, by any means, but you wouldn't want to spend a lot of time there."

"Go sit down now."

We went into the other room and sat on the couch covered by the Hudson Bay blanket. The room was an odd collection of furniture: the long deep couch that looked ideal for naps, two Windsor chairs that I guessed either David or his father had made, a coffee table that rocked when I put my feet on it, a worn wing chair next to a brass reading lamp. None of it seemed to be Anne or Jack's except the piles of books and magazines throughout the room. I saw a pair of slippers appear on the stairs, legs, a torso and finally Jack's head. He whistled when he saw me.

"Looks like you got clotheslined," he said. He reached out and shook Montana's hand. "Jack Siegrist."

"Hi, Jack. I'm Montana Wildhack."

He sat in the wing chair and extended his long legs.

"Here's the ice pack," Anne said, coming into the room and handing me a dishtowel and the pack. Jack squeezed her hand as she stepped over his legs and sat in the Windsor chair. I shifted on the couch so I could hold the ice pack on my left eye and see them with my right.

"Story time, Dennis."

"Jack!" Anne said, leaning over and swatting him.

"What? Come on, Anne, you want to hear this even more than I do. When was the last time someone came to visit us after being clotheslined and thrown in jail? I want to hear what happened. Dennis?"

"Where do you want me to start?"

"Start with how you got thrown in jail."

I began with the gig for the Simms High School cheerleaders. Montana picked up where I left off, and Anne and Jack were quiet for a few minutes after we finished.

Later Montana and I ate in the kitchen while Anne told us the itinerary for their trip to Boston tomorrow morning. She'd talked to the editor she worked under at Houghton Mifflin; he didn't have any current openings, but knew of one in children's literature and another in the textbook department. Jack had spoken with three midsized law firms looking for a young litigator with trial experience.

"What are your plans now?" Anne said. "Are you going to be around when we get back?"

"I don't know. It depends what happens with the criminal charges. I can't go anywhere until that's cleared up."

"What did Hugh say?"

"Just that he'd call in a couple days."

"Jack, what do you think?"

"I can't imagine the court will do much. It's a first offense, the arresting officer's your own brother. A fine, maybe probation. I doubt you'd have to serve any time, although it depends on the judge."

"That's very reassuring, Jack," I said.

Montana excused herself to use the bathroom, and as soon as she'd left the room, Anne leaned toward me and said, "So when did Montana show up?"

"Thursday night."

"Just like that."

"Pretty much. She broke up with her boyfriend last week and she wanted to get out of town for a few days. She had a frequent-flier ticket, so she decided to fly out and then drive back with me."

"And?"

"And what?"

"And what's happening?"

We could hear Montana turn off the bathroom fan.

"Just tell me one thing and save the rest for later," Anne said. "Are you with her or not?"

"What do you mean, with?"

"You know exactly what I mean. Yes or no?"

"Yes."

"I need to finish packing," she said when Montana returned. "Do you want an ACE bandage for your ribs? I think there's a heating pad around here somewhere if that would help."

"No, I'm fine," I said, smiling.

"What?"

"Nothing."

"Take another Tylenol before you go to bed, all right?"

"All right. Thanks, Anne. What time do you leave tomorrow?"

"We fly out of Billings at ten-fifteen, so we should probably leave here around seven. "

"Wake us up before you leave, if we're not already up."

I got three beers from the refrigerator and sat at the kitchen table with Montana and Jack. Up on the road, I saw taillights flash as someone braked for the curve.

"Do you miss your brother?" I said to Jack.

He glanced out the window toward the barn, and I suddenly wished I could retrieve my question like a bone and bury it. "I miss the idea of him as my brother," Jack said, looking at the bottle in his hands and picking at the label. "The idea of what you want your brother to be as opposed to what he actually is. Or what he wants you to be. I really didn't spend much time with David after I was about sixteen. He was always smug toward me, even when he was little. He knew he was going to inherit the ranch one day, and he enjoyed lording that over me. 'What are you going to do when you grow up, Jack? I know what *I'm* going to do.' That kind of thing. He had his entire life mapped out by the time he was twelve. He'd grow up here, learn how to run things, go to Bozeman for four years, get a degree and have fun, meet a nice girl he'd eventually marry and have kids with and take over the place when Mom and Dad retired to Arizona. Although at that point they talked about retiring to Flathead Lake until they lost interest in facing another winter.

"Thanks to David, I knew from day one I'd never get the ranch, which was fine, but it pissed me off that he held that over me. It had nothing to do with merit; it was simply a matter of who was born first. And maybe because of that I threw myself into school and reading, which had never been that important to anyone else in the family. My parents went to college but they're not intellectuals; my dad will only read *Reader's Digest* condensed novels because he says he doesn't like all the descriptive parts. He wants plot and to hell with the rest of it.

"But my parents had ranching friends in Two Dot who'd sent all their kids back East to college, and one of them suggested to my parents that they send me to boarding school. I applied and got accepted. Probably because I was such an anomaly as a sheep rancher's son from Grass Range, Montana. When I left, David told me he didn't see why Mom and Dad were wasting all that money on me when I could go to school in town like everyone else. He said the same thing when I went to Dartmouth. What was wrong with Bozeman? Missoula was out of the question. That was for hippies and druggies according to David.

"I think he'd begun to feel trapped. Dad quit three years early, and suddenly instead of being able to take off whenever things were slow, knowing Dad would take care of it, David was responsible for everything, year-round. He was out here alone, no girlfriends, no real friends closer than Roundup, doing what he'd always planned on doing except now it wasn't so wonderful."

"Did he admit that?" I said.

"No, but you could hear it in his voice. He was lonely. Spend a few days out here and you'll see how quiet it gets. It's oppressive. You can easily go a week without saying a word, and the only people you see are driving by up on the road.

"By that point, David thought I was pretentious because I'd gone to Exeter and Dartmouth, lived in Boston and rarely came home. Because it really wasn't home for me anymore. Except for a couple summers, I hadn't lived here since I was sixteen. I thought David was provincial for insisting you had to be a fool to live anywhere else but Montana. There was only this obligatory connection as brothers. We'd call one another a couple times a year and say hi, how are you, you're still alive, good, yeah, everything's fine, job's great, busy all the time, how's the ranch, great, well, talk to you later.

"And then I got a call one morning and found out he was dead, and I was hit with this incredible sense of guilt that I should have done something to be closer to him. He was the only sibling I had. He wouldn't visit me, but I could have visited him here, gone fishing or hunting with him. Something. You either find some way to remain connected or you let it slide. I let it slide. Personally I would have liked to have been connected like you and Anne are, but to be honest, I really never made the effort."

"It might not have made any difference," I said.

"Maybe not. But you'd like to believe it would have. You know what I mean?"

"Yeah, I know what you mean."

I heard the furnace click on and the hum of the refrigerator. I wondered if David's record collection was a way of filling the oppressive clicks and hums of the empty house and taking the edge off being constantly alone. Had he hated that silence or was Jack mistaken and was it something David enjoyed? Was it too late for Miles and me to be connected beyond the obligation we felt to ourselves and my parents as brothers, or could we still turn that around? Right now I really didn't care. As for the silence, I was here for a while and could find out for myself.

"Time for bed," Jack said, wiping the curled scraps of the beer label into his hand and standing up.

"Thanks for letting us stay here, Jack," I said.

"Happy to have you."

I went into the bathroom off the kitchen and looked at myself in the mirror. The swelling in my left eye had gone down enough that I could raise the eyelid slightly and see a sliver of red film shine along the bottom. When I walked into the bedroom, Montana had taken off her boots and was sitting on the edge of the bed. She looked tired, her head and shoulders bowed.

"How was his brother killed?"

"Hunting accident."

I switched off the overhead light and turned on a small lamp sitting on the night stand; it gave off a warm orange glow. The room smelled damp and musty like a summer house. Rain pounded the roof. I raised Montana's chin so I could kiss her, holding her face in my hands. She reached for my T-shirt and pulled me toward her. I knelt on the floor between her legs, running my hands down her throat, shoulders, breasts. I unbuttoned her blouse, going slowly, not wanting to rush any of this. I unhooked her bra and cupped her small breasts, kissing her nipples. Montana wrapped her arms around my head and held me, breathing into my scalp. I moved down her torso, unbuttoning her Levi's and tugging them off as she raised herself off the bed. I slipped out of my shirt as Montana lay back across the bed. I ran my hands up the length of her calves, still kneeling, dipping my head to her thighs and moving up them with my mouth. Montana lifted her legs and dropped them over my shoulders, crossing them at the ankle. She drew a sharp, quivering breath as I found her with my tongue. She twisted her hips, pressed her heels into my back, grabbed at my hair.

After a while I sat back and stood up. Montana lay on the bed, watching me. She held out her hand and I pulled her up to a sitting position. She undid my pants, and I stepped out of them. She touched me, kissed me, ran her hands down the backs of my thighs. Then she stood up and told me to lie on the bed. I reminded her to be careful of my ribs. She smiled. I lay on the bed. Montana moved to the foot of it and slipped her blouse and bra off her shoulders, letting them fall to the floor. She knelt on the bed and moved toward me, sliding her hands up my legs. In a moment she was gliding above me, slowly at first, then more intently. I held her tightly, wanting her closer. She took stuttering breaths and buried her fingernails into my skin. My nerve endings ran with electricity until I shuddered and emitted a shower of sparks up inside her. I imagined Montana's insides glowing with a bright silvery light and thought what a beautiful life this can be.

Thirteen

On Thursday morning a cerulean sky and the sun lofting up over the eastern hills, massive and orange. Montana and I were walking west toward Forest Grove. The gravel road curved and climbed. A sedan with Idaho plates drove slowly past, the family of four turning to stare. At the crest we stopped and looked back. The ridge of the hills to the north was densely covered with pine trees that soon thinned and became pale green grass that dropped steeply to the road or plateaued across the triangular outcrops of shale that sat heavily above it. The white house and red outbuildings looked tiny below us, the nearby creek visible only by the thick brush that choked the banks of its winding path. Across from it was a wheat field that rolled away to the south, bordered on both sides by dark fallow fields, rising and falling all the way to the horizon and a faint pencil line of trees.

Hugh Erskine had called late Wednesday afternoon and said he'd spoken with the district attorney, who was willing to drop the felony charge and proceed only with the misdemeanor. I'd probably receive a suspended sentence and small fine, but Hugh was hoping to avoid going to trial.

"You're a hot ticket around here, McCance. Everyone at the office saw your name in today's *Gazette* under the weekly court appearances and wants to know what happened. There's a rumor going around that you went berserk out on the highway when you got pulled over with a fifteen-year-old girl in your van. Supposedly it took two deputies to restrain you. Several people heard you have a serious coke habit, but at lunch I learned it's actually a drinking problem and that your parents didn't go to Whitefish but took you to a drug/alcohol rehab clinic in Kalispell. At any rate, you're now infamous around here."

"Suddenly my life seems very simple."

"I thought you'd enjoy hearing that," Hugh said. "Hang in there and I'll get this taken care of."

After a while Montana and I headed down the other side of the hill. The homes were farther and farther apart, most of them weather-beaten trailers with elaborate wooden decks or porches and satellite dishes nosed at the sky. It began to depress me. All of it. The narrow aluminum homes, the harsh open country. How did these people live out here? Who did they talk to? I was beginning to understand what Jack had meant when he said the silence became oppressive. I hadn't slept well since we'd arrived, and I'd been waking up shortly after dawn and walking for two hours before breakfast. Montana would try to coax me back to bed, then reluctantly join me. I kept thinking this was going to make me feel better, that walking in the country would help me shake off the gray funk that had settled over me, but it didn't. Instead I resented the fact that I was even here. I should have been halfway to Austin by now, or at least in Laramie with Montana's parents. And if we'd ended the gig in Simms early, I might not be here waiting to find out if I'd be convicted of resisting arrest. Miles might have been eating a glazed donut believing he had another twenty minutes before he kicked my ass. Or maybe if I hadn't popped off in the kitchen about how Dad had gotten him hired, he might not have felt compelled to arrest me. Of course, if I went back far enough, I could say that if I hadn't dropped out, all of this might have been avoided, although Miles still might have thrown me in jail, just to let me know how little he thought of me and my new status in the family. Somehow the whole thing felt inevitable. Sooner or later it was going to happen, and I was going to be on the losing end.

I wondered what would become of Miles. I didn't believe for a minute he was happy being a deputy and thought if he didn't have his house to work on, he would be completely lost. Maybe I was wrong. Maybe he was carving out a space for himself that he was happy to occupy, spending his days alone in a patrol car and returning home to work on the house. The house would save him. He'd always have a string of projects that would never be finished, aware that without one he'd feel desperate, panicked, the same way I'd feel if I never touched my drums again. Without it you realized how little you had to hold on to, how little else you wanted to do. Who knows, maybe one day a local shop teacher would quit or retire and Miles would get a job at a junior high or high school. That might save him, draw him into the community. I didn't see that happening if he continued being a deputy. I could picture him deciding in a few years that he had too many neighbors living too close and moving even farther from town. He would become more and more remote, driving into Prairie View only for work and supplies. Friendships would slip and his social circle would contract until it no longer existed. I would return home less often, and Miles and I would become even more distant, strangers to one another. My children would ask about him. They'd want to know why I never talked to him, why they never saw him. I wouldn't have any good reasons, only vague replies that wouldn't satisfy them or me. My mother would never get over it, and whenever I was home she would press for any sort of reconciliation, however minor. By then my anger would have hardened into irrational stubbornness, and I'd tell her I was open to it, but Miles had to take the first step. Which he would never do.

I was suddenly furious at the idea of Miles never apologizing or trying to make amends and I thought, Fuck it. *I'll* go talk to him.

I turned to tell Montana that we had to head back to the house, but she wasn't next to me. I stopped and looked for her. She was squatting on her heels fifty yards behind me, watching something in the grass. I walked back up the road.

Montana stood up, about to tell me what she'd been watching, then saw something in my face and said, "What's wrong?"

"I'm going to go talk to him."

"Miles?"

"Yeah. But we have to go back right now." I was afraid of losing my nerve before we got there.

"Let's go."

At the house I circled the kitchen phone for several minutes before picking up the receiver. Then set it down. Just pick it up and dial, for Christ's sake, I thought. When I picked up the receiver again, I sensed Montana behind me and I turned to find her standing in the doorway. I hung up and glared at her.

"Why don't I wait outside," she said.

I dialed Miles, assuming he wouldn't be home. Why would he be? Most people worked on Thursdays. I let it ring five times, taking shallow, trembling breaths. I was about to hang up, almost relieved, when Miles answered and said hello. I was trying to catch my breath and couldn't speak for a moment. He said hello again, irritated.

"Miles," I said. "This is Dennis."

"I know."

"Are you, uh . . . are you going to be home this week?"

"I'm home right now. Why?"

"I thought I might drive out."

"I'll be here."

"How long?"

"Till five."

"Okay," I said. "I might be out later."

I hung up and walked out onto the deck, trying to calm myself. Montana was sitting in a lounge chair leafing through a magazine. "He's home."

"Do you want me to go with you?"

"No, not to the house," I said. "Maybe I could drop you off downtown and you could look around for a little while."

"Sure."

Shortly after eleven I turned into Westwind Estates and parked on the road at the end of the dirt driveway. Miles was leaning over the band saw in the open garage, and he gave no sign that he saw me. I climbed out wearing my sunglasses to hide my eye and walked up toward the house in the streaming sunlight. Miles set aside two pieces of wood and walked down to meet me and for a moment I felt sick with fear that this was a terrible idea and that he would be no more forgiving now than he had been in the past. Then he turned his head slightly and spit a chocolate stream of tobacco into the dirt, and I saw what looked like a large violet birthmark on the left side of his face, starting at his temple and spreading into his hairline. It took me a second to realize that I'd done that to him. I hadn't believed it was possible for me to hurt Miles, and I felt an odd surge of pride and wonder. We said hello and stood looking at one another. Miles hooked his thumbs in the pockets of his jeans. I crossed my arms and immediately remembered Miles once telling me to never do that during any type of confrontation because if it came to blows, you wouldn't be able to punch or block in time. After a moment, he said, "What's on your mind?"

I cleared my throat. "I wanted to tell you that I moved out of the house and that Mom and Dad aren't going to help me out anymore. I thought you'd like to know that. And I'd appreciate it from now on if you'd let me make my own mistakes. I don't need you telling me how to run my life."

"All right."

I looked over at the empty lot to the south covered with yucca, then back at Miles, his narrow blue eyes still trained on me. "I'm sorry about your head. I didn't mean to hit you, really. Actually, I did mean to hit you. But the only reason I did was because you pissed me off. Whenever you play the hard-ass with me, it really pisses me off. I'm just trying to figure out what to do with my life like everybody else, Miles. I'm not trying to make anybody mad. I'm just trying to figure a few things out. All right?"

"All right," he said.

"That's what I wanted to tell you."

"OK."

I looked up at the house, not sure how to end this. "Listen, I don't want to take up your time. I'm sure you're busy." I started to back away, then stopped. "Did you finish the floors?"

"I finished a week ago," Miles said, smiling with pride. "They look so good, I haven't brought up the furniture from the basement. I may even wait another week. You want to take a look?"

"No, I have to get going," I said reflexively. Then I wished I'd said yes. I'd spent so much of my life trying to get away from Miles that it would take time to learn not to be afraid of him.

"OK," Miles said. "Maybe some other time."

"Sure."

"Take care, Dennis."

"You too," I said, backing away, thinking I should shake his hand, then slowly turning and walking down the driveway. I climbed into the van and started the engine. Miles was still standing in the driveway. I whipped a U-turn and he lifted a hand from his pocket and raised it as I drove away.

On a bright Monday afternoon, Montana and I were sitting on the deck at the ranch feeling smug. Over the last four days, we'd written our first song without a single argument.

Montana was sitting across from me on a folding chair strumming chords on her guitar. "You want me to sing it again?"

STRANGER TO THE TRUTH

> You bring me roses
> And pink champagne on ice
> You take me dancing in the evening
> and the next day you still treat me nice
> But all my friends say that a man like you
> Sounds too good, that he could never be true
> They keep saying I'm a stranger to the truth

She stood up after the second verse and chorus, singing louder and with more force as if she were playing to a crowd, her legs set apart, twisting a little on the balls of her feet.

> Now I'm out with all my friends
> 'Cause you tell me you're too tired
> So imagine my surprise
> When I see you dancing with her all inspired
> I follow you to your house and see shadows
>   on the walls

It hurts to know you've lied, it makes me
    want to see you crawl
Now I'm wishing for the days when I was a
    stranger to the truth

Well, they got agents training round the
    world for the FBI
They got their gumshoes and they've got
    private eyes
But I don't need my own sleuth
'Cause I'm no stranger to the truth

"What do you think?" Montana said.

"I think it's pretty damn good."

"That's what I was thinking. Do you think we're biased?"

"I'm not," I said. "Are you?"

"Not at all."

"We need to go into town today."

"Why?"

"We're completely out of food."

"It's been nice not seeing anyone else, hasn't it? No one even calls here."

"I unplugged the phone when we got back on Thursday."

"No wonder no one calls. "

"Should we go into town?" I said.

"Now?"

"Is there something we need to do here?"

"I thought we could try and work on another song."

"You're feeling creative?"

"Yeah. Aren't you?"

"Maybe."

Up on the road, I saw a pale blue truck moving quickly past the splayed foothills and idly thought it looked like the ranch pickup. I followed it with my eyes and when it turned off the road toward the ranch, I was suddenly nervous. I stood up and walked out toward the turnaround.

"What's wrong?" Montana said.

"I don't know," I said, reaching for her hand.

I saw Anne driving, and I stepped back from where we were standing as if to delay her approach. She parked several feet in front of us and through the windshield I could see that her face was red and swollen from crying. My blood seemed to pool in my hands and feet so that my limbs felt hollow and shaky, and I thought, Dad's dead.

Anne turned off the engine and stared down at the gauges. When she looked up at us, there were tears on her cheeks and her eyes were full of despair. She climbed heavily out of the pickup, not closing the door, and stood with one hand on the hood as if to steady herself.

"Dennis," Anne said. "Miles was killed yesterday morning."

Fourteen

A story had been roughly pieced together by the sheriff and slowly given shape by my parents as they spoke at length with Tammy Wyland and repeated it, first to one another hoping to make sense of it, and then to Anne and Jack. So that by the time I heard the story, it was detailed and refined, and I knew that it would be altered and added to with each new telling for a very long time.

Miles had decided to move outdoors and work on the yard. He leveled the backyard with a neighbor's Bobcat, and on Saturday he and Tammy laid fat strips of sod from the back door to the base of the thirty-foot sand dune that rose behind the house. When they finished, they sat on the dune drinking beer while Miles explained his plans to build a horseshoe-shaped garden with a fish pond in its center at the south end of the yard. He had the next day off and before Tammy drove home, they made plans to go antique shopping at ten o'clock.

The following morning Miles dragged the garden hose out to the lawn and stood watering it. At about the same time, his only neighbors to the north, Mr. and Mrs. Connell, left their eleven-year-old son, Jeremy, at home alone and went into Prairie View to do their weekly shopping. Moments after they left, Jeremy slipped into their bedroom and got the key to the gun cabinet that he knew his father kept in the dresser with his underwear and socks. He took his father's Winchester lever-action 30-30 rifle from the cabinet, loaded it and walked out to the backyard with a half dozen empty pop cans. He set them on the fence posts along the south end of the yard and didn't see anyone through the white flowering yucca that grew in the hundred yards between the two homes. Jeremy walked back to the opposite side of the yard, dropped to one knee and raised the rifle.

He fired twice. The sheriff hypothesized that Miles heard the first shot and turned toward the sound. The second shot hit him just under the jaw and exited out the back of his head. In the other yard, Jeremy, panicked that a neighbor would hear the shots and tell his father, quickly gathered the cans and put the rifle and key back where they belonged. Then climbed on his ten speed and pedaled over to his best friend's house two miles away while Miles lay on his back in a growing pool of blood and water in the center of his lawn.

I listened to Anne and could see all of it, but I could also see this: Miles getting up from the grass and heading inside to grab his coat and keys and pick up Tammy in town. Because an eleven-year-old boy named Jeremy Connell couldn't kill Miles. Even with his father's rifle. I could see the bullet slam into Miles's throat and leave through the back of his skull, but it didn't mean Miles was dead. I couldn't see that. An eleven-year-old boy could not kill Miles in his own backyard and then pedal over to his best friend's house to play. It wasn't possible. Not Miles. You didn't fuck with Miles. You instinctively knew that about him: Don't fuck with this guy. He may have been shot through the head, but he wasn't dead. I'd have to see him to believe that. I'd have to see him dead. There was no other way to believe it.

Later when we had packed and loaded everything into the Angstmobile, Montana and I climbed into the van and followed Anne through the rolling countryside. An image formed in my mind of Jeremy Connell walking back to the opposite side of the yard carrying the rifle, turning around, dropping to one knee, raising the gun butt tight to his shoulder and looking through the sight. And squeezing off two quick shots. Did *he* believe it?

I parked behind Anne in front of my parents' house. Jack was reading on the porch swing, and he stood up and walked out to meet us. I shook his hand, and Jack looked at me as if to say, I know you don't believe it because I didn't believe it either when David died.

For a moment I felt as if we were stranded on the front walk, unsure what to do next. Anne quietly suggested I go upstairs and see my mother. We began to move again. I walked up the steps. Inside the house was still. I walked through the dining room and stood on the sun porch at the back of the house for a moment, staring blankly at the carriage house before going through the swinging door into the kitchen and finally upstairs to my parents' bedroom. The door was slighly ajar, and I stood and listened at it for a moment.

"Tom?"

"No, it's Dennis." I paused before placing my hand on the door and slowly pushing it open.

The curtains and blinds had been drawn, and it took a moment for my eyes to adjust to the darkness. My mother was wearing a white nightgown and sitting up in bed, clutching her stomach with one arm and pressing a fist to her mouth. I sat on the edge of the bed. She held me tightly and began to sob bitterly. When she stopped crying, she wiped her eyes and held my hands. I glanced up at her face. It was pale and puffy and had the look of fatigue that has nothing to do with sleep. Her eyes were swollen and defeated. I looked down at my hands that she was now rubbing hard with her thumbs.

"I heard you drive up," my mother said. "Your van makes a lot of noise. That's how I can tell when you're home from your gigs. I hear your van."

I nodded. The rubbing was painfully irritating.

"I've been in bed since we got back," she said. "There are so many things I have to do, but I don't seem to have the energy. Your father finally went to the office because he couldn't take sitting around with nothing to do. I understand but I don't seem to have any energy, Dennis."

"That's all right. You don't have to do anything."

"I just don't seem to have any energy."

"It's okay, Mom."

"I just need to rest for a while." My mother closed her eyes, still sitting up. I waited a few minutes before easing out of the room and going down to the kitchen. I was getting a glass of water when I heard someone walk into the room, and I turned to see who it was.

"Dennis."

"Dad." My father's posture, which had always looked so aggressive, now looked exhausted: His head seemed to be sinking, his shoulders buckling, his arms reaching out for support. The skin around his jaw was slack and there were dark circles under his eyes. "Do you want a glass of water?"

"Sure."

I handed him the glass in my hand and got another one from the cabinet and filled it. My father leaned against the kitchen sink. I hiked myself up on the island counter and waited for him to say something. When he didn't, I said, "How was Whitefish?"

"It rained the entire time we were there," my father said. "After three days inside, I told your mother, 'Put your raincoat on. We're going for a ride in the boat.' 'In this rain?' I said, 'That's right. We're up here on a lake for two weeks, and by God we're going to get out on the water.' We lasted ten minutes before we headed back to the dock. That was the only time we got out. Next year we're going to Hawaii."

I stared at the tile floor, thankful for a moment of relief. When I looked up, I saw the grief in his eyes and it pulled me up short.

"He was watering his lawn," my father said quietly, gazing at me. "I never worried about him getting shot as a deputy. That's part of the job. My dad was shot three times in twenty-five years as a cop. You can't worry about that. Your mother did, but what can you do about it? It goes with the job. You understand that when you take it. People may try and shoot you. If he'd been shot on the job, I could explain it to myself. But I sat in my office for the last four hours without being able to make any sense of this. He was watering his lawn, Dennis."

For the first time in my life, I believed my father was asking me for an answer to something he couldn't explain to himself, something that didn't fit into his ordered view of the world; an explanation for how someone as strong and self-reliant as Miles could be as vulnerable to this sort of random violence as anyone else. I didn't have any explanations, only the thought that Miles had always been drawn to violence, that the air around him seemed charged with it, and maybe he'd actually been more prone to it, more open to it than the rest of us.

At that moment my father seemed more human to me than ever before, no longer invincible and full of certainty, but someone who had been badly shaken by something that he might never be able to explain to himself.

"Where's the, uh . . ."

"The service is going to be at Saint John's tomorrow at three. Father DeVries."

I knew this from Anne. "How about the reception or whatever you call it, afterward?"

"Here, I guess."

I cleared my throat. "I think we should have it out at Miles's house."

My father looked closely at me.

"I know that sounds odd under the circumstances, but I really think that's where it should be. That house is Miles's proudest accomplishment. He loved that house. The happiest I've ever seen him was when he was giving Anne and me a tour of it. I think it should be out there. I think he'd like people to see it."

"I'll talk to your mother about it."

"OK."

"Is she still in bed?"

"Yeah."

"I'm going to go up and check on her."

I was still sitting on the counter when Anne stuck her head in the doorway and said they'd decided to go out to dinner because no one had done any shopping. She ran upstairs to see if my father wanted to go with us and came down to say he wanted us to bring something back.

When we returned from dinner, my father took me aside and said my mother thought it would be fine to have people drive out to Miles's house afterward. I wanted to show Montana the house before it was full of people, and we drove there in the Angstmobile. The sun had set moments before and flooded the western skyline with rich warm color. We had our windows rolled down, and whenever Horse Trot Road swooped down to the river floor, we could feel the cool breeze coming off the Missouri.

"Would you ever want to live here?" Montana said.

"I used to think so, but now I'm not so sure. I don't feel like I belong here anymore," I said. "Would you ever want to live in Laramie again?"

"Too close to home. My dad told me on the phone the other day that he's taught at the U now for twenty-six years. He started out teaching freshmen anthropology when he was twenty-eight and planned on going to a university in a bigger city as soon as he had a couple years of experience."

"What happened?"

"He fell in love with my mom."

"They couldn't leave after that?"

"Nope." She laughed.

I turned into Westwind Estates and passed a speed limit sign so riddled with bullet holes that it was impossible to tell if the number was 15 or 25. Miles's two-tone pickup was parked in front of the garage.

"Does this feel strange to you?" Montana whispered at the front door.

I slipped the key in the lock. "I feel like he's away on vacation, and I'm just dropping by to check on the house."

I opened the door. The front room was dark and smelled of wood dust. When we walked inside, our steps echoed on the floor and I knew the room was still empty. I felt for the light switch next to the doorframe.

"Turn on the lights," Montana whispered.

"I'm trying to," I said. "Why are you whispering?"

"I don't know."

I found the switch and flipped it on. The floor was pristine, long strips of hard northern maple that made me think we should have taken off our shoes. I imagined Miles walking proudly around the house in his bare feet. I watched Montana stride across the room in her black heeled boots and found myself looking to see if they left marks. Nope, thank God. Miles would have killed me.

"The acoustics in here should be great," Montana said. "No carpet to suck up the sound." She began singing "I Fall to Pieces." I listened and thought, I wish I could do that. Montana abruptly stopped. "Where's his furniture?"

"In the garage."

"Hmm." She looked around the room and spotted the stereo. "Care to dance?"

"I'd love to dance."

"See if you can turn the lights down."

I stood ready at the light switch until Montana put on an album, and I turned them out.

"That's down, all right," she said. "Now where are you?"

The front windows picked up the yellow glow of a neighbor's yard light. Montana stood waiting in the center of the floor as Patsy Cline began singing "Sweet Dreams." My hands glided around her hips and pulled her close. She wrapped her arms around my shoulders and hummed with her mouth next to my ear; it raised goose bumps on my scalp. After we'd danced through one side of the album, it occurred to me that I hadn't thought of Miles at all despite being in his house. I wondered if the ligature that bound us as brothers was so tenuous that within a week there would be nothing left of it. I didn't want to believe that, but at the same time I couldn't help remembering what I'd felt when Anne climbed out of the truck and said, "Dennis, Miles was killed yesterday morning."

I was suddenly overcome with shame and began to weep, silently at first and then harder until my entire body shook. Montana held me closer and whispered, "It's all right, Dennis, it's all right."

"All I felt was relief," I sobbed, "that it was Miles and not Dad. That's all I felt, Montana."

"It's all right, Dennis, it's all right."

I woke the next morning to the sound of running water and checked the clock: 5:35. A few minutes later I heard someone go down the stairs and out the front door, and I lifted the blind and looked outside. My mother was walking toward Dingfelder Park, wearing her running clothes and moving her arms in slow sweeping circles.

I dressed and walked over to the park. The sun was visible only as orange light seeping into the cobalt blue of dawn. The grass was wet with dew and darkened the toes of my shoes. I couldn't see my mother but knew this was where she was running. In a few minutes I saw her on the opposite side of the park with her familiar shuffle and prizefighter's arm action. I watched her until she was only fifty yards away and then inexplicably stepped behind a tree. My mother ran past without noticing me, her eyes staring several yards in front of her but focused inward.

I waited for her to run by two more times before I stepped out onto the asphalt path. For a moment I thought she wasn't going to recognize me unless I said something, but twenty yards away she slowed to a walk and looked at me. Her face showed no sign of surprise at finding me waiting for her in the park shortly after dawn, and I wondered if her capacity to be surprised had been blunted by what had happened. Looking at the depth of sadness and passivity in her eyes, I felt that it might be a long time before my mother allowed herself to be surprised again. She continued walking on the path and I fell in next to her.

"I thought if I ran, I might be able to stop thinking for a while," my mother said, breathing deeply through her nose. "I haven't done anything but lie in bed and think for the last three days. I fall asleep for a few minutes and then wake up and start thinking again. This morning I woke up at four-fifteen and lay there for an hour. I finally decided I had to get up and do something. Anything to stop thinking. I hoped this might help."

"Did it?"

She shook her head. We made room on the path for the park gardener, who motored by in his green cart and nodded from behind the cracked Plexiglas windshield, a morning cigarette clenched between his front teeth.

"What's going to happen to us as a family, Dennis?"

"What do you mean?" I said, shocked that my mother would ask me that question.

"I feel like it's falling apart," she said.

"No, it's not."

"I think it is," my mother said. "Even before this happened. You and Miles never got along and then you have this horrible fight out on the highway and Miles ends up throwing you in jail. Anne's so unhappy living out on the ranch that she can't wait to be back in Boston. And now I don't know what's going to happen to you. I feel like we're going to lose you, Dennis." She reached for my hand and squeezed it. "I'm afraid you're going to move away and we're going to lose track of your life."

"That's not going to happen," I said angrily. But as soon as I said it, I felt something sink inside me. I knew that I'd never been more distant from my parents than this summer. I didn't know if that was because of the lies I'd told or if we really were beginning to drift as a family, but I suddenly saw how easy it would be to move away and slowly lose track of one another's lives.

"I'm so afraid that it will," my mother said. "I can't help thinking about all of these things. Why didn't you feel you could tell your father and me about law school? Was it something we did or failed to do? Why didn't you and Miles ever get along?

Why do you get along so well with Anne but not Miles? I don't know, Dennis. It makes me physically ill to think of you and Miles hating one another."

"I never hated him."

"What was it, then? Why couldn't you get along? Was that so much to ask? And now there's never going to be any chance of it. As your mother that tears me up inside. Why couldn't you get along, Dennis?" She was crying.

"I don't know," I said. "For a long time I was too young to understand him. I was in ninth grade worrying about being the first chair drummer and preventing Nick Gooch from stealing my girlfriend while Miles was graduating from Bozeman, trying to find a teaching job. I . . ."

"You had a girlfriend in ninth grade?" She wiped her eyes with the cuff of her sleeve.

"Yeah." We'd been forbidden to date until high school.

"I didn't know that."

"It's not important."

"Who was she?"

I saw that my mother was enjoying this. "Cynthia Walsh."

"Cynthia Walsh," she said, frowning. "Was she the clarinet player with the swayback?"

"Cynthia played clarinet but she didn't have a swayback. The girl with the swayback played flute."

"I don't remember Cynthia Walsh."

"It was awhile ago."

"I didn't mean to interrupt you."

"I think we reached a point where our images of one another stopped growing. To Miles I was always the eleven-year-old smart aleck trying to avoid mowing the lawn. By the time I was old enough to understand what he was doing, he wasn't around much. And when he was, I was afraid of him. He'd come home from Bozeman and immediately start in on me. Why wasn't I helping out more around the house? Why wasn't I mowing the lawn or shoveling the sidewalks? I was always having to defend myself. To be honest, I didn't really know him. We never had a normal conversation. But I think it was going to get better."

"Why do you say that?"

"I went out and saw him last Thursday. We talked and I just think it was going to get better. It felt like we'd gotten past a barrier. I don't know. But I think it was going to be better."

Several yards in front of us, an overweight jogger in a plastic suit and sweats, his pink bald head shiny with sweat, ground to a halt, clutched his knees and groaned, "Christ Almighty."

"Hang in there, champ," I said as we walked past.

"Champ, my ass," the jogger panted. "Call 911."

My mother and I looked back in alarm and saw the man start off again.

"Are you still planning on moving to Austin?" my mother said.

"Yeah. I know it doesn't make a lot of sense to you and Dad, but being a musician is the clearest picture I have of myself." I laughed. "No, it's the only picture I have."

"How important is Montana to you in all of this?"

"Very."

"What is her real name again?"

"Just call her Montana, Mom. When you meet her it'll make sense. It fits her."

When we were walking up the front steps, my mother turned to me and said, "I feel a little better now, Dennis."

"I'm glad."

Two miles south of Praire View, where the homes end and the open land begins its undulating run at the Little Belt Mountains, Memorial Cemetery appears as a manicured oasis among the swirling yellow grass that surrounds it. A sign bolted into the stone entrance reads: NO TRESPASSING AFTER DUSK WITHOUT PERMISSION.

I rode under the archway in the backseat of the limousine led by the domed hearse and three Cascade County Sheriff patrol cars with flashing blue lights. The procession passed out of the sun and curved up a gentle rise where the elms formed a shadowy tunnel over the road. An elderly woman wearing a straw hat and orange gardening gloves looked up from the headstone she was clipping and watched us pass. The limousine eased to the side of the road and parked. No one in the backseat moved. Thirty yards away a green canopy on retractable aluminum poles that shone in the sun stood over the empty grave. The mound of earth alongside the hole had been covered with a large square of artificial turf. I imagined the funeral director, Mr. Sikorsky, standing on it in the four-door garage of his funeral home, bending over his putter like a question mark stroking dozens of dimpled golf balls at a styrofoam cup while his assistants combed the obituaries. I saw our driver glance at us in the rearview mirror. I looked at Anne and Jack sitting on the jump seats and at my mother and father sitting next to me and said, "Ready?" My mother nodded behind her oversized sunglasses and gripped my hand.

I stepped out into the June heat. Cars were parking behind us on both sides of the road, and I heard doors closing and saw people solemnly nodding hello to one another. A long line of cars was still pouring through the entrance where a deputy sheriff directed them with a drum major's flair.

Mr. Sikorsky appeared and silently guided me, my father, Jack and three of Miles's friends to the gleaming casket. We shouldered it across the road in the shade and out into the glare of sunlight. I could feel my heels sink into the grass, but the casket still felt too light for me to believe that Miles was inside it. We set it on a metal gurney and joined the rest of the family under the canopy. I stood on the edge of the group, turned at an angle toward them. Several of the women were fanning themselves with the funeral program. I looked at my relatives and realized the last time I'd seen them together was at Anne and Jack's wedding reception in town. The highs and the lows. Forget the fourth of July and Thanksgiving. You couldn't get everyone to agree on a convenient picnic site for the former and no one had enough chairs to seat everyone for the latter. But let someone marry or drop dead and by God we'll be there. Provided it was within driving distance.

Father DeVries was reading aloud from the Bible. I could feel the sun on my back and a single thread of sweat dropping along my ribcage. I looked across the canopy at Tammy Wyland standing beside Anne. Tammy was dressed completely in black, clutching her purse with both hands and standing so rigidly that I thought the slightest touch would cause her to collapse. Looking at her, I was struck by an idea that she had probably known and seen Miles more clearly in the short time they'd been together than anyone in the family; had understood and accepted him because she didn't have the fixed ideas or expectations of who he was or what he should be doing that family members have. Maybe that wasn't fair to my parents and Anne, but I knew that for me, Miles had always existed on the periphery of my life, a reproving presence who occasionally stepped into it with anger and violence to snatch me by the throat and tell me I was fucking up again. Even now I felt Miles hovering on the periphery. And thought that he would be for a long, long time to come.

Father DeVries had stopped speaking and bowed his head. People were looking to the west where an honor guard of deputy sheriffs stood in a row. One of them grunted an order. They snapped their rifles up and aimed at the heartless blue sky. Another grunt and they fired. I saw Tammy flinch and begin to sob. Anne put an arm around her. They fired again, and I saw my mother's chin drop to her chest.

When they fired a third time, a picture formed in my mind of the bullet hitting Miles in the throat and knocking him to the ground, a gaping hole in the back of his skull, his blue eyes staring vacantly at the sky. This time he didn't get up from the grass but lay there, blood draining out of him and water from the garden hose running over his body until Tammy found him two hours later. I was trembling. I looked at the casket, its meaning now clear to me, and thought, I'm sorry I never got to know you.

I was standing in Miles's house before the front room windows in the late afternoon sunlight with my mother's dapper eighty-one-year-old father, Patrick Quinn. Chairs had been brought up from the garage and were now occupied by family and friends balancing paper plates on their knees filled with cold cuts and casseroles. I saw my uncle John spit an olive pit into the palm of his hand and drop it onto his plate. I turned back to my grandfather, keeping an eye out for Billy and Montana. Earlier that morning I could tell she was uncomfortable about attending the funeral with my family. I'd assured Montana that she didn't have to go at all, but she said no, she wanted to be there. I called Billy and asked if Montana could go with him. Billy said sure, he'd be happy to take her.

"Do you notice how everyone's saying that at least he died instantly, with no pain?" my grandfather said. "That seems to be a common hope about death, that it be instantaneous and painless. *Boom*, you're finished. Personally I want more advance notice. Thirty or forty minutes at a minimum. An hour would be even better."

"How's that?" I said.

"You need time to get the priest in and say your last confession. Receive the last rites. Set things right. Otherwise you're staring at a considerable stretch in purgatory. At best." He fingered his silk tie.

"I don't know, Patrick," I said, shaking my head. "I guess I'd like to think He wouldn't hold it against you if you didn't have time."

"Who wants to gamble on that?"

I shrugged. "Sometimes you don't have a choice." I saw a black Coors van pull up at the bottom of the driveway. "Will you excuse me, Patrick? I need to go see a friend."

"I need to eat, anyway," my grandfather said. "By the way, you're dressing much better these days, Dennis."

"Thanks." I went outside and weaved my way through the cars parked in the dirt driveway, nodding hello to people heading up to the house. I saw Montana standing at the side of the van in a navy blue summer dress Anne had loaned her. She saw me and walked over, her eyes full of sympathy. "Are you okay?" she said, holding me and kissing my cheek.

Billy had climbed into the van, and he popped his head out of the open doors and said, "Can you give me a hand, Dennis?"

"What have you got?"

"So I was going to send flowers or one of those plastic platters you see at Safeway with vegetables and dip, but then I thought, Wait a minute. What they'll really need is beer. So I brought a keg. Here, grab the dolly. Just a minute. Why don't you carry the tap."

Billy placed the damp silver keg on the dolly and walked backward toward the house. Behind us someone honked twice. Then again.

"I think it's your buddy George," Billy said.

I looked over my shoulder and saw the Suburban. George waved his hand above the roof. I handed Montana the tap. "I'll be right back."

As I went around the front of the Suburban, I could see George behind the wheel in a pressed white shirt with a silver cow skull on his bolo tie. I realized he must have been at the funeral. I shook his hand through the open window.

"I'm sorry about your brother," George said. "I know you two didn't get along, but he was still your brother and it's a goddamn shame, cowboy. A real goddamn shame."

I nodded. "Do you want to come in?"

"I can't. I meant to catch you at the cemetery afterward, but I couldn't find you. I promised Barbara a week ago I'd take her out to dinner tonight. I just wanted to come out and say hello. You take care now and give my sympathy to your folks."

"I will. Thanks for driving out, George."

I wandered back up toward the house near the fence line. The day was still hot and there were tufts of cotton floating in the air from the gnarled cottonwoods. Several windows had been opened in the house, and it gave off a steady hum of voices. A tanned couple in their thirties was standing on the front porch. As I walked by on my way to the backyard I heard the woman say, "I know, but what was he *doing* when it happened?"

"I heard he was mowing the lawn," the man said.

"*Mowing?* Who ever heard of someone getting killed mowing the lawn?"

"My grandfather died shoveling his driveway."

"I'm sorry to hear that, darling."

"It was a long time ago."

I went around the corner of the house and found dozens of people in the backyard, plastic beer cups in hand. The keg had been placed in the shade of the house, and I poured myself a beer. I surveyed the crowd on the lawn and spotted Anne and Montana standing together at the foot of the sand dune.

"McCance."

"Hugh," I said, pivoting and shaking his hand. He had beautiful white hair combed high off his forehead and red, mottled cheeks that sagged. A light sheen of perspiration had formed on his sunburned face, and he'd loosened his shirt and tie. "Beer?"

"Never touch it," Hugh said. "Your father just tried to rustle up some real alcohol for me, but there wasn't any to be found. I told him it raised serious doubts about the validity of his Irish heritage. Let's go over here for a minute. I have some good news for you." Hugh drew me to the north side of the house where there were fewer people. "I spoke with our esteemed district attorney a few minutes ago, and he's willing to drop all charges after what's happened. He wants to run it by the sheriff first— the courts feel a lot of pressure from the cops to protect them from assault, as if that's not part of the job—but the DA doesn't think it's a problem. I told him from the beginning this whole episode was a family matter anyway, and that your brother just happened to be in uniform when it occurred."

"That's great news," I said. "Thank you very much, Hugh. I really appreciate it. Send me the bill."

"Consider it *pro bono*," Hugh said, lighting a cigarette and coughing.

I stood in line at the keg. The buzz of voices inside the house and on the lawn had risen in volume with the discovery of the beer. I looked for Montana by the sand dune but didn't see her. I was next in line at the tap. A local attorney I vaguely recognized filled my cup and offered his condolences. I thanked him. I went to find Montana and heard a man say, "That's the brother?"

I saw my father standing in the sun, squinting down at a small elderly woman who was cupping one of his hands and patting it. My father leaned forward so the woman could kiss him on the cheek. She gave his hand a final pat and headed for the shade.

"Who was that?" I said as I walked up to him.

"My first client, Harriet Snow. She had a German shepherd

that took a chunk out of a neighbor kid's leg. I argued that the neighbor had been taunting the dog and knew better."

"How'd you do?"

"We won. I charged her fifty bucks. Two weeks later the dog bit the postman and another neighbor on the same day, and they put it to sleep." My father turned his back to the sun. "I was talking to Billy Smitherman inside. He was asking about the house, wondering what's going to happen with it. Has he said anything to you about it?"

"No," I said, taking a drink and peering over the rim of my cup to gauge his state of mind.

"Personally I wouldn't mind seeing him live out here if that's what he's interested in. It's a nice home and you two have been friends for a long time. Talk to him about it. He was uncomfortable bringing it up to me, but tell him if he's interested, we'll try and work something out."

"All right."

"Your mother said you're still planning on moving to Austin."

I said I was.

"That's what you really want to do?"

"Yeah," I said, pausing. "When I decided to go to law school, I was hoping to discover that being a lawyer was what I really wanted to do. Not because you ever pressured any of us to become one, but basically because I envied the fact that you knew what you wanted to do since you were sixteen. You still love doing it and you make a great living. That's a wonderful gift. Truly. But it wasn't there for me. After that first semester, I couldn't imagine doing it for the rest of my life. For you it's a vocation. For me it would have been a job. I finally admitted to myself that what I've really wanted to do all along is play in a country band. I'm good at that. It's the one thing I do well. I may never make any real money at it, but I love doing it and right now I feel like that counts for a lot."

My father looked down at the strip of sod he was standing on and pressed its uneven seam with the ball of his foot. He looked across the lawn and put his hands in his pockets.

I took a drink and waited.

"I would have liked to have seen you become a lawyer," my father said. "Of the three of you, I think you would have been the best one. I used to think Miles would be good because he was aggressive, but he got mad too easily; he would have had a tough time refraining from punching people. Sometimes I'm amazed that I can. My initial reaction about you as an attorney was that you weren't tough enough. I really believe you have to be tough to be good. Now I think you would have been. You wouldn't have backed down. I like that."

We were both looking across the grass toward the empty lot to the north. The triangular shadow of the house was at our feet.

"When are you planning on leaving?" my father said.

"Probably tomorrow."

"Why don't you stick around for a couple days. Your mother would like that."

"All right."

Later I went searching for Montana. I found her near the keg, nodding at a young attorney who had one arm propped against the house and a hand on his hip. I could hear him giving a blow-by-blow account of a deposition he'd taken that morning. He paused and pursed his lips when I put my hands on Montana's hips, rested my chin on her shoulder and whispered, "Let's get out of here."

"Okay." She stuck her hand out to the attorney. "Good luck in court."

"I doubt we'll go to trial."

Montana paused. "Well, whatever." I laughed. When we were around the corner of the house, she looked over her shoulder and said, "God, to think you could have turned out like that, Dennis."

"Wouldn't you have loved me as a lawyer?"

"I like you much better as a dropout. Where are we headed?"

"Down to the river."

"To swim?"

"If you want to."

"Sounds good."

Dozens of vehicles were parked on both sides of the road under the cottonwoods for a hundred yards. We passed a truck with a pair of boots poking out of the passenger window, their owner asleep and snoring, a Stetson straw tipped over his face. Up on a neighbor's back deck, a man in a white apron and polka dot shorts yanked the domed cover off a smoking Weber and yelled inside, "They're beautiful!" He wielded the cover like a shield and cheerfully waved his spatula at Montana and me through the swirling black column.

"Anne wants us to stay with them on the ranch for a couple days before we leave."

"When do you need to be in Austin?"

"Oh, we've got plenty of time, Den," Montana said.

We turned off the road onto a sandy path that wandered through the sharp-pointed yucca in the shade of the trees. Montana stopped to take off her flats. I undid the knot on my tie and began pulling on the tip, the thin end sliding up the front of my shirt and disappearing into my collar: magic. I looked up and saw Montana laughing at me. The path let out onto a narrow strip of beach that sank abruptly into the Missouri, placid and green. On the opposite shore the cottonwoods grew to the edge and dropped their reflections across the river. Above the tree line like a second tier were the amber flat-topped foothills. Then nothing but high arching blue.

I took off my shirt, shoes and socks and gazed out at the water. "What's your approach here, Montana?"

"Well, I don't know about you," she said, pulling her dress over her head and dropping it on the sand. Then slipping out of her bra and panties and grinning over her shoulder at me. "But I'm a diver."

Montana took two running steps and I watched her long thin body arc through the air and into the river, a silver globe rising where she entered and thousands of white bubbles trailing her as she streaked beneath the surface.

I dropped my pants and dove.